"It's not that I envisaged another for a husband, Sir Hugh. I had rather hoped not to envisage a husband at all."

"I'm sorry for that, my lady, and I know this has been a difficult day, but I will not defy the king and neither should you." He inhaled before continuing. "I hope that you can get used to the idea of our marriage, and with that, I would ask if I... May I court you?"

Eleanor was momentarily speechless, flummoxed by this man's question.

"You want marriage and courtship, at the same time?"

Hugh stepped closer and caught her hand lightly in his. "I do..."

He raised her hand to his lips and softly kissed the back of it, sending a ripple of awareness shooting up her arm. He then took a step back, his eyes never leaving hers, inclined his head and turned on his heel and walked out of the solar.

Author Note

King John was not the first nor the last tyrannical, unpopular and frankly incompetent monarch in England's history. However, what made his reign significant was that his poor governance led to the kingdom's terrible reversal of fortune. His campaigns against France, especially the disastrous Battle of Bouvines, resulted in a huge loss of his dynastic territory in mainland France, and was never regained. His difficult and often bitter estrangement with his barons culminated in their rebellious revolt and demand he sign the Great Charter of Liberties, better known as the Magna Carta, which he eventually did in the summer of 1215... And which he later reneged on.

It's in the spring of that tumultuous year this book takes place. A time of division and civil unrest. A time of lawlessness and terrible hardship, when the burden of heavy taxation had taken its toll. And it is in the fictitious area of Tallany in Northumberland that the story is mainly set, reflecting the divide felt throughout the kingdom. It is this that the heroine, Lady Eleanor Tallany, finds herself on an opposing side to, as the hero, Sir Hugh de Villiers, whom she is forced to marry, is unreservedly a king's man. Can they find a way to come together against the odds, or are their differences too great a challenge?

I hope you enjoy their story!

MELISSA OLIVER

—

The Rebel Heiress
and the Knight

HARLEQUIN® HISTORICAL™

ISBN-13: 978-1-335-50562-0

The Rebel Heiress and the Knight

Copyright © 2020 by Maryam Oliver

Recycling programs
for this product may
not exist in your area.

This edition published by arrangement with Harlequin Books S.A.

For questions and comments about the quality of this book,
please contact us at CustomerService@Harlequin.com.

Harlequin Enterprises ULC
22 Adelaide St. West, 40th Floor
Toronto, Ontario M5H 4E3, Canada
www.Harlequin.com

Printed in U.S.A.

Growing up in Richmond upon Thames, **Melissa Oliver** used to walk past the old Harlequin office as a teen and wistfully sigh that one day her dream of writing for them would come true. Amazingly, it finally has and now she can bring all those stories out onto the pages of her books. Melissa lives in southwest London with her gorgeous husband and equally gorgeous daughters, who share her passion for castles, palaces and all things historical.

The Rebel Heiress and the Knight
is Melissa Oliver's debut title.

Look out for more books from
Melissa Oliver coming soon.

Visit the Author Profile page
at Harlequin.com.

To Jack for your love,
support and belief in me.

And also, to my editor,
Charlotte Ellis, without whom none
of this would be possible.

Chapter One

North of England, spring 1215

Three days! Three arduous days and nights she had kept him waiting, giving him excuse after excuse as to why she couldn't grace him with her presence. And still there was no sign of her.

Hugh de Villiers kicked the rushes on the floor of the great hall and exhaled in frustration. No, it seemed more like three long months that Lady Eleanor Tallany had been defiantly ignoring King John's missive demanding her at his court. To add insult to injury, she'd continued to ignore subsequent demands, resulting in King John dispatching Hugh and his men to these godforsaken northern wilds to meet with the enigmatic heiress.

He'd suspected that the lady would rather leave than face the contents of that missive, and had men posted around the castle keep, but no one had left. If she had been in the castle all this time she was still here.

Inside.

Hiding somewhere.

God give him strength!

He watched the far end of the hall as the steward of

Tallany Castle, Gilbert Claymore, walked towards him, wringing his hands and looking grim. Hugh gritted his teeth. This behaviour was both ridiculous and offensive in equal measure. Who did Eleanor Tallany believe she was that she could so insult and flout her Sovereign's wishes and demands?

For Hugh, it was a matter of unquestionable fealty to King John, and if it meant softening his liege's somewhat erratic and volatile behaviour. Hugh was honour-bound to his King, his allegiance never in doubt even in these uncertain times, with the country on the brink of civil war. Yet here he was, put firmly in his place, his patience worn thin by this woman for no understandable reason.

'Well, what is it this time, Claymore?'

'My lady sends her apology, Sir Hugh, but she cannot meet with you this morn as she has a…a malady.'

'Another one, eh?'

'Her head gives her pain today, but she bears it with fortitude and grace.'

'Indeed. And yet only yesterday you were telling me of Lady Eleanor's remarkable competence in the running of her estates. Impressive in itself, but all the more so with her litany of maladies.'

Hugh raised his brow. Really, the steward must take him for a fool.

'My lady is usually of good health.'

'Well, then, it must be our presence that distresses her so.' A muscle flickered in his jaw. 'Damn it, man, my time here should be of short duration. I need to get back to court.'

'And would my lady have to accompany you?'

So that was what was bothering Lady Eleanor. That she would be made to come to court. Why?

Even Hugh, having spent many years on campaigns

in France, knew of this widowed heiress and her desire to be left alone. Her lack of presence at court fuelled further gossip and rumour.

'That I cannot answer, since I don't know the contents of this missive nor what King John's intentions are.'

Not strictly true, since Hugh had another mission, as well as to deliver the King's demands to this frustrating woman. Hugh also had to find and capture a group of outlaws and their leader, Le Renard—or The Fox, as he was apparently known in these parts. The gang had not only stolen levies intended for the Crown, but also more worryingly had helped and abetted the Northern Rebel Barons. Traitors, who openly opposed and defied the King.

'Tell your lady that the sooner we hear King John's command, the sooner we can all go back to whatever it was we were doing. My men are restless, Claymore, as am I. And this situation cannot be endured any more. I believe I have been more than patient. I will go to Lady Eleanor's solar and drag her down here myself. Either way, the King's missive must be read today!'

Eleanor looked out of the small arched window from her solar and rubbed the back of her neck and winced. This time the pain was real. She wished the King's men and the so-called hero of the disastrous Battle of Bouvines—this Hugh de Villiers—would leave, but that was a fool's wish. They wouldn't leave until they'd got what they wanted: her. And she couldn't avoid them any longer.

She had stupidly believed that if she ignored King John's summons, he would forget about her, as he had done these past few years since her husband's death from dysentery.

Ah, the solitude of those years and the freedom that

had come with being in her ancestral home rather than bound by the shackles of court was something she had enjoyed—relished, even.

Eleanor had finally been doing what her father had taught her, despite being 'just a woman'. Managing her vast lands and looking after her people to the best of her ability. Yet it seemed now that was all to end.

Since the King's men had arrived Eleanor had sought to find a solution, a way out of her predicament, but all she had achieved was incensing the men instead—which was not something she had intended. But she didn't want to know the contents of King John's missive. Whatever he wanted from her, it would not be good. Nothing he demanded ever was. And now Eleanor had no idea about how to proceed.

Either way, she could never leave Tallany, nor its people, to fend for itself in these difficult times. That was what had made Eleanor secretly ally herself with the Northern Rebel Barons some months back and give them the assistance they'd need against a king bent on destroying everything she believed in. Dangerous on her part, but necessary, nevertheless.

Mayhap that was the reason why the King's men were here. Mayhap they knew of her treason. But surely no one save her few loyal men knew her part in that…

No, this was about taking her back to court—or, worse still, keeping her at the Tower, just as before her disastrous marriage. A shiver ran through her.

Eleanor wished she had more time. She had always known that her destiny was not hers to determine, but for her freedom to be snatched away so soon made her feel powerless and vulnerable.

She turned and caught her steward's eye as he entered the chamber. He nodded once and walked out again. No, she could no longer avoid the King's men and their commander, Sir Hugh de Villiers.

The hall fell silent as the steward of Tallany Castle and its mistress, followed by a couple of older women, walked onto the dais with purpose. Hugh shut his eyes in relief and sighed. Finally she had come. He could get this over and done with and leave this place.

He opened his eyes just as Lady Eleanor turned to face him and his breath caught. A heady scent of flowers and blended mixed spice teased his senses. He hadn't given the widow herself much thought—hadn't known what to expect of her—but it certainly had not been the lovely vision in front of him.

He looked her up and down, mesmerised. Oh, yes, a face and body that could send a man to purgatory! Her hair was pulled back and bound underneath a linen veil held by a silver circlet, but he could just glimpse dark glossy strands. Her eyes were dark too, and framed by lashes that curved at the ends. And her pink lips were lush and inviting…though not inviting *him* anywhere, as they were compressed into a thin line.

He glanced up and saw that she was glaring at him. A look of pure contempt flashed in her eyes before being masked. She stiffened, tilted her head and gave a curt nod.

What in God's name was he thinking?

He gave himself a mental shake and stepped forward, making a perfunctory bow.

'Lady Eleanor, it is an honour for me and my men that you grace us with your presence and I'm glad to see that your health seems much improved.'

'Indeed? And you must be Hugh de Villiers?'

'At your service, my lady.'

The lady, however, raised her eyebrows and looked down her nose at him.

'I rather doubt that, Sir Hugh. We both know why I am commanded here.'

He stood there staring at her open-mouthed, stunned by her rudeness.

'Do we, Lady Eleanor?'

'As you well know, sir.'

So she preferred plain talking, did she? Very well.

'My lady, mayhap if you had come to court when the King summoned you, this might have been avoided,' he said tersely.

'*This*,' she said through pursed lips, 'could never have been avoided.'

'Perhaps not, but it would have saved my men and I having to journey here and interrupt your…busy life.'

'Are you mocking me?'

Whatever Hugh had been expecting in Eleanor Tallany, it certainly hadn't been this hostile woman in front of him now.

'Not in the least, my lady. I'm merely pointing out that had you been gracious enough to submit to King John's demands, all this unpleasantness might have been avoided. You must know that he is not a man to be defied.'

'How easy it is for you to say, but this "unpleasantness", as you call it, could never have been avoided. It serves to determine my future.'

Hugh frowned at her. 'A future decreed by your King.'

They stared coldly at each other, waiting for the other to back down, as the hall descended into an awkward silence.

'Well, then,' she said finally, keeping her frosty gaze locked on his. 'Perhaps we should find out what this future holds, shall we?'

Hugh watched as Eleanor waved her hand for the missive to be read and the Tallany priest, Father Thomas, stepped forward and bowed to his mistress before cutting open the seal of the parchment scroll.

Hugh ground his teeth together. By God, she was infuriating! And to think he had been stirred by other thoughts that her beautiful face and comely body had aroused just moments ago.

He closed his eyes and exhaled deeply, reminding himself that it wouldn't be long until he left this godforsaken place. All he had to do was give whatever King John's message to this woman, catch a group of outlaws and then he could leave and get back to his life as a soldier. The sooner the better.

Father Thomas's voice filled the great hall as he read the missive, but not for one moment would Eleanor betray her fear to this Hugh de Villiers or to any one of the King's men. Her trepidation was entwined with a sense of outrage at having her home, her corner of England, invaded by these unwanted interlopers, and her apprehension about King John's edict was making her heart beat a little faster, but she didn't look away. Whatever the King had to say, wanted to accuse her of, she could face it. She would do it with her head held high.

Mustering all her courage, she straightened her back and stared boldly at the man who threatened her peace… Sir Hugh de Villiers.

He was bemused and baffled by her, she could tell, and attempting his own brand of indifferent haughtiness to match hers. She glared at him, putting every pent-up feeling of frustration, resentment and anger into it, but he merely smirked at her and dismissively shook his head, as if she were a petulant child.

Seething, she thought she would love nothing more than to march up to him and wipe that look off his face, but that was beneath her. Besides, it would only prove to Hugh de Villiers that he had the right of her character. Not that Eleanor cared what he thought! Really, he was quite insufferable. Although it should come as no surprise. No doubt the King was surrounded by such ambitious sycophants as this man. Just like her loathsome late husband, who had been not only ambitious and greedy but many other unpleasant things she would rather forget.

Eleanor was thankful that at least she was now free from that obligation and no longer had to bow to the demands of a husband. She shuddered at the thought of that! Yes, she must be thankful for the precious freedom she enjoyed—but for how long? She dreaded with what the King wanted with her. If only she were somewhere else…

As if reading her mind, Hugh de Villiers threw her a wry, detached look, probably wishing he were far away too. She wanted to be anywhere but here in her great hall, having to listen to Father Thomas. She'd rather be knee-deep in pig manure, or stitching a dozen linen shirts, or mulching a dozen barrels of apples for cider, or…

An audible collective gasp echoed in the hall and snapped her to attention. She tried to recall the few snatched words she'd heard moments ago. Had she heard correctly or could it be her imagination?

What had Father Thomas just said?

'Lady Eleanor Tallany…as decreed by King John… marriage…'

By God, she hoped she *had* imagined it. But she knew instinctively that she hadn't.

Marriage? *Marriage?* But to whom?

Heart pounding, Eleanor glanced around the room. Her eyes landed on Sir Hugh de Villiers, who looked ashen.

No, no, no! Please, not him. There had to be a mistake! 'Pardon me, Father, what did you say?' she whispered as she turned to face her kindly priest.

A shadow of concern shrouded his eyes. 'Our Lord and Sovereign King John has decreed a betrothal between you, my lady, and…' Father Thomas gulped. 'And Sir Hugh de Villiers. The bringer of this joyous message.'

Her breath caught in her throat as her eyes darted back to Hugh de Villiers, horrified. A ringing noise in her ears drowned out all other sound in the room. She could feel sweat on her brows; her palms clammy. Dear Lord, this could not be happening! Not again.

She closed her eyes, trying to find an inner strength, her inner calm. Faintly she could hear someone calling her through the dull roar in her head.

'Lady Eleanor?'

It was Father Thomas's soothing voice from far away. 'My lady?'

She opened her eyes and searched his old lined face for support and assistance.

'Do you understand what this means, Lady Eleanor?'

She dug her fingers into her palms, embracing the sharp pain. She took a deep breath, rolled her shoulders and straightened her spine.

'I do!' she ground out in a clear voice, and the hall erupted into cheers—except, it seemed, from her husband-to-be.

Hugh de Villiers strode towards her; his jaw clenched tight, and knelt in front of her, bowing his head. Just as quickly he got up and without a backward glance stormed out of the hall.

Hugh paced outside the inner bailey of the castle, almost colliding with a hapless boy carrying a wheel of cheese from the buttery. He barked at him to be careful and then put up a hand in apology for his own overreaction. He stopped abruptly and exhaled slowly, trying to control his foul mood. He never lost his temper, but after days and nights of frustration, waiting for this woman who had so sorely tested his patience, he felt he just might give in to it spectacularly.

It had to be a jest—it had to.

Hell's teeth!

What was King John thinking?

Marriage to Eleanor Tallany?

He knew he should feel honoured at having such an heiress bestowed upon him, but he didn't want a wife. His experience had taught him that women were not worth the inevitable heartache, and the only ones he allowed into his life were those who followed camp and warmed his pallet at night.

He was not interested in marriage. Hugh was a soldier, a knight, and a life serving his King was all he wanted. And yet he was obliged to follow this command. He would be a fool to refuse—not that he could anyway. But why had John not told him of his intentions? It would have saved Hugh the embarrassment of gaping at that priest and muttering that there had to be a mistake. Not a great start in front of the woman who would soon be his wife...

Knowing King John, he would be delighting in his surprise and would declare that this rise in fortune was a befitting honorarium, elevating Hugh's status after having once saved his Sovereign's life. A debt that John no doubt felt he owed him. But he didn't. Hugh had only done his duty as a knight to protect his King—which he would always do.

And yet for John to bestow this unexpected gift upon him did show his trust in him. And it would also bind these northern lands to the King for good, allowing one of his own men to be guardian of a huge area of the north.

Hugh stopped in his tracks and thought through the implications of these tidings properly. He realised that, despite his reservations, the idea of finally having a home of his own, somewhere he could put roots down after being on the road since the age of twelve, was something he did secretly long for. Not that he had entertained that idea in a long time. But he would have to take a wife. One that King John wanted for him.

Lady Eleanor Tallany…

A woman like her—imperious, wilful, rude and superior—was certainly not what he wanted.

Only he had no choice in the matter.

Hugh raked his fingers through his hair, knowing that he'd better find his betrothed and make amends for his unpardonable behaviour earlier—not that she would make it easy for him.

Hugh had a funny suspicion that nothing was going to be easy with Lady Eleanor Tallany.

Eleanor was pacing back and forth in her solar, trying to think of a way through this unholy mess. She still couldn't believe it. A husband? A husband who would try to control her, use her and abuse her as before. Saints above! She couldn't do it again.

Of all the things she had imagined, a husband was not something she had thought the King was going to force on her. Not at this time of civil unrest. But of course it made perfect sense to attach her to one of his own men—especially in an area of England that was largely sympathetic to the rebel cause. As was she.

This man—this Hugh De Villiers—didn't seem that enamoured of the idea of marriage to her anyway…which was surprising, given the way he had looked at her before formal introductions had been made. Given that marriage to her would make him powerful and rich.

Eleanor's shoulders slumped as she sighed. Their initial meeting couldn't have gone any worse than it had. Not only had she erred by making the man wait for days before granting him an audience, she had also behaved badly when they'd met. She shouldn't have done it. She shouldn't have been so belligerent. It had not been well done of her—and in front of all his men and her people...

But something inside her had just snapped when he'd gazed at her from head to toe. So she'd thrown him icy daggers, held herself rigid and clasped her hands tightly to stop them shaking, trying not to betray the apprehension she'd been feeling.

Eleanor might have assumed that Hugh De Villiers had known of the King's wishes and was sizing up his new chattel, but he'd seemed just as shocked as she when Father Thomas had read out the missive.

No, the way he had looked at her was the way so many men had before. He was no different from her cruel first husband or from the guards at the Tower, who had taunted her, tried to touch her. No different from any man who had wanted her and her land and wealth. Except that he was different—or soon would be. She would once again belong to a man, along with everything she possessed.

If only she could prevent the marriage...

Could she refuse?

There was rap on the wooden door and her old maid Brunhilde opened it to allow Hugh de Villiers to enter.

Eleanor turned to face him. 'Well, Sir Hugh, I take it that this was a surprise for us both?'

'Just so, my lady.'

'However, it is an unwelcome surprise. And I can see this…betrothal is just as unpalatable to you as it is to me.'

'What gave you that idea, my lady?'

The fact that you stormed out of the hall after the missive was read.

'Am I wrong?'

He shook his head. 'I never thought to be… Well, I never thought to take a wife.'

For some reason his honesty suddenly made her feel hollow.

Now, where had that thought come from?

'And I never thought I would be bound to a husband again.'

'Yes, but your destiny was always to wed, Lady Eleanor—as well you know.' He raised an eyebrow.

'And as *you* well know, Sir Hugh, I *was* wed.' Not that her first marriage had been much cause for celebration, but this man didn't need to know that. 'So, you'll excuse my reluctance at the thought of going through it again.'

He moved closer, his eyes fixed on hers, making her feel uncomfortable. Perhaps she shouldn't have said that. Her unruly tongue always got the better of her. She waited for him to respond, but he didn't. Instead he smiled knowingly.

She swallowed, trying to steady her nerves. He was so very tall, imposing and handsome. Had she missed that earlier? No, of course not. She had just ignored the fact that he was attractive. Ignored his height and those broad shoulders that filled his grey tunic. Ignored the way his dark hair fell over his forehead, covering a scar that split his eyebrow. She had also ignored the way his green eyes crinkled at the corners—and definitely ignored the way his lips broke into a lop-sided grin as they had a moment ago.

She groaned inwardly. Yes, he was attractive, but in an obvious way. No doubt he knew it too. Well, his easy smiles would have no effect on her.

'I had thought, or rather hoped, that I might be forgotten—especially now that I'm an old widow.'

'An "old widow"? You cannot be more than twenty, my lady.'

'I'm one and twenty, sir.'

'You're right—that is ancient.' He chuckled, shaking his head. 'And as for being forgotten…? That would not be possible.'

Eleanor rolled her eyes and walked to the arched window, peering outside. 'No, not with all the riches I bring.'

'That is not the only thing, my lady.' He followed her. 'Tell me, are you always so forthright in your manner?'

'I speak as I find,' she said, with her back to him.

'Even though it is not usual for a lady of your standing to be so…blunt?'

Eleanor heard him move towards her and knew he was no doubt standing behind her. 'I suppose you might say that I do not possess the necessary maidenly manners that I'm sure you're used to, Sir Hugh.'

'You surprise me. *Why* do you not possess those maidenly manners?'

'There was never any need,' she muttered, turning around to face him. No need for good manners with a brute of a husband whom she'd come to despise and the King he'd served so faithfully—as did this man before her.

'Is that so?' he said as she shrugged her shoulders. 'You would need them if you came to court, my lady, instead of burying yourself up here. Why don't you?'

Lord above, how had this man managed to get himself

in the position of interrogator? He was good—dangerously good. Eleanor would have to watch her step with him.

'I was indisposed.'

'Ah…and is that why you ignored the summons of your King?'

'Of course not. You must appreciate that I have not been well,' she said.

He inclined his head. 'Indeed. I am glad to see you in good health now, my lady.'

Eleanor exhaled slowly, surprised that she had been holding her breath.

'Well, Sir Hugh, what are we to do about our… predicament? You know King John as I do not. How do we get out of this unwanted marriage?'

'There is no way out of our *"predicament"*, as you call it. Once King John sets his mind on something he is not easily swayed.'

'Surely there must be something we can do?'

'Would you refuse your King?' He looked shocked—affronted, even.

'Sir Hugh, I am named after the King's mother, and my own mother served as one of her ladies when she was Queen. My family have always been loyal subjects, so you will understand if I don't honour your question with an answer.'

'Very well—but be under no illusion. There is no question of refusing the King's request for our betrothal. He would think it a huge insult and it would be in your interests not to persist with that, my lady.'

There was no denying the mild warning that laced what he was saying. Yes, Eleanor was right to be cautious with Sir Hugh de Villiers. Still, she couldn't resist a little probing of her own.

'Do you always do everything the King bids?'

'Naturally. I am sworn to him. I may be a soldier, and not an ideal husband, but if this is what King John wants, then so be it.'

'As easily as that?'

'It has to be,' he said softly, watching her as she bit her lip, turning away.

How? How was she going to get him to understand that this was an impossible situation for her to be in?

But she knew that no amount of explanation would change the course her life was taking.

He was still staring at her. 'So, my lady, are we in agreement?'

'No…no, we are not.'

'Lady Eleanor, the King will have you marry another if not me. And I hope that I am better than other prospective bridegrooms.'

True—he had a point. If not him then it would be another of King John's cronies.

The hopelessness of her situation exacerbated the anger she felt. 'I wonder what it is that has made the King want to honour you in this way, Sir Hugh? Could it have something to do with your valour or your courage or some such? Your heroic actions at the Battle of Bouvines?' she said dismissively.

He looked somewhat taken aback that she had heard of this. 'Who knows? John may believe it a fitting way to honour my *"valour"* and my *"courage"*,' he said, matching her sardonic tone. 'But you would have to ask the King, my lady. He does need to secure these lands with someone he can trust.'

'You, I suppose? And through marriage you'll acquire all of Tallany…including me?'

He winced, looking uncomfortable. 'So it would seem. And as far as Bouvines is concerned, when any knight witnesses his King unhorsed and about to be taken for ransom, or even killed, there is no question of what he must do. As such, I only did my duty.'

'As you are now?' she retorted. 'In that case there really doesn't seem any way out of this unwanted marriage.'

'No… I'm sorry that I'm not what you envisaged, but I will endeavour to be a good husband.'

Eleanor rather doubted that—especially if Sir Hugh knew to what extent she had conspired against King John. Besides, she didn't want another husband who would come to own her, possess her and make her feel totally powerless. Not again.

She screwed her eyes shut and looked away. 'It's not that I envisage any other for a husband, Sir Hugh. I had rather hoped not to envisage a husband at all.'

He studied her for a moment, making her wish once again that she'd kept her mouth shut.

'I'm sorry for that, my lady, but I will not defy the King and neither should you.' He inhaled before continuing. 'I hope that you can get used to the idea of our marriage, and with that I would ask if I…may I court you?'

Eleanor was speechless momentarily, flummoxed by this man's question. 'You want marriage and courtship at the same time?'

Hugh stepped closer and caught her hand lightly in his. 'I do…'

He raised her gloved hand to his lips and softly kissed the back of it, sending a ripple of awareness shooting up her arm. He then took a step back, his eyes never leaving hers, inclined his head and turned on his heel and walked out of the solar.

Chapter Two

It had been a miserable week, leading up to the wedding, and by this time tomorrow Hugh would be married to the elusive Lady Eleanor Tallany. Today they were out riding together through the woods, by the demesne lands. The old deciduous woods harboured a purple blanket of flowers on this warm spring morning.

Hugh sighed and glanced over to Eleanor, sitting on top of her grey palfrey. She looked magnificent, if not a little pale, wearing a green woollen gown edged in silver thread, a cream-coloured veil and a silver circlet. With her haughty expression, her back straight and the folds of her dress draped to the side of her horse, she looked regal.

'Which way would you suggest this morning, Lady Eleanor?'

'Whichever way pleases you,' she said stiffly, then as an afterthought turned her head and smiled at him. The smile didn't quite reach her eyes.

He pushed down his frustration. 'I'd rather your opinion, as you know these lands much better than I, but no matter. How about riding north? The steward informs me that it is an area of great natural beauty and offers a splendid view from the hill.'

She shrugged. 'As you wish.'

'What I wish is for you to tell me more.'

'Tell you more about what, Sir Hugh?'

About yourself, about your life…

He took a deep breath. 'About anything you want. Tell me about Tallany. The land, the villages, the people who reside here.'

She turned her head sharply and swallowed, but when she spoke her voice resumed its flat, vapid tone. 'Ask the steward—Gilbert Claymore. He will furnish you with any information you need. Now, shall we put these horses through their paces?' She raised her brows and smiled.

Ah, again that false smile pasted on her face. He groaned inwardly. This was going to be another bad day; he could feel it in his bones. It would be as bad as yesterday, and the day previous to that. In fact he would happily swap this past week for a campaign, fighting a dirty, difficult battle, rather than have to endure another day supposedly courting his betrothed before their marriage.

Which was ridiculous, as he didn't know anything more about Lady Eleanor than when he'd first met her. If anything, she had been more animated and truer to herself that first time than she had been since.

She avoided him, ignored him, or at best offered short answers to anything he asked, just as she had only moments ago, and all with polite deference.

Eleanor Tallany was more frustrating now than when he had been made to wait for her. And this woman was to be his wife. His *wife*, for the love of God… And it was patently obvious that his attempt at courtship was just as objectionable to her as the prospect of marriage to him.

Courtship? Well, that was entirely laughable.

Hugh had hoped that by courting Eleanor he would get her to soften her stance and allow him to get to know her, but she welcomed *that* as much as bloodletting! Which was, no doubt, just as excruciatingly painful.

And as if that wasn't bad enough there was the unwelcome pull of attraction every time he set eyes on her. He couldn't understand it. She was everything he loathed in anyone, least of all a woman: haughty, tempestuous and insolent. But it was there every time he encountered her. Even that chaste kiss in her chamber, meant to seal their betrothal, had had him wanting more. And he had only kissed her gloved hand, for pity's sake!

Hugh had glimpsed Eleanor when she was with her people, her steward, her handmaid, and knew she could be open and warm, her smile genuine. Nothing like the smiles she threw his way.

Damn... All he wanted was to get to know this woman better so that they could build some sort of understanding. A foundation for their imposed marriage. Notwithstanding the fact that Eleanor was a demand on his time with the business of finding and capturing Le Renard and his gang of outlaws. Not that Hugh was close to finding The Fox...yet.

He had to give them credit. The gang had outfoxed them all... They had managed to let loose some of his men's horses in the middle of the night; with only a few having been retrieved. And a few nights ago they'd made a dent in the food supply by stealing wheat from the village mill, meaning there was little left to make bread with. Highly embarrassing with the wedding feast tomorrow.

But most humiliating of all was the outlaws' appropriation of a few of King John's guards, who had travelled here with Hugh. Not only had those men been found tied around a tree in the village keep outside the castle, but they had been left dressed in women's clothing. There for all to see.

Yes, it had been a very bad week indeed.

He gave himself a mental shake, trying to snap out of these morose thoughts. He turned his head. 'This is a fine morning, is it not, Lady Eleanor?'

'I beg your pardon—did you say something?'

'No, nothing of importance.'

'My apologies, Sir Hugh. I was deep in thought.' She looked over again to meet his gaze, all wide-eyed innocence.

'And would you like to share those thoughts, my lady?'

'I was pondering the unfortunate circumstances surrounding the attacks from these outlaws. Are you close to finding them?'

He felt a sudden annoyance at himself and his rare incompetence in finding a few clever outlaws. Really, though, his mind had been otherwise preoccupied. It was not every day a man was about to enter into an unwanted marriage with a woman who no doubt preferred the company of a three-legged goat to her betrothed.

'Not yet, but I will catch them. Sooner or later they'll make a mistake and I will be ready when they do.'

'It's all so strange. We never had difficulties like this before. Well, not since my father's death. It makes me quite fearful to know there are dangerous outlaws nearby.'

Hugh shot her a sideways glance, trying to understand her interest. 'It is after all why I am here, my lady, to secure these lands. You have nothing to fear.'

'My thanks, Sir Hugh. What would I do without you otherwise?'

Her voice was toneless and that fake smile was pasted back on her face, setting his teeth on edge. He swore an oath under his breath. How long was she going to proceed with this pretence of being a polite, docile and biddable wife-to-be? Frankly, at this moment anything would be preferable company than this shell of Eleanor Tallany—even that three-legged goat.

Hugh knew he needed to shed some of the mounting tension from his body. 'Lady Eleanor and I will continue our ride alone,' he said to the few retainers and her maid, who had accompanied them.

Her handmaid, the ever-faithful Brunhilde, caught her mistress's eye for confirmation. Eleanor gave a single nod.

Hugh and Eleanor rode towards a stream, allowing their horses a quick drink, and fell back into silence. He jumped down and strode to her palfrey and extended his arms, offering to help her down. But she declined, shaking her head.

Hell's teeth! He had been right to believe this was going to be another miserable day.

Hugh marched to the stream in exasperation and splashed some water over his face, then took off his gambeson and tossed it on the saddle. It was a remarkably warm morning for a spring day, but that was not why he needed to cool off.

He turned and met Eleanor Tallany's impassive gaze, and sighed as she turned away. He had wondered whether perhaps her change in behaviour was due to her fondness for her first husband, Richard Millais, but he'd dismissed that after something she had said. It certainly didn't fit with what Hugh had known of Millais's reputation for debauchery and cruelty, but who knew with women.

Who knew Eleanor Tallany? Certainly not him. His one and only experience of a close relationship with a woman had left him with a bruised heart and wounded pride.

He reminded himself once again that he hadn't wanted this either, and shared with Eleanor her sentiments about this forced marriage, but he was honour-bound to make it work. And, notwithstanding the unwanted attraction he felt for Eleanor, Hugh found her beguiling.

Why had her behaviour changed so much since that first day when they'd found they were to be betrothed? He'd given her all the assurances he could that he would be a good husband, but it had raised no response from her. He'd tried every possible means to get her to talk to him but had failed. She was void of any emotion. In fact, the only emotion she had ever displayed was the anger and defiance she'd shown when they'd first met.

Well, now…perhaps he could somehow unleash that anger again and break through her mask? He didn't know why it mattered, but he knew that somehow it did. He glanced briefly at Eleanor, still looking haughty, and the corners of his lips slowly rose.

He mounted his horse and rode to her side. 'As I said, Lady Eleanor, there is no need to worry about these outlaws or anything else,' he said dryly. 'Now that I am here you can rest easy and need not concern yourself with the running of Tallany any longer. It's time for a change.'

Her back stiffened instantly. 'Sir Hugh…?'

'This place needs a man in order to implement some changes around here.'

'As do I, I suppose?'

'Why, yes. As a matter of fact, I believe you do.'

She turned away. 'I have managed perfectly well without anyone else.'

Hugh sensed that she was trying to conceal the irritation in her voice and that her perfectly placed smiles were beginning to crack. He should have thought of this earlier, but now he'd had enough.

'Ah, but you don't have to. Not now that I am here and can manage everything as it should be.' He smiled at her with what he hoped was a look of smug arrogance.

'Everything as it should be? I can assure you that my steward Gilbert and I have managed perfectly well, even during difficult times, and—'

'Oh, I am sure, my lady, that you have done your very best. As much as you could,' he mocked. 'For the villages, the tenants and all the lands…being just a woman.'

The pink hue in her cheeks and neck heightened as she breathed out, no doubt trying to control her temper. He raised an eyebrow and smiled, vacantly.

'Just a woman, Sir Hugh? Is that all I am?' she asked through gritted teeth.

They cantered uphill and emerged into a clearing—a change from dense woodland to an expanse of rolling fields.

He inclined his head, bowing slightly, without any need to say more.

'I see. How very insightful of you. I bow to your superior knowledge, but I would ask you not to be too hasty in your assumptions about me or anything else.'

He sensed that it would only be a matter of time—a very short time—before his goading would make Eleanor snap, give in to her anger, and hopefully reveal her true self.

'I don't see why. I'm here to save Tallany, after all, and right all the wrong.'

'I must say I don't know how we coped without you!' she muttered, pinning her gaze to the landscape around her.

'And now you don't have to. As I said, you won't have to worry any more.'

'What a relief.'

'It is, isn't it?' He grinned.

'Naturally, since my pretty little head can't cope with much.'

'Just so, my lady.'

'And now that you are here to save us from perdition, what exactly would you have me do once we're married?'

Hugh raised his brow at her in amusement.

'Never mind.' She turned her head away.

Hugh noticed her hands, covered as always with crochet gloves, clasping the reins tightly. This was better. Much, much better. Her spurious mask was finally slipping. Just a little more and she would be back to being herself.

Eleanor exhaled slowly and looked away, trying not to show that Sir Hugh's boorish rudeness was affecting her. But it was impossible! She was finding it hard to contain her anger and annoyance any more, along with her feeling of helplessness at this imposed situation. Her head was swimming with all the changes that would be forced upon her once more.

Hugh de Villiers seemed to be enjoying this. Enjoying mocking her—which was confusing. He had been a model of the courteous, gallant knight this past week, starting with that surprisingly gentle kiss, which had taken her off guard. It might have been merely on the back of her hand—her gloved hand, at that—but she had felt it all the way down to her toes.

Not that she cared a jot about that or any of his placating words. Not again. Eleanor knew how with, the snap of her fingers, a man could change his temper in an instant.

This past week had been incredibly trying and difficult. Not only had Eleanor needed to conceal her dangerous involvement with the outlaws, but she had been reconciling herself to the prospect that soon, once again, she would be someone's wife.

Coming to terms with her impending marriage also

meant that Eleanor had had to suppress and disguise her true character, fearful of what her betrothed would do if he found that instead of being meek and deferential, she was sharp-tongued, headstrong and with a mind of her own. Richard had told her many times she was a termagant that every husband would come to despise, heiress or not.

Bitterness, anger and fear coursed through her. She resented this. These feelings that she had thought to have buried long ago. And she resented being made to marry once again against her wishes—to marry another handsome young knight who thought far too much of himself.

'Would you see it beneath yourself to take a challenge, Sir Hugh?' she asked. 'This would be in the hope that you might change your mind regarding the limited constraints of being *"only a woman"*.' She held her head high, not daring to look at him.

'You are not in shackles, Eleanor.' He flashed the lazy, lopsided smile that made him even more absurdly attractive.

'Is that so?' She inhaled sharply, trying to hang on to her temper.

'What is this challenge you wish to propose?'

Eleanor knew that she shouldn't allow herself to rise to whatever scheme this man was devising, but it wasn't easy. She should, instead, turn the conversation back to gaining any useful information Hugh de Villiers had about her outlaw friends, which would serve them better. Not that that topic of conversation was any safer. Still, she could steer it in the way she wanted whilst not risking losing her temper.

She turned her gaze to the gently rolling hills before her. Beautiful, she thought wistfully. She had grown up here and knew every blade of grass and branch of tree.

These were *her* lands, her ancestral lands, but they would soon belong to him. As would she...

'Well, my lady?'

'A race to the third oak tree over there—you can see it in the distance.'

'I do see. But...a race? On horseback? With you?' He smiled slowly, raising a brow.

She continued to stare out into the distance with what she hoped was a steely gaze and did not even bother to look at him. With the answer he'd given he'd made her even angrier, if that was possible, and now he chuckled in response. He was laughing at her again.

'Perhaps you are scared to be bettered by someone like *me*?' she said. 'Well?'

'You're not serious, my lady?'

'Deadly so.'

'Hardly a fair contest, Eleanor... Come, let's forget all this.'

He spoke so gently that it vexed her all the more.

'Do you accept or not?' She scowled, finding it hard to remain composed.

'Very well, if you insist. But let it be noted that I did warn you. I hope you will not be too disappointed when I win.'

'We will see, Sir Hugh. We will see. Quickest to the oak I mentioned, by any means.'

'Then call it, my lady.'

He brought his destrier round beside her palfrey, towering over it, and grinned at Eleanor, taking her hand in his and pressing it lightly.

She snatched it back. 'Now!'

Eleanor pushed forward, galloping away to get a fast start before realising that he had held back, allowing her to get ahead.

His laughter roared behind her as she sped out in front. Of all the confounding, patronising and infuriating males! She continued to speed ahead before seeing him in the periphery of her vision as he cantered effortlessly past her. No, she would not allow it. This was her race to win! She had to.

Eleanor kicked her young horse to get him to go faster, trying in vain to get closer to Sir Hugh's lead. Both horses stretched and galloped fast, weaving in and around trees and bushes and criss-crossing each other, masterfully led by their riders.

She glimpsed Hugh's mocking smile and his nod of approval, then saw him tear a bite out of a piece of wheaten bread. Next, he pulled his flagon from his saddlebag and began drinking out of it.

He was eating and drinking now? At a time like this? Of all the insults!

She couldn't believe his arrogance. She could feel the slow rise of a red mist of fury building within her as she grabbed onto the reins even tighter, her knuckles turning white. How dared he treat her so? Talk to her so? Behave so? Detestable man. She would show him!

Hugh continued to race ahead, pushing his destrier faster, but not as fast as usual—he had to make it look as though it were a fair contest. He had been taken by surprise with Eleanor's challenge, which he had found both entertaining and endearing. He'd heartily enjoyed getting a rise out of her, and found that the more annoyed Eleanor became, the more he couldn't resist goading her. The way she spoke in outrage, defending herself, had almost made him stop and apologise. Almost.

He glanced around at the sound of her grey palfrey at

his side with a ready smile, but froze. Eleanor wasn't riding him any more.

Sheer panic and guilt spiked through him as he abruptly turned his horse around and scanned the surrounding area in the hope of finding her. This was his fault. He shouldn't have pushed her this far and agreed to her outrageous challenge.

Suddenly, in the distance, he could just make out a crumpled heap beside a tree on a hilly mound. With a sharp kick he led his horse back, but this time at his usual faster speed, riding to the motionless heap.

Hell's teeth! It was Eleanor, face-down in the long grass. He dismounted and bolted towards her.

'Eleanor?' he bellowed. 'Eleanor, please say something!'

Sick with worry, Hugh prayed she was unharmed. But as he reached her, lying there motionless, something sprang up, caught his foot and sent him hurtling forward, down the mound.

It was *her*—Eleanor—and there was nothing wrong with her! She had deliberately tripped him up and now he lay with his face in thick dry mud, feeling both embarrassed and humiliated. He groaned, wiping his cheek.

Eleanor quickly got back on her feet, and she raised her eyebrows briefly at him before turning, hitching up her skirts and running towards her horse, which she had whistled for and was now galloping back towards her.

Just as she reached the animal, and was about to mount it, Eleanor felt a sharp tug on her arm and a firm hand clasped around her waist, pulling her back. She fell with a thud, unceremoniously, into the arms of Hugh—who was no doubt furious.

'Oh, no, you don't. Tell me, are you always this adept at deception?' he asked.

'When there's a need…' She wriggled, trying to free herself, but to no avail. He was too strong for her.

'I wondered where that prickly woman I'd first met had gone under all that finery and false smiles…but here you are!'

'Let me go!' she demanded as he gripped her firmly.

'I don't think so, my lady. That was a shameless trick you pulled back there.'

'You deserved nothing less.' Eleanor was allowing her anger to bubble over, but frankly she didn't care.

'Is that so?'

'Yes, damn you.'

'Dear me, you're not very ladylike. Where did you learn to curse like that? It seems you really were telling the truth, Eleanor, when you said you possessed no maidenly manners.'

'Let me go.'

'No, I will not—now, hold still.'

Eleanor gasped and froze. Had Hugh de Villiers really uttered exactly the same words that her late husband Richard had used before…before doing the terrible things he'd done to her?

A small sob escaped from her lips as she screwed her eyes shut. So be it. There was little she could do anyway, whatever this man intended to do to her. He was much stronger than she.

Suddenly she realised he had let her go. Nothing she had been expecting had happened, so very slowly she opened her eyes and found Hugh looking at her strangely, his brows furrowed. He was openly studying her, trying to find answers to the questions swirling in his eyes.

'Come, Eleanor, let me help you mount your horse,'

he said gently, holding out his hand, his eyes never leaving hers.

She nodded curtly, not trusting herself to speak, and placed her hand in his.

They rode back in silence as Hugh's head was still reeling. What in God's name had happened back there?

Hugh glanced in Eleanor's direction and frowned. How could he have misjudged the whole situation as badly as he had? He'd only meant to stop her from riding away. One minute they had been sparring, Eleanor matching him in every sense, word for word, and throwing the nonsense he was saying back in his face, and the next...

He shook his head with frustration as they rode. Eleanor had challenged him to a race on horseback and, to his utter surprise and amazement, had ridden well. Even more surprisingly, and somewhat amusingly, she had resorted to cheating and subterfuge to get ahead, catching him off guard. He certainly hadn't been expecting that.

But then again her challenge had been a race to reach that oak tree first by any means. Ha, by any means indeed!

Without understanding why or how things had developed as they had, he felt guilt and remorse wash over him. Saints above, there was only one thing for it.

He swallowed before speaking. 'Lady Eleanor, I owe you an apology for what happened back there. I didn't mean to cause you any distress.'

'I believe there is really nothing to apologise for, Sir Hugh. Please, let us not dwell on it.'

'As you wish.'

Oh, but there was. He'd upset and distressed her. And, whilst it was one thing for him to tease and annoy someone, he would never willingly cause hurt. He might now be a celebrated knight, a soldier used to combat, but he would never intentionally hurt another. He took his oath to protect others very seriously.

And that was what confused him. For Eleanor to think, however briefly, that he might ravish her, or even force her against her will, was worrying and extremely shocking.

What kind of a man did she think him to be?

Of course that posed the question of what kind of a man she'd known before. It raised doubts about the very nature of her marriage to Richard Millais, a supposed leader of men. For her to react to him in the way she had…

He shook his head absently.

'Did he hurt you?' The words slipped out before he could decide whether it was a good idea to ask Eleanor about her marriage. 'Richard Millais? Did he hurt you?'

He met her steady gaze as he slowed his horse to a slow trot beside her. She opened her mouth as if to say something, and then shut it.

'It is perhaps best if we leave the past firmly in the past, Sir Hugh.'

He didn't want to let it go but what else could he do? He could hardly push her to talk if she had no desire to confide in him.

'Very well, Eleanor. Instead, allow me to ask where you learnt to ride like that? You are most impressive.'

'For "just a woman"?'

'Ah about that… I believe I owe you an apology for that too.'

'For saying what you believe to be the truth?'

'No, for purposely provoking you.' He watched her frown, saw confusion etched in her face. He quickly continued. 'I want to get to know you, Eleanor. We're to be married tomorrow and I still know nothing about you.'

She raised a brow. 'And you thought that would be your best approach?'

'No! Frankly, it was a mistake.' He sighed deeply. 'Although I suppose we *are* now talking more freely, as a betrothed couple should—not that I have any idea about betrothed couples.'

He could see that her eyes softened as they met his.

'Have you always been a soldier, Sir Hugh?' she asked.

'Since I was a young lad, squiring for Lord Anderville. Then I joined the Earl of Oxford's mesnie and eventually gained my spurs.'

She tilted her head. 'And you rose up the ranks until that fateful day you saved the King's life?'

Hugh shrugged. 'Whatever you may have heard about me, you must know that pitched battles are messy and unpredictable.'

She raised her brows. 'You surprise me.'

'Because of my supposed valour and heroism? I may be a strong, able soldier, Eleanor, but so are countless others. There is much to say about luck with any kind of one-to-one combat.'

She looked surprised. 'And skill, presumably?'

'Yes, and skill. But even then it's not always enough… Many brave souls never come home.'

'I know.' She nodded. 'There were many of our local men who didn't come back from Bouvines. The battle that sealed England's troubles.'

He stared at her, impressed that she had such an astute understanding about the current political situation. 'It certainly fuelled the King's problems with the Rebel Barons,' he said.

'And our Sovereign's problems affect us all.' She paused before continuing. 'Anyway, I thank you for your apology, and in the same spirit I would like to offer mine. My behaviour was unbecoming for a lady.'

'Ah, but then you do not possess the necessary maidenly manners, don't forget,' he said. 'Really, there's no need to apologise, Eleanor. I think it remarkable, given the provocation, that you didn't hit me over the head rather than challenge me to a race on horseback.'

'Which I won.'

'Which you cheated at!'

They'd both spoken at the same time. Hugh chuckled softly, shaking his head as Eleanor's eyes filled with a brief spark of humour. She had spirit, this woman who would soon be his wife.

They continued to ride back, and soon in the distance Hugh could see the figures of the retainers and Eleanor's maid, Brunhilde, waiting for them.

'Sir Hugh.' Eleanor broke the companionable silence. 'My marriage to Richard was...nothing less than a disaster.'

'I did wonder.'

'Did you?' she muttered, shaking her head. 'When I told you that we needed to find a way out of this imposed marriage I meant it.'

'And I meant it when I told *you*, my lady, that it's not possible. Believe me, if there was a way, I would have done everything in my power to bring it about.'

'But I... I'm not a woman fit for marriage.'

Was that what Millais had told her? That she was not fit to be a wife? Hugh felt himself getting angry on her behalf and thought he would wager that it had been the other way around. It would have been more likely Richard Millais had been unfit to be anywhere near Eleanor Tallany or any other woman, from the little he had seen of the man.

He pulled the reins to bring his horse to a halt, prompting Eleanor to do the same.

'Eleanor, I understand your reluctance for this marriage but allow me to reassure you.' He inclined his head. 'Let us not talk of disastrous pasts but hopeful futures.'

She didn't say anything, just continued to gaze at him, looking no doubt for sincerity in the words he had uttered. He realised then just how much Eleanor needed to be reassured.

'Very well, then. So be it, Sir Hugh.' She shrugged. 'As you wish.'

The ghost of a smile played on her lips. But it was a real smile, nevertheless, as she repeated the words he had said moments ago.

Yes, indeed, Eleanor Tallany had spirit. He returned her smile, feeling his mood lift for the first time since… well, since learning of his betrothal.

'Thank you. And I know it would also be the wish of King John.'

Eleanor's smile vanished. 'Of course, Sir Hugh. Now, shall we catch up to the others?'

She rode ahead, leaving him wondering about everything that had transpired between them. One thing was for sure: their morning together riding had been unlike any other they had yet shared.

Chapter Three

The great hall of Tallany Castle had not seen such revelry for a generation. Sumptuous tapestries hung from the stone walls and trellis tables were festooned with flowers and lush foliage. Trenchers groaned with pheasant, beef and chicken, cooked in a myriad of spices, with almonds and figs, served with wine from Eleanor's ancestral lands in Gascony. This was followed by sweetmeats, sugared quince, potted fruit and ginger biscuits decorated with honey and edible spring flowers.

The room was filled with the hum and chatter of wedding feast merriment and the ode of a troubadour broke through the noise.

Eleanor looked across and caught Sir Hugh—now Lord of Tallany, her husband—looking at her just as she was putting the last of a crumbly ginger biscuit in her mouth. She instantly looked away when she noticed his lips curving upwards to form that lop-sided grin of his.

She must stop stealing looks at Hugh—it was not as though she wanted his attention. Yet she could hardly avoid him now that they were married—something she had done ever since they had arrived back from their horse ride yesterday morning.

Eleanor could hardly think of it without feeling mortified. She hadn't meant to betray her emotions on that ride, but Hugh was evidently good at getting under her skin.

It made her feel uneasy that he had the ability to get past her defences. Husband or not, he was still the King's man. She must keep him at an arm's length and not allow him to get too close to her. For one thing, he mustn't find out about Eleanor's involvement with the outlaws. It was imperative that she did not jeopardise either her safety or theirs, and the important work they were doing to undermine King John's rule.

The other thing… Ah, the other thing was the sense of dread she felt about what would follow this wedding feast—the wedding night.

She gave herself a mental shake, pushing those unwanted thoughts out of her head, and then watched, surprised, as a knight with the standard of Lord Edmund Balvoire entered the hall. The man looked around and tapped the sealed missive in his hand before presenting it to Gilbert at the side of the hall.

Now, what did that slimy toad Balvoire want at a time like this?

Eleanor watched with interest as Gilbert brought the missive to Hugh, who caught her eye and nodded briefly.

'Is all well?' she asked, as Hugh frowned after reading through the missive. 'I hope there is no trouble?'

'No more than usual, Eleanor. It seems that the outlaws and their leader…this Le Renard, or The Fox, or whatever he likes to call himself…were sighted a few days ago on Edmund Balvoire's land. They stole all the silver levy intended for the Crown.'

'That's terrible.' She hid a knowing smile behind her goblet as she took a sip of wine.

'It's more than terrible. Balvoire will petition the King for more aid.'

Hugh's voice was low and its tone unlike how she'd ever heard him use before.

'I will find them soon—and Lord help them, especially Le Renard, when I do!'

She gulped down her wine too hastily, making herself cough, and she placed her goblet back on the trestle table.

'Apologies, my lady,' he whispered, patting her back. 'Come, let's not talk of this and we shall enjoy our wedding feast instead.'

But Eleanor perceived the tension emanating from Hugh and reminded herself that she had to be very careful. Danger was all around her; one false move would prove fatal.

The troubadour's ode had finished, to a cheer of approval, and immediately the musicians struck up a familiar melodic tune.

Lord Hugh, as he had now become, rose suddenly and bowed, holding out his hand. Eleanor rose too, unsure, and curtseyed before accepting his hand, their featherlight fingertips barely touching. They descended the dais together to begin the wedding dance, with their guests cheering and banging their goblets on the tables.

Hugh and Eleanor came together, held hands above their heads and circled each other, forming the elegant shapes of the dance.

'You seem distracted,' she said, and swallowed as a momentary pang of guilt spiked through her. She knew she was the cause of Hugh's troubles.

'I'm sorry… I believe I am.'

She bit her bottom lip, 'And I believe it is customary for a husband to make small pleasantries on such an occasion. Even if it is for the benefit of his guests.'

Eleanor raised a brow, hoping to cajole him back into being his usual self, forgetting that she had barely spoken to him since the horse ride.

Hugh blinked in surprise and a slow smile spread on his face. 'True—but allow me to say, for your benefit alone, Eleanor, how lovely you look on this…happy occasion.'

They continued to circle each other in the wedding dance, every brush of his fingers, every lingering gaze playing havoc on her senses. It was annoying that he was so attractive—his dark hair curling slightly at the back, his broad shoulders filling a wine-coloured tunic that was edged in silver thread and nipped in at the waist by a leather belt and a long dark surcoat over that.

He towered over the entire hall, and those keen, sharp eyes didn't seem to miss a beat. Even the scar that split his left eyebrow in two gave him a certain powerful edge. Once again she felt nervous about everything—about later—and once again she pushed her thoughts away, lifting her head to face him.

'I must say that for a big, tall soldier you are surprisingly light on your feet and graceful in your moves.'

'Would it surprise you even more to know that, despite the impediment of my big, clumsy appearance, I actually enjoy dancing, music and merriment.'

'It would—just as it might surprise you to know that I do not.'

'Ah, but your lack of appearance at court and your terrible maidenly manners give that away, don't you think?' he murmured, making it impossible for her not to betray a giggle. 'That's better. You've been so quiet since our ride yesterday. I had wondered how to coax you out of it.'

'By not repeating *that* disaster.'

'Saints above, no! Lesson well learnt. I must say that

temper of yours, Eleanor, is certainly something to behold, but it must only be unleashed very sparingly.'

She forced back a desire to laugh. She was indeed surprised to find that Hugh was such an elegant dancer, but more surprised that he could tease her about her quick temper during their ride. He was trying her to put her at ease and it was almost working. But it shouldn't. It couldn't!

She must remember that Hugh de Villiers was King John's man and would always be…just as her first husband Sir Richard had been. He too had been young, virile and handsome. He too had been charming, kind and understanding at the beginning…

She remembered when she'd first met Sir Richard Millais and how she'd almost swooned at his smile and his gallantry. How lucky she'd felt, believing him to be her golden knight, come to save her from loneliness and uncertainty after her father's death. But it had all been a lie. A huge, terrible lie. She had been so naïve…

Richard had been no heroic knight—more the devil incarnate. He had resented the fact that it was through her that he had gained all his riches and he had made her know it. And he'd had no need of her clever mind, sharp tongue or wilfulness. He'd wanted to break her in and teach her what it meant to behave like a real lady: docile, dutiful and obedient.

Of course, she'd refused to oblige. The more Richard had taunted, belittled and punished her, the more she'd stood her ground and taken whatever he'd proscribed without wavering. He'd wanted her to cry, to plead for mercy from him, but she'd deprived him of that. She'd never betrayed any fear of him, had never shown him any emotion, whatever he'd done to her. No tears—never any tears.

Eleanor flicked her eyes back to Hugh's watchful gaze, saw wordless questions forming in it. After a short moment he sighed and took her hand again, turning her in time to the beat of the music.

'I am afraid I have not been honest with you, my lady,' he murmured softly as he stepped to the side and moved behind her.

'Oh? How, exactly?'

He was standing close behind her. Very close. Close enough for his breath to tickle the side of her neck.

'Have pity on me, Eleanor,' he whispered into her ear.

'What do you mean, my lord?'

He spread his long fingers around her small waist and lifted her in one swoop, turning her swiftly so she was in his arms. The guests clapped and cheered from all sides, tapping their goblets on the table.

'You'll promise that you will be gentle with me, won't you?'

Ah, that lopsided grin again. 'Gentle?' she repeated.

He set her down slowly, so that his handsome face was close to hers. She looked away, confused, hardly able to breathe.

He guided her face back to his, his green eyes melting into hers, and shrugged. 'Don't forget I'm a novice husband and will need help and guidance from my new wife.'

He was doing it again—trying to put her at ease, trying to make her feel less anxious. No doubt he believed it would make her a more biddable wife.

Eleanor flushed. 'Somehow I think you will fare well, my lord.'

'I hope so, as I have been unlucky so far. But under your excellent tutelage…who knows?'

'Who, indeed?'

Eleanor knew, though… She knew that she couldn't

trust this man; his silky words and easy smiles were not going to work on her. Why would they?

Hugh de Villiers was trying to appease her, probably because it was their wedding night and he wanted her to be willing when he took her to bed... And if she wasn't willing? Would he take her anyway, as was his right?

Again, her nerves mounted.

He had promised her hopeful futures that would drown out disastrous pasts, on their ride back yesterday, but she didn't really believe him. Hugh might be a knight, a modest hero of the Battle of Bouvines, believing in some dusty chivalric code, but he was not her hero.

Heroes didn't exist. She'd learnt that a long time ago.

Hugh drummed his fingers on the trestle table, wondering how long he'd have to watch the fool juggle and tell customary lewd jokes about the wedding bed. Eleanor had left the hall moments ago, with her maid Brunhilde at hand to help ready her for the bedding ceremony, blushing as she did.

Hugh sighed. As much as he was eagerly anticipating this part of the evening, he couldn't help feeling a sense of trepidation.

On the one hand, he wanted to bed Eleanor. The desire he felt for her every time he saw her, spoke to her or—God help him—touched her, as he had during their dance, was making him feel like a callow youth. When she had walked into the chapel earlier he'd had difficulty taking his eyes off her.

Eleanor had looked stunning in a green velvet gown, with her hair tightly bound under a gold circlet and a delicate veil. He'd had a ridiculous notion to touch and brush away the wisps of dark chestnut hair that had escaped, but had restrained himself.

And when they had been dancing, the warmth of her scent…flowers and spicy soap…had wrapped around his senses and he'd had the strongest urge to kiss her, but again he'd restrained himself. When he'd lifted her into his arms he had been overcome by a need to explore her body, yet naturally he had not.

Damn!

It was not just her captivating beauty that he was attracted to, but her quick intelligence as well. She was strong, resilient, and from all accounts extremely capable. She certainly challenged and intrigued him.

Yet, for all that he knew she hid a vulnerability that made him feel the need to protect her, even though he barely knew her. Eleanor had been hurt in her previous marriage—that much was evident from the haunted look in her eyes. All of which would make this night far more difficult.

Hugh needed to reassure her that she had nothing to fear in him. He wanted Eleanor's trust, even though trust was something he found not just difficult but impossible—especially with a woman.

After all, the woman he had loved body and soul all those years ago, Alais Courville—the woman he had hoped to spend the rest of his life with—had played him false so completely that all his hopes for their future had been burnt to dust. Her betrayal had been so breathtaking and so devastating that it had left him with a bitterness that could never be erased. Never again would he allow anyone to get close enough to trample on his heart as Alais had done.

Though of course that had nothing to do with Hugh wanting to bed Eleanor. But once he had done so he would take a step back and leave her to her own devices. It wasn't as though she wanted any real intimacies, and he certainly didn't want to get too close to her.

He would be the kind of husband Eleanor would welcome—respectful, yet distant, courteous, yet remote. He didn't want anything more. Then he could get back to business, serving King John by capturing Le Renard and his outlaws.

Even the missive that had arrived earlier from Lord Balvoire, with its serious implications, had not really penetrated his mind. His thoughts were solely on his new wife and this night. Yet how to proceed?

He tossed back the ale in his goblet, swiped his mouth with his hand and jumped to his feet. He must proceed slowly and with care...

Hugh knocked on the wooden door of his new chamber and ambled in just as Brunhilde was drawing the heavy curtain around the bed, leaving only a small opening visible, Eleanor evidently behind it. He stood against the stone wall with his arms crossed over his chest and nodded at Father Thomas as he swung a censer, blessing every corner of the room and wishing the married couple joy, fertility and much happiness.

The guests who had staggered behind Hugh to the solar were outside in the antechamber, craning to catch a glimpse, but Father Thomas and Brunhilde ushered them away, closing the door.

Hugh and Eleanor were finally alone, and this was their wedding night.

Hugh drew the curtain around the bed slowly and found Eleanor sitting upright in the large feather bed, wrapped in a deep blue coverlet. She looked up at him and stole his breath.

If he had thought her lovely before, it was nothing compared to how she looked now. He had never seen her luscious long hair unbound, framing her face. He watched, entranced, as her lips parted and she bit her bottom lip nervously. Her brown eyes held flecks of gold and amber in this light, but also a veil of anxiety and barely disguised fear.

Hugh had two choices here. He could get into bed and make Eleanor his in every way imaginable, as was his right, blotting out all vestiges of the man who had been there before. Or… Or he could do something for her.

He could wait.

He knew what he wanted to do. Lord above, he knew what he *should* do—if only to legitimise the marriage— but then, this proud, terrified woman was like no other. He sensed that her past experiences, whatever they were, could not have been good, and if he wasn't careful they would determine their future…badly.

Hugh gave himself a mental shake and smiled. 'I hope it has not been too exhausting a day for you, Eleanor?'

'I am well, as you can see,' she said in a flat tone. 'Are you well, my lord?'

'Mmm? Yes, of course.'

No, he damn well wasn't. He dragged his shaky fingers through his hair and swallowed hard.

'Are you sure, my lord?'

'Yes—and call me Hugh. I cannot get used to anyone "my lording" me—especially you.'

He sighed, trying to drag his gaze away, then sat at the edge of the bed and swallowed, his mouth suddenly dry, as he watched her. He caught a tendril of her loose, unbound hair and wrapped a silky lock around his fingers.

'You seem more nervous than I… Hugh.'

'I am.' He smiled. 'Tell me, what do you want to do?'

'Do?' Her eyes widened in confusion. 'What do you mean?'

He shrugged. 'This is our private time together, Eleanor, and what we do is no one's business but our own.'

She frowned, meeting his eyes. 'This is our wedding night. It wouldn't be legally binding if we didn't...'

'True... But no one need know. We don't have to do anything you don't want to.'

He watched as Eleanor's jaw visibly dropped and she pushed forward, meeting his gaze.

After a moment she shook her head, looking away. 'No... I thank you for your consideration but, no. I'd rather get this over and done with, if you don't mind.'

'Very well.' He cautioned himself to proceed slowly. 'But remember you promised you'd be gentle with me, Eleanor.'

She rolled her eyes as he slid his hand to cup her face, tilting it and tracing her soft pink lips with his thumb. He bent his head to hers, his lips so near that there was only warm, wet air between them. He let the moment stretch agonisingly, allowing Eleanor to pull away if she wanted to. Hugh's mouth curved into the ghost of a smile as she moved closer, before he pressed it to hers and kissed her softly.

He noticed from the corner of his eye that her hands reaching out from beneath the covers were still gloved.

'You wear those even in bed?' he whispered against her lips.

'What?' She looked up, dazed. 'Oh, yes. These allow the applied balm to...to make my hands soft.'

'Fit for a lady.'

'I suppose...' she murmured, and she pressed her lips to his, surprising him.

She was like sunbeam and silk, his prickly, haughty wife, and she was very tentatively kissing him back.

Hugh felt her gasp as his tongue gently coaxed the

seal of her lips apart. Every part of him, every sinew of his body, was aware of her—the feel of her, the delicious taste of her. Spurred on by her response, he deepened the kiss. It seemed the lady was enjoying this as much he was. And he clamoured for more.

An unexpected yearning grew in the pit of Eleanor's stomach and moved deep into her core as Hugh's mouth covered hers, kissing her in a way she could never have imagined.

This was madness!

She felt the touch of his fingers along her collarbone before his lips left hers to kiss the column of her neck. He lifted his head, desire blazing in his eyes. A wordless question. It was a question Eleanor could not answer even as her wayward body craved more.

Hugh dipped his head and claimed her lips again, his hands cupping her jaw gently. Saints above, what was happening to her? Eleanor felt as though she was losing herself, gradually and slowly losing sight of everything around her.

Yes, indeed, madness!

She longed for more…longed to explore this sensual pleasure she had never known existed. Her previous experiences had centred on cruelty and dominance. This was nothing like that, but even so a voice from deep inside her was warning her about the loss of control…how things could spiral quickly into the unknown.

This was happening far too quickly and it had to cease.

Eleanor opened her eyes and slammed the palms of her hands onto Hugh's chest, untangling herself and scrambling to the other side of the bed before he had a chance to grasp what had happened. She sat with her back to him, listening to his breathing from behind her.

Dear God, what had she done?

She screwed her eyes shut and groaned inwardly. Yes, she had felt her body betray a thrill of excitement, and in her muddled head she knew that she had actually enjoyed kissing Hugh— unbelievable as that was—but Eleanor couldn't do it. It repelled her, frightened her… And yet would it…with Hugh?

She shook her head. No, she didn't want to know. And what could she do anyway? Her body was not hers. Hugh had every right to make his demands and force her to submit, even though he had suggested they might wait.

Her back stiffened and her fists clenched as she waited for his inevitable outburst of anger.

It didn't come.

Instead, Eleanor heard him sigh deeply, get up and walk around to the ornately decorated coffer. She glimpsed Hugh from under her lashes as he tapped a tattoo on the surface with his fingers before grabbing two silver goblets and pouring ale from the silver jug into each. He was there in front of her in two big strides, pressing a goblet into her hands.

'Thank you…' she muttered. 'I… I prepared the wedding ale myself, with added spices and honey,' she said, looking at her feet as she turned the goblet in her hand.

'It's delicious,' Hugh said as he took a large gulp.

Tension crackled between them as the silence stretched.

'Eleanor, look at me, please.' He gently lifted her chin with his fingers. 'I apologise for my…eagerness.'

She pulled away from his hold and took a sip from her goblet. 'There is nothing to apologise for.'

'It seems there is—and it also seems that I'm making quite a habit of it.'

She shrugged, hoping her expression was one of indifference, but her head was in a haze of confusion. It was both unexpected and puzzling that Hugh should apologise for her woeful lack of wifely duty. Yet here he was, apologising to her again after doing so yesterday. Could she remember any man—knight or nobleman, least of all her husband—ever apologising about anything, ever? And yet Hugh de Villiers didn't think it beneath him to do just that.

'Eagerness on one's wedding night is natural, Hugh. My reaction is not.' She sucked air through her teeth and continued. 'But you should know that…that intimacy disgusts me.'

There—she'd said it and now he knew. Perhaps he would find other women to warm his bed whilst she looked the other way.

He raised an eyebrow but said nothing, willing her to say more.

So she did. 'It's…it's not your affliction, but mine. I told you yesterday that I'm not fit to be a wife. I'm unnatural, Hugh.'

'I take it that is what Millais said to you?' he said. 'Well, I want you to know that he was wrong. Very wrong.'

'Even so I… I'm damaged. I carry terrible scars.'

Eleanor left those words hanging between them, feeling so uncomfortable talking about the past that it made her squirm.

Hugh looked at her with compassion, without a trace of pity, as if he understood how deep those scars ran.

'I appreciate your honesty, Eleanor but I am not Richard Millais. You must understand that you should never have experienced what you did with him. And if anyone was unnatural it was Millais, not you.' He lowered himself slowly to one knee, placed his goblet on the floor and took her hand in his. 'Listen to me, I have never forced an unwilling woman into my bed, Eleanor and I'm not about to start now. I want you to give yourself freely to our union. And until then, if I have to wait…well, then I will wait.'

'And if I don't?'

'It's a risk I'm willing to take.' He shrugged. 'My hope is that you might come to realise that the intimacies you find so disgusting may actually be the opposite.'

Eleanor shook her head in disbelief but said nothing.

'We need time…time to get to know one another.' Hugh smiled before continuing. 'So from now on I will sleep on a pallet that I will ask my squire to smuggle in from somewhere. I will make him swear an oath of secrecy. No one need know.' He stood up and stretched out his arms.

'You believe I will come to your bed willingly when I can never give you my heart?' She shook her head. 'My castle, my lands and my wealth may now be yours—even my body—but my *heart* will never be.'

She watched as Hugh froze, his eyes narrowed and his lips pressed into a thin line. This was exactly the sort of outspoken behaviour that had incensed Eleanor's first husband, leading to the punishments he'd inflicted on her.

'I don't believe I have ever asked for your heart, and nor shall I be offering mine in return.' He took a deep breath before softening his voice. 'You are a shrewd, intelligent woman, and we both know that our alliance has been brought about against our wishes by King John. But it has happened and we must make the best of it.' He paused before continuing. 'So allow me to court you. Properly this time.'

She gaped at him in disbelief, not quite trusting anything he said. Hugh de Villiers seemed kind, and understanding, and apparently nothing like her late husband—but he was still a man used to getting his own way.

Could she trust that he would not force her when she didn't come to him willingly? Until she knew him better there was no way of knowing. She was not so naïve as to swallow all his rational words now, when they might become irrational later, once he'd realised she would not change her mind about coming to the marital bed. What then?

Eventually she nodded cautiously. 'Very well, my lord.'

'Good.' He took a sip from his goblet. 'And I think I have just the thing for us to do—unless you'd prefer to go to sleep?'

Sleep?

Did Hugh de Villiers really believe that she could sleep easily knowing he was sharing the room with her? Even on a separate pallet, with the bed curtain shut tightly, he would still be there…sleeping in the same chamber… near her.

She gulped. 'No, I'm not ready for sleep yet.'

'Good. Well, in that case, we shall do something else.'

She blinked several times. 'Do something else?' she repeated, confused.

He smirked as he strode to the coffer and pulled out a medium-sized rectangular object covered in woollen cloth. 'Apart from my horse, my sword and gaining my spurs, this is my most prized possession.'

She watched, intrigued, as Hugh placed the object on the bed in front of her.

'Have you ever heard of chessmen?'

She frowned, shaking her head. 'You want to play games? At this time?' This wedding night was getting stranger and more unexpected at every turn.

'Ah, but chess is far more than just a game, Eleanor,'

he said, pulling the cover off a beautifully crafted black and red two-toned board. From another woollen sack he pulled out intricate mini-statues and placed them carefully on the board. 'It is about strategy, skill and outwitting your opponent. King Richard was a patron of chess, as were his father and grandfather before him.'

'I didn't know that.'

'It's true, nevertheless. And the Earl of Oxford encouraged all of us to engage in the game, believing that it was one of many skills a good knight should acquire.'

She met his eyes and smiled despite herself. Now *this* was a challenge she would certainly welcome to test her mettle.

She brushed her hand across the smooth chequered board. 'It's beautiful. Where did you get it from?'

'More like who did I win it from!' He winked. 'And, before you ask, it was from an over-confident Poitevin knight who claimed to be the best player in Christendom, and he had won it from a Moor in Granada. Naturally I had to repudiate that claim.'

'Naturally...' She bit back a sudden urge to laugh at the absurdity of this evening.

'Are you ready for a challenge, my lady?'

'Certainly—how do you play?'

He sat on the bed opposite her, on the other side of the board, and crossed his legs. 'Now, pay attention, Eleanor. These are lowly pawns and they can move one square forward and capture one square diagonally and only ever other pawns. Never anything else.'

She smiled. 'Very lowly indeed.'

'But very useful, which is why they're often referred to as the infantry. And they can be successfully promoted.'

'To King?'

'No piece can do that, my lady. There is only *one* King.'

'Indeed...'

He placed a further four pieces on each side of the board. 'These here are two rooks, two chevaliers—or knights—and two bishops. And naturally only one King and Queen apiece.'

Eleanor listened intently as Hugh explained the way in which each piece could move forward.

'And the aim of the game?' she asked.

He chuckled. 'The final aim is, of course, to trap the King and check him—a checkmate. I believe it comes from the Persian phrase *shah-mat*. Meaning the King is ambushed.'

She looked at him with disbelief. 'How do you know all this?'

'Well, if one wants to become a master at something it is imperative to gain as much knowledge and under-standing as possible, don't you think?'

'Yes... But are you? A master?'

'You'll just have to find out, my lady.' He winked. 'All I will say is that even King John has not found a way to pass me, and he has been playing since boyhood.'

Hugh played chessmen with the King!

'Is that so? Well, we'll have to see about that.'

'Fighting talk.' He nodded approvingly. 'I like that. But I warn you... This can be a very slow game and it can take days for an outcome.'

'Surely we have the time?'

'We do.' The corners of his lips curved. 'And while I think of ways to outwit you at night, by day I can focus my mind on the thankless job of finding the outlaws and The Fox, on top of getting better acquainted with Tallany. Your move, Eleanor.'

'I can move the pawn just one square?' she asked. He nodded. 'How can you be sure of capturing the outlaws?'

'Much as in chess, I will need my skill to outmanoeuvre them. Eventually they'll make a mistake—even a small one. And when they do, I'll be ready. Once I capture Le Renard and his outlaws everything, I believe, will fall into place.'

She swallowed. 'I see...'

'Don't worry. I'll find them. Trust me, Eleanor.'

Trust him? Of all the things to say.

There was so much to think about, so much to ponder on, that it made her head spin. Her new husband seemed intent on getting to know her, but she wouldn't allow it. She couldn't! It would be far too dangerous.

'I can see already that this may prove to be a long challenge, Eleanor. I hope you're ready for it?' he teased.

Yes, she'd play this game—but that didn't mean he would get any closer to her. Hugh would now be doubling his efforts to capture her outlaw friends, which meant she had to be very vigilant.

What would he do when he realised that the outlaws he sought were the same outlaws that she secretly aided? A shiver went down her spine. There was no way of knowing how he would react. Especially if he discovered that not only did Eleanor help the outlaws but that she was also one of them!

She was, in fact... Le Renard. The Fox he was searching for.

She exhaled slowly. 'Yes, I'll be ready.'

One thing was for certain: he must never, ever find out.

Chapter Four

Clank, clank, clank. The quarterstaff of Hugh's opponent struck out and nearly caught him, but he was too quick and moved swiftly to one side. He briefly looked around the clearing, breathing in clean, fresh air mingled with industrious graft and sweat, and exhaled.

The area around the castle yard was gathering small pockets of curious villagers who were milling around the periphery, watching the combat training in progress. Archers and swordplay in one corner, and targets struck on horseback in another.

Hugh darted to the left and took a few steps back, getting ready to make his own attack as beads of sweat trickled down his face. This was good—very good. Focusing on his training would provide a much-needed balm to his soul. He was a knotted coil of frustration, and the opportunity to expel some of his pent-up energy was welcome indeed.

It had been an inspired suggestion of his to play chess night after night for the past two weeks with Eleanor. He'd watched her, bemused, as she'd become more and more engrossed in their game, her intelligent eyes focussed, the cogs in her head turning. He was impressed that she was so adept at learning and playing the game at the same time. She was giving him a real challenge.

Their evenings were unexpectedly congenial and pleasant, filled with light banter. He sensed that the rare glimpses he'd had of his wife were the real Eleanor and he wanted more… Yet as soon as their game was suspended for the evening she would retreat behind the bed curtain, shutting him out. It was as if she remembered to go back to being distant and reserved when they weren't playing chess—which was becoming increasingly frustrating and disheartening.

Her reticence and awkwardness *must* have something to do with Richard Millais. Hugh could only guess what Eleanor had gone through at the hands of her first husband—not that she'd actually confided any of it to him. But the hopelessness and anguish that had been stamped on her lovely face on the fateful night of their wedding was something he could never forget.

'I'm damaged. I carry terrible scars.'

The fact that Millais had taken sport in inflicting pain upon a woman he'd been supposed to protect and care for made Hugh want to dig the bastard up and tear him limb from limb.

God's teeth! When he thought of the haughty, imperious woman he had first met, understanding now the pain and hurt beneath that strong exterior, he couldn't help but admire her. She wore her scars like armour—to protect herself.

There was nothing for it. All he had to do was prove that he was worthy of her and different in every way from Richard Millais.

Ha, all he had to do…

So much easier said than done…

Despite all his attempts to get to know her since their

wedding, Eleanor still seemed quite indifferent to him. She had been friendly but guarded since that night, and definitely out of bounds.

Lord above, but it was killing him. Night after night of sleeping in the same chamber, listening to her move and murmur in her sleep, listening to her breathe behind that heavy bed curtain… It was slowly driving him mad.

Hell! There was only one thing for it—he had to woo Eleanor. And for a man who had never had to do very much for women to fall at his feet, it was not going to be easy.

'You're a man of few words, old friend, but this is ridiculous. I have been here for a day and you have barely muttered a word. Unless grunting is a word, that is.'

Hugh dodged another scathing blow from the quarterstaff and looked up to meet the amused blue gaze of his friend Sir William Geraint, a man who had taken his knight's oath the same day as Hugh and had been like a brother and a good friend since.

'And you, Will, were always one for a conversation even during combat. You're more suited to the women's bower chambers,' he retorted.

'True.' William smirked. 'I am known for my gallantry.'

'So you say.'

'So I have always been told by many a good lady.'

'Not to mention the bad.'

'Ah, but I'm too much of a chivalrous knight to cast aspersions on any woman's character.'

'That is because you're not too fussy about whom you bed,' Hugh said as his feet skidded in the dirt.

'I have standards, whatever you may believe, Sir Hugh.' Will made an exaggerated mock-bow.

'It's Lord Hugh de Villiers of Tallany to you.'

'So it is.' Will grinned. 'You've landed on your feet, Hugh, you lucky bastard.'

'The battlefields at Bouvines were not so lucky for many, Will.'

'True, but at least some good has come out of it. And it couldn't have happened to a better man. I'm happy for you, Hugh.'

They continued to circle each other, twisting and turning their weaponry, striking and blocking attack and defence in easy, fluid motions.

Hugh looked up. 'My thanks, old friend, but it wasn't an easy landing.'

'How so?' asked Will.

Maybe the fact that Hugh had yet to bed his wife after almost three weeks of marriage!

'For one thing I have not found and brought to justice the outlaws and their leader, Le Renard.'

'You will. It's only a matter of time.'

Yes, Hugh had to be patient, it seemed. Patient until he eventually rooted out the outlaws. But there had been no sighting of them since before the wedding. For one reason or another they had not surfaced anywhere, meaning it would not be easy to track them. And in any case his mind was so preoccupied with other things it was difficult to focus and throw his usual zeal into it.

He sighed, thinking once again about his marital problems. It seemed patience was not only needed with the outlaws, but also when it came to Eleanor. Thankfully it was a virtue that he not only possessed but also harnessed in order to use it in very difficult situations—like the ones he'd faced since his betrothal.

He gave himself a mental shake and focussed on trying to win this combat with his tricky opponent. 'I need to set a trap, Will, and then I'll get them.'

He thrust forward with his quarterstaff and was met by a defensive swipe by Will. They were close again, nose to nose.

Hugh shook his head. 'The problem is that Le Renard and his men seem to have melted away into the forest. Disappeared into the night.'

'Then smoke them out. In fact, the missive I've brought from our King may be the answer.'

Hugh swerved round him and made another swipe. 'Oh? How so?'

'New taxes, Hugh.' Will expelled a breath and engaged with his friend's quarterstaff. 'Tax levies that John desperately needs and your outlaws may want to steal back. This could be exactly the way in which to entrap them, don't you think?'

'I do.'

Hugh swivelled his staff round and over his arms. He thrust forward, attempting to strike a blow to Will's ankle, but his friend foresaw his intentions and jumped in the air, avoiding it.

'Now, is that any way to show your gratitude? A low move even for you, Hugh.'

'I just wanted to see whether you're still as quick on your feet as you used to be.' Hugh chuckled.

'Glad I passed the test. And now that I've helped you with your outlaws, what is the other matter that troubles you?'

Hugh frowned. 'I don't recall saying I had other troubles.'

'When you recounted your difficult landing, you said, "for one thing…" Implying that there is another thing.'

'You know, Will, you're damned annoying.'

'Yes, but I have the right of it, have I not?' Will raised

his brow and tarried with the combat. 'Come now, man, I'm waiting.'

'You can wait until hell freezes over.'

'Dear, oh, dear—and there was I thinking that marriage to an heiress as fair as yours would mellow you. It seems I was wrong.'

'I'm warning you, Will. I don't welcome this topic of conversation.'

'Oh? And why not?'

They circled each other, toe to toe.

'Just leave it.'

Awareness suddenly trickled through Hugh, making him turn to find Eleanor walking around the edge of the castle yard with her maid, mingling with the villagers and handing out parcels from her basket.

She stopped and met his gaze, giving him a curt nod but seeming reluctant to move away.

Will paused and followed the direction of Hugh's smouldering gaze. He whistled, shaking his head.

'Don't you dare say anything,' Hugh hissed under his breath, moving forward for another attack.

But he was met with Will's quarterstaff. 'I'm not saying a thing,' Will said, pushing back against Hugh's weapon.

'Good!'

'But if I was…'

'Will…' Hugh's voice held a low warning which was soundly ignored.

'If I were to offer advice…'

'Which I would not want,' Hugh muttered out of the corner of his mouth.

'Which I would still offer, as your friend…'

Hugh took a step back and lunged forward with force, taking Will by surprise. He lost his footing and fell backwards on the ground with a thud. Will glared at his friend and rubbed the back of his head as Hugh strode towards him and held out his hand, pulling him back on his feet.

'Unsporting.'

'I know, and I'm sorry. I… I wasn't thinking.'

'Clearly.' Will looked at his friend and then back at Eleanor, still watching them from afar. He sighed. 'I would say allow for more time there as well, Hugh.'

'Are you ready to continue?' Hugh asked, ignoring him.

They began their dance again, engaging their weapons against each other.

'Although a marriage like yours has little to do with whom you actually marry and more to do with what you gain,' said Will. 'But I can see that for whatever reason it matters to you.'

'Hell's teeth, Will—are you still talking?'

'Tell me why you care?' Will asked. '*Tell* me.'

'I need to woo Eleanor.'

'Pardon me?' A slow, mischievous smile spread across Will's face. 'Well, well, Hugh… I never thought to see the day when a woman didn't swoon at the sheer sight of you.'

Hugh bit back an oath.

'Tell me, though… For what purpose do you need to woo Lady Eleanor? You're already married to her!' Will stopped for a moment and tapped his chin with his fingers. 'Ah…let's see, now… My guess would be that your lady wife is impervious to your charms.' Will defended himself against another scathing attack and continued. 'And now you wish to win your wife's heart?'

'No, I'm not interested in that!' Hugh spat. 'I just want to win her trust. I want to reassure her that not all men are like her cruel bastard of a late husband.'

And he wanted to take her to bed so that he could learn all the secrets of her body…but he couldn't voice that even to his close friend. For one thing it wasn't Will's concern, and for another a marriage that wasn't consummated could lawfully be dissolved—which was a perilous situation for both Hugh and Eleanor…not that he didn't trust his friend.

'You're in luck that I am here.' Will grinned.

'Heaven help me…'

'As I said before, you need to allow your lady to get used to you, but in the meantime you can use sweet honeyed words and *talk* yourself into her affections.'

Hugh frowned. 'Sweet honeyed words?'

'Better still, deploy a minstrel or a troubadour to bleat on about your chivalric qualities, or mayhap compose a poem of courtly love?' Will stepped forward and struck his weapon out. 'Apologies. Not words of love but words of…*trust*, was it not?' He smirked. 'Courtly trust—well, there's a novel idea.'

'You believe this to be a jest?' asked Hugh.

'On the contrary.'

'Flowery words are not going to affect Eleanor.'

'Very well—what about a gift for your lady?'

'A gift? For an heiress?'

'Really, Hugh, what is the matter with you? All women like to receive gifts,' Will said, attacking again. 'A jewel, a trinket, or a ribbon for your lady's hair?'

Hugh stopped momentarily and with his quarterstaff raised the leather cord with its silver and ruby pendant from around Will's neck. 'Like *this* little trinket? Remind me who gave this one to you of your many paramours?'

A dark shadow flashed across Will's eyes before he smiled and shook his head. 'A gift given in thanks and I've always liked it.' He shrugged. 'But it wasn't from any paramour. Anyway, we're not talking about me, but you.'

'Are we?'

'Yes. I am thinking that you should give a gift to your heiress—call it a wedding gift.'

Hugh's brows furrowed before he lifted his head and nodded. 'Much as I hate to admit it, it's not a bad notion.'

'Glad to be of help.'

'Not a jewel or a trinket, though but possibly…animals.'

'Animals? Seriously?' Will shook his head. 'I give up…'

In one single fluid movement Hugh swiftly turned, fell to his knee and swiped his quarterstaff at Will's ankles, taking his legs from under him. Then he got back to his feet and kicked Will's quarterstaff away, pointing his at Will's chest.

'You should.' Hugh panted as he made a mock bow. 'My thanks, old friend. It is always a pleasure to thrash you. Now, do you submit?'

Will grimaced as he rubbed his arm. 'I allowed you to win, you know. I wanted you to look good in front of your lady wife.'

'Of course you did.'

'By the way, your arm is bleeding.'

Hugh shook his head dismissively as he helped Will to his feet and turned to face his wife.

Yes, he needed to woo her.

Eleanor's breath hitched in her throat as she watched in secret admiration as Hugh strode towards her after his victorious sparring with Sir William.

She had on many occasions watched men train in combat with keen interest, secretly learning different techniques. The male form was hardly a novelty, and held little surprise for her, and yet she had to admit that a thrill had run through her at the glorious spectacle of her husband and Sir William stripped to the waist and training with so much skill.

They had been evenly matched, both as strong and athletic as each other. But even so Eleanor had never, ever seen a man so well built and muscular as Hugh. A sheen of sweat glistened on the bulging golden muscles that rippled across his chest, his back…and, Lord above, his arms! Oh, but his arms were so…

'Good morning to you, Eleanor.'

Hugh bowed and smiled that lop-sided smile that managed to send butterflies to her stomach.

'Hugh.' She nodded, her mouth suddenly very dry. 'Congratulations, that was well fought.'

His grin deepened, revealing a dimple. Had she missed that? Yes, it was more than likely, since Eleanor hadn't dared to look at him properly.

She glanced away, only to notice a trail of blood down his left arm. 'That needs to be cleaned up.'

'It's nothing, really.'

Eleanor wanted to insist, but found it hard to get the words out. Really, there was so much of her husband on display she didn't know where to look.

'Your friend Sir William seems nice,' she said.

'Nice?' Hugh laughed, raising his brows. 'Gallant, chivalrous, courageous or even valiant are amongst Will's favourite epithets.' Hugh raised his voice so that Will would hear.

Eleanor smiled. 'You seem close.'

'He's like an annoying younger brother but, yes we're close. Both of us poor landless knights. Well, I mean that is until recently for me…'

Eleanor looked away, feeling a little embarrassed, and was relieved when Sir William finally caught up with them, fully clothed now and sketching a formal bow, breaking the awkward silence.

'Good morrow, Lady Eleanor, how fine you look.'

Eleanor inclined her head. 'And how finely you fought, Sir William.'

Will smiled graciously. 'But, alas, not finely enough. However, gallant, chivalrous and courageous I may be I can never better Hugh. Your husband, my lady, is a legend amongst men.'

'A legend, you say?'

'Indeed.' Will grinned as Hugh turned and glared at him. 'And his talents are not restricted to the tourney or the battlefield, oh, no…' Will shook his head. 'His courtly manners are appreciated far and wide.'

'I'm sure they are, Sir William,' Eleanor said, trying to suppress the bubble of laughter that was forming at Hugh's reaction. His eyes were firing daggers at his friend. She decided to join in with the teasing. 'In fact, I have witnessed the extent of Hugh's exceptional skill in dancing.'

'Ah, yes, so nimble and light.' Will chuckled. 'And have you heard Hugh's singing voice, my lady? *No?*' he exclaimed, when Eleanor shook her head. 'But you must. It is a voice that would make a troubadour renounce his talent.'

'Stop talking all this nonsense, Will!' Hugh snapped.

'A modest man, you see, and one with so many hidden talents. One day you must ask him to recount the verses he has scribed, my lady.'

'Take no notice of him, Eleanor,' Hugh said, rubbing his shoulder.

'What was it again, Hugh? *Ode to the Heartless Thief*? Or was it *Ode to the Greenest Leaf*? I cannot remember.'

This time Eleanor could not contain her laughter.

'Haven't you got somewhere you need to be, Will?' Hugh growled.

'Indeed—I must break my fast. And don't forget what I said, Hugh.' Will winked at his friend and turned to address Eleanor. 'I will say, my lady, that Hugh the Legend is not one to make a fuss, even if he is bleeding.'

'It's nothing. Just a graze,' Hugh said dismissively.

Eleanor shook her head. 'No, it needs cleaning up and I'll do it myself. Good morning to you, Sir William.'

'My lady.' Will bowed over Eleanor's hand and flashed a grin at Hugh, who scowled back.

Chapter Five

It had been a mistake. A colossal mistake to insist on cleaning Hugh's wound herself.

Eleanor had become aware of her error the minute he sat opposite her on a bench in their solar, watching her with a guarded intensity that had almost robbed her of her breath.

Now the silence stretched, with only the noise of the crackling fire in the hearth breaking through.

Really, what had she been thinking, offering to clean Hugh's wound? Someone else could have done it and spared her the embarrassment of being in such close proximity to this man.

This man?

She had to stop thinking of Hugh as no one of consequence when the reality was screaming at her. He was her husband, and even though for now it was in name only, he *was* her husband. A very large, very looming, very real, half-naked husband.

She gulped and bent her head lower, concentrating on the task at hand rather than contemplating Hugh's sinewy taut, muscle-bound body.

Ever since their wedding night Eleanor had been anxious, knowing that her new husband would finally make the demands of her that she dreaded but expected. Instead they had continued playing chess, which he had taught her with unreserved patience. And during those moments Eleanor would lose sight of who she was with and enjoy the intricacies of the game, pitching her ability against his.

But it was more than that, and if Eleanor was honest with herself she'd say that she actually enjoyed Hugh's company as well. He treated her like an equal, respecting her views even if at times they disagreed about an issue. Yet she could not help but feel shy and unsure around him when they weren't playing.

As Lady Eleanor Tallany, and even when she dissembled as The Fox, she had purpose and confidence—but as a wife she did not.

Annoyed with herself, and the direction of her thoughts, Eleanor thrust her fingers into the pewter bowl of warmed honeyed water on the small trestle table and continued to wipe the wound clean with strips of linen.

Hugh coughed, dragging her attention back to him. 'Eleanor? I think… I believe it is done.'

'Mmm?' she muttered. 'I beg your pardon?'

She continued to wipe the wound. Rubbing it briskly, back and forth.

'I believe it's now sufficiently clean, don't you?' His eyes crinkled in amusement.

It was that blasted kiss! That astonishing, disturbing and yet melting kiss that Eleanor was so confused about. But she had more important things to think about, for the love of God—like how she could distribute food to the people who needed it and give back the silver stolen by the outlaws from Lord Edmund Balvoire to his poor beleaguered people.

She swallowed. 'Yes, so it is. I try to complete a task well.'

'That is a comfort to know. Thank you.'

A smile tugged at the corners of Hugh's lips, making her think once again of that kiss.

Oh, for goodness' sake!

Her reaction on their wedding night had been instinctive and visceral, even though she'd known that their kiss would lead them to fall into what might be considered normal and binding for a marriage contract. But Eleanor just hadn't been able to go through with it, and she was not stupid enough to believe the situation could endure indefinitely. Eventually something would have to break through the impasse.

If she was honest with herself, Eleanor was no longer as wary of Hugh, even though she had barely slept after his surprise offer on their wedding night. He had kept to his word and stayed firmly outside the bed curtain, but she could hardly pretend that curiosity wasn't getting the better of her. She seemed to be aware of him whenever he was near...or far.

His low voice interrupted her conflicted thoughts. 'I'm glad we have this opportunity to talk, actually, Eleanor, as I've been puzzling over something you said last night.'

She frowned. 'Oh, what is that?'

'I cannot help but feel that, despite Tallany being a prosperous estate, the village and its people do not seem to actually reap the benefits. Is there a reason for this?'

Eleanor lifted her head and met Hugh's inquisitive gaze. The fact that her new husband was interested in Tallany, and its vast area of land, was to be expected—especially as he was its new lord—but that he should also seem concerned about its people was something so incredible that she was momentarily speechless.

She drew in a deep breath. 'I believe that could be a consequence of the losses in France and the aftermath of Bouvines.'

'I see—or rather I do now,' he muttered, shaking his head. 'I have been away from England for so long that I had not realised that our recent failures on campaign had affected people as drastically as they have.'

Eleanor raised her brows and wondered whether Hugh really *did* see. Did he realise that the situation had been further exacerbated by the King's heavy tax scutage? Evidently not.

'Surely you knew something of what was happening back home?' she said.

'Only what was happening at court.' He grimaced. 'When you're away, all you think about is how to get through each situation, each crisis, each battle. You never stop to realise that the outcome, whether good or bad, success or failure, affects us all.' He sighed. 'I suppose that is one explanation as to why the country is plagued with so much lawlessness.'

'Indeed.'

The plight of ordinary people was the very thing that had made The Fox and the outlaws such a necessity in Tallany. Yet Hugh's incessant pursuit of them, and in particular Le Renard, was now making it incredibly difficult and dangerous to carry on as before. So Eleanor had reluctantly suspended their activities temporarily, fearing for their safety and her own if they were found out.

'I suppose you could say that when people are desperate they're forced to use any means to survive,' she couldn't stop herself from saying.

'Yes, that's natural—commendable, even—as long as it's within the confines of the law, Eleanor, otherwise we descend into a breakdown of order altogether.'

She wanted to say more, wanted to argue her point, but she kept her mouth shut. She dared not expose herself and give rise to suspicion.

He threw her a sideways glance. 'Having said that, I do, however, want you to show me how we can help Tallany's people as best we can.'

She stared at him before nodding slowly. 'Very well, my lord. I would be happy to.'

Eleanor did her best to stay detached and distant, but she could feel her resolve slipping. The truth was she couldn't help but like Hugh, however hard she tried not to. It was all so unsettling—and, frankly, she had other things to be unsettled about. Such as making sure her husband never found out about her involvement with the outlaws as Le Renard. Or the work they did to help Tallany.

She turned to fetch a cloth to dry his skin, wanting to change the topic of conversation. 'You're lucky that I don't need to stitch this up,' she said wryly. 'My stitchwork leaves a lot to be desired.'

'Is that so?' He quirked one brow. 'By your own admission, Eleanor, you have no court manners, you cannot dance, and now it seems you're poorly skilled at that bastion of female proficiency: stitching.'

'Well,' she said, smoothing the wrinkles out of her kirtle, 'it's true, nevertheless.'

'I wonder whether you are a little too disparaging of your own talents,' he said, stretching out his arm.

'I promise you I am not.' She turned and picked up a small bowl filled with thick translucent paste. 'May I apply Brunhilde's salve? It smells like something a cat might drag into the kitchens, but it has amazing healing properties. Your wound may not be big, but I wouldn't want it to fester.'

Hugh's lips curved, revealing his dimple. 'Go ahead.

And nicely diverted, my lady, but I can tell you that I am not persuaded by you in the least.'

Oh, dear, if only he wouldn't smile at her like that.

'I am very honoured that you wish to champion my woeful lack of maidenly talents, but I promise you I'm a hopeless case,' she said with a sigh as she rubbed the salve into his wound, feeling the smooth skin of his arm beneath her fingers. The sensation of touching him made her aware once again of his closeness.

'Then tell me, what are you good at?'

What *was* she good at? Not much—only the ability to survive.

As Lady Eleanor she organised the castle and worked efficiently as its chatelaine, but she also mobilised her people at times of crisis. And as Le Renard she fought for her people to have back the basic necessities that were constantly being stripped from them. She had been both master and mistress of Tallany but not any more.

She flicked her eyes upwards and met the gaze of its new master. A master just as capable as she. And Eleanor couldn't help but begrudgingly respect Hugh, despite his being King John's man.

What *was* she good at? Nothing of value for someone like Hugh.

She wished at times that she was able to reveal herself to him. She wished she could show him her dextrous, quick skills as an archer and watch his awed response when she succeeded in hitting her mark with precision again and again. But that was not something he could admire in her. No one except a select few knew of those skills. And even if Hugh were to find out, she was sure it would fill him with nothing but contempt and disgust for her.

She got up to move. 'Wait a moment whilst I fetch some fresh strips of cloth to bind it.'

Hugh's hand snaked out and caught her wrist. 'You didn't answer my question, Eleanor.'

Heat scorched her skin where his fingers touched her. 'I would have to say that I am not good at much,' she said.

'I rather doubt that,' he said, shaking his head. 'You're good at caring for Tallany and its people.'

'Possibly.'

'Oh, absolutely. I saw you giving out parcels in the village earlier. I'd wager you were handing out provisions, foods and other such stuff.'

Eleanor tilted her head and regarded him. 'We look after each other here in Tallany. Without that we have nothing.'

'True.' He nodded at his wound. 'Just as you're looking after me now, I suppose?'

'I suppose...' She shrugged, not meeting his eyes as his thumb traced a line from her wrist to her fingers, stroking each one. Each roughened and callused one...

Oh, God! In her haste to tend his wound she had removed her gloves.

'May I ask why it's been necessary to hide your hands, Eleanor?'

She tried to pull away, but he held her hand firmly in his. 'They're rough, ugly, and not befitting the Lady of Tallany.'

He frowned. 'I disagree. They're hard-working, caring hands—perfectly befitting the Lady of Tallany.'

Eleanor opened her mouth to say something, but couldn't think of anything. Instead she felt breathless as an undefinable frisson passed through her.

Hugh's gaze met hers as he continued to gently stroke her hand, then fell briefly to her lips. She felt herself moving closer to him. But just as she was almost in his arms a sudden knock at the door jolted them apart. A servant walked in, bowed, then retrieved the bowl of dirty water and put a fresh one on the small trestle table.

Eleanor exhaled slowly. 'I think, my lord, that we're finished here,' she said, turning sharply on her heel.

This simply would not do. She could not afford to lose sight of her situation and of where her husband's fealty lay. The stakes were far too high and far too dangerous—which meant that she must not allow herself to get drawn in by Hugh or get too close to him.

And far more important than any of that…

She must stop thinking about that kiss!

Hugh was wound so tightly he could barely concentrate, let alone focus on a simple task such as eating his meal, even though his stomach was empty.

He glanced around the busy hall as people tucked in to the delicious trenchers of food—strips of pheasant with dark quince and spring lamb cooked in a nutmeg-spiced sauce—and wondered where his appetite had gone.

He poured himself another mug of ale and threw it back, swiping at his mouth before pouring another. He had no idea about that or anything else, so addled were his senses by the woman sitting next to him. The woman he should be wooing but found himself avoiding this evening.

Hell!

What was the matter with him? He couldn't stop thinking that just when she had been almost in his arms she'd jumped away, faster than a frightened doe. And it had been nothing to do with any interruption. The desire he'd felt had intensified even after so many hours and he couldn't stop thinking about it. Annoyingly, Eleanor seemed to invade his thoughts far too much of the time for his peace of mind.

'What is wrong with you this evening?' Will hissed, on the other side of him.

'Nothing.' Hugh scowled over his mug without looking up.

'There I was, under the firm belief that I was to witness the finer points of courtship, but clearly I was wrong.'

'God's breath, just leave it alone.'

Will ignored him and pressed on. 'Most people would agree it strange—odd, even—that a man should begin to court a woman *after* he has wed her, but then you were never one to follow convention too strictly, were you?'

'Lower your voice, for the love of God. Someone may hear.' Hugh indicated Eleanor's direction with a slight tilt of his head.

'I am intrigued to know what that may be worth.'

'Your head remaining attached to your body.'

Will grinned. 'Fair enough,' he said, tossing back his ale. 'But for pity's sake get on with it. You are supposed to be wooing your lady.'

'I am doing so.'

'Beg pardon—my mistake,' Will said sardonically. 'Really, Hugh, you have been silent all evening. Talk to her, make her laugh—do something.'

'What am I? A performing jester?'

'That would preferable than this brooding, my lord.'

With that said, Will turned his back on his friend and started a conversation with a few men sitting adjacent to him.

If only it were that easy. He *had* been talking to Eleanor, and he *was* getting to know her, but every time he thought they were becoming close she would pull back and remember that she wanted nothing to do with him.

Earlier, he had been surprised to discover it was actual hard work that had resulted in those callused fingers which she tried to hide and not because she was some sort of pampered heiress. The more he got to know her, the more his interest and attraction for her grew. He certainly admired her—but, damn it, he desired her too... and that was beginning to cause all manner of discomfort within him.

'Hugh? Does your arm still pain you?' Eleanor asked, placing her hand briefly on his shoulder to get his attention.

'No, it's fine,' he said gruffly, staring at the mug in his hand.

'Are you sure?'

'Perfectly.'

'Is there something I can do for you?'

He almost choked on the ale he was drinking.

Something she could do?

Lord above, but he could think of many things she could do and that he would love to do to her...

No, no, no. That would not do! He had to stop these thoughts.

Even her voice tonight held a certain sensual, husky tone that was probably a figment of his imagination. His curious mind wondered still on the cries of breathless pleasure that he might evoke if he could only kiss her and...

'Did you...did you just growl at me, my lord?'

Hugh turned his head and finally met Eleanor's eyes, fixing a half-smile on his face that felt strained even to him. His gaze lingered on her mouth as she caught her plump bottom lip between her teeth. She was holding a few strips of meat dripping in their tender juices between her fingers.

'I'm hungry, that's all.'

Impulsively, evidently without thinking, Eleanor fed him the morsel she had been holding and wiped a little of the sauce from the side of his lip. Her fingers grazed his teeth, so close that he could have nipped them if he had wanted to.

He didn't... Instead, frozen, he watched her for a heart-beat. Then, before he knew what he was doing, he held her wrist in place and licked the sauce off her long fingers.

Eleanor's eyes widened in shock, awareness no doubt catching up with her, as he pressed his eyes shut and ex-haled sharply, realising his mistake.

To spare her blushes, and his own, Hugh abruptly got to his feet, inclined his head and turned on his heel, catch-ing Will's eye, who shook his head as he left. *Damn!*

Ambling through the hall, Hugh exchanged greetings and small talk with the boisterous groups of his men mill-ing around. He chuckled at a jest, slapped Gilbert Clay-more on the back, and nodded in agreement with whatever the old steward had said without retaining a word of it.

Nonchalantly he slipped out of the crowded, noisy hall, hoping no one had noticed his discomfort.

The moment Hugh stepped outside his smile slipped and he let out a shaky breath. Closing his eyes, he leaned his forehead against a stone wall, welcoming the rough, cool feeling against his skin.

Dear God, what was *wrong* with him?

Hugh returned to their chamber much later, after clear-ing his head and putting in place a few things that he had planned with Will for the morning. The room was drenched in the moonlight seeping in through the arched window, and the open shutters were letting in the frigid night air. He smiled to himself. How like Eleanor to go against normal convention and allow the cold into their chamber whilst the fire was still smoking and spluttering in the hearth.

'Hugh, is that you?'

He turned and saw the shadowy silhouette of his wife sitting on the bed. The thick, heavy bed curtain pulled and tied back.

Now, *that* was a surprise. That curtain had been shut firmly, pushing him out, since their wedding night.

'Aye. Go back to sleep, Eleanor.'

'I couldn't sleep. I was worried.'

'I'm sorry.' Even to his own ears his voice sounded flat.

'You have nothing to apologise for,' she said softly.

Hugh sighed. 'I don't know how, but I constantly misstep around you. It must be that I never expected to be married—especially to a someone like you, my lady.'

'Behind the heiress it's just me.' She shrugged. 'I'm only a woman, Hugh—remember?'

He smiled, recollecting their ride out together, many weeks ago now. But, no, Eleanor Tallany was not 'only a woman'. His heart quickened at the thought. She was far, far more. She cared about her people...*their* people. She was not just the chatelaine of Tallany but its heart and soul.

'I had hoped for a rematch, Hugh, and had even set up the board with all the pieces.'

His lips twitched. 'I'm sorry to disappoint you but I'm in no state for a game of chess. My skills would be woefully lacking.'

'Ah, but that would be my perfect opportunity to finally gain the upper hand and beat you.'

Was Eleanor teasing him? Again?

'The shame that you'd take advantage of a man in his cups...' He grinned as she chuckled softly. 'Although you will get your opportunity to beat me, Eleanor, never fear. I cannot think of any other, apart from Will, who has challenged me as much as you. Our matches have been closely fought. You may not believe that you have any talents—which is nonsense, anyway—but in this you most certainly do.'

The laughter died on her lips and Hugh sensed that she was blushing—not that he could see.

He gave himself a mental shake. 'Anyway, what were you worried about? Surely not about me.'

'Of course I was. Where did you go?' She leaned forward, rubbing her eyes.

'Mmm? I had business to attend to.' He looked around the room. 'Eleanor, where is my pallet?'

'I… I had your squire remove it,' she said, biting her lip.

What? His brows met in the middle as he frowned quizzically. 'Why?' He swallowed taking a hesitant step towards her. 'Eleanor?'

Her eyes widened as she covered her mouth with her hand. 'Oh, no—I didn't mean… Saints above! You thought that I wanted to…?'

'Calm yourself, my lady. I have given you my word regarding *that*,' he said. 'But mayhap you will enlighten me as to exactly where I should sleep?' He crossed his arms over his chest and leaned back against the coffer.

'Well, here in the bed, of course.' She patted the coverlet. 'It's big enough for both of us.'

He stared at her blankly.

Lord above, was she trying to kill him slowly?

Apparently Eleanor was still talking. 'And, to be honest, I hadn't realised that your pallet was so lumpy.'

She was watching him, trying to gauge his response, but he wasn't giving one.

She sighed and he saw her shoulders slump. 'I'm sorry. Should we fetch the pallet back? I thought you may sleep better on the bed.'

Ha! As if he would be able to sleep *now*! If he had believed that sleep had evaded him merely because he was in the same room as Eleanor Tallany, God alone knew what his nights were going to be like lying next to her. It was going to be akin to slow, excruciating torture.

Heaven help him, though. He had given his word and even if it would kill him, he would wait until his wife came to him.

'No, it's fine.' He dragged a shaky hand through his hair. 'If you feel comfortable for us to share a bed for… er…sleeping purposes, then I'm happy to oblige.' He swallowed down what else he'd be happy to do.

She smiled and lay back on the bed as he sat down to take off his shoes and stretched his arms to remove his linen tunic. As he was pulling off his braies she shot back up, her arms either side of her, apparently ready to fly out of the room if she had to.

'What are you doing?' she asked.

A bemused grin lit his face. 'My lady, I never sleep with a stitch of clothing.'

'Do you mean to tell me that all this time you have been sleeping…?' she said, waving her hand in the direction of the corner of the chamber where once the lumpy pallet had been.

'Naked as the day as I was born!' He chuckled. 'Don't tell me you haven't sneaked a look?'

'No! No, I haven't.'

'I can believe it. Well, to spare your blushes I will keep my hose on. Would that suffice?' He sighed as she moved to the other side of the bed.

'Yes, but I… I didn't realise that you…without any…'

'So, it would seem. Would you prefer it if I slept elsewhere, Eleanor?'

'No! That's not necessary. Surely we can muddle along as bedfellows. We are married, after all.' She shifted uncomfortably.

He gave her an eloquent look and shook his head as he sat on the bed. 'Very well, wife, I will bid you goodnight. And, Eleanor?' He noticed she gulped as her gaze lingered on his bare chest and shoulders, just as before when she had tended to his wound. 'Thank you for thinking of my comfort.'

She gave a curt nod before pulling the coverlet higher and turning to sleep with her back to him.

Well, then, this was interesting… From the vivid curiosity he'd glanced in Eleanor's eyes mayhap she wasn't as immune to him as he'd initially thought.

After what seemed many hours, tossing and turning, Hugh was about to drift off to sleep when he felt Eleanor tentatively lay her hand on his shoulder. Just as quickly she removed it.

'Is everything all right?' he asked, in a muffled, sleepy voice.

'It's nothing… Hugh, I wondered if you were awake…'

'Hmm…? I am now.'

'I'm sorry. I didn't mean to wake you up but I can't get to sleep,' she murmured.

'Can I help you with anything?'

'Well, yes, you can ,' she whispered.

That got his attention. His eyes flew open and slowly he turned his head and met her quizzical gaze. 'Oh?' he croaked. 'What would you have me do?'

She was biting the inside of her cheek, clearly finding whatever she wanted from him difficult to ask for. Well, now… His heart beat a little faster. Could she…did she want the same thing as him?

She rubbed her forehead with the back of her hand. 'Actually, I don't believe what I desire from you will be conceivably, remotely possible…' She lay down again with her back to him.

Hugh darted to the other side of the bed, reaching for her. 'Whoa, wait—wait… Why not let me be the judge of that.' He gently turned Eleanor around and stroked her cheek with his callused knuckles. 'Well, Eleanor?'

He raised his brow, putting his weight on one elbow and waiting eagerly for her to respond. He sent a silent prayer, willing her to say the words he longed to hear from her.

'I don't know that I should…' She shuffled beneath him, clearly flustered.

'Oh, you should—you definitely should,' he murmured.

Please, just say it!

'I'm not certain that it's an entirely appropriate thing for me to ask you.' A crease appeared between her brows.

'Oh, it will be. Ask me anything, Eleanor—nay, demand it of me. As you reminded me earlier, we're married.'

For the love of God, just say it!

'Yes, of course… Well, it's just that I…'

Hugh's heart was hammering against his chest now.

'Just say what it is you want from me.' He stroked the length of her velvety hair, then along the side of her shoulders and down her arm. Reaching for her hand, he clasped it and gave it a squeeze of encouragement. 'Go on, Eleanor.'

'Very well. You see, there is something that has been on my mind all day…'

'There has?' he ground out, hoping that he was still somehow breathing.

'Yes?'

Just say it, please!

'I want… I mean, if it's not too much trouble, I want to ask you to teach me…'

'Anything—anything at all.' Hugh leaned in closer.

'The impressive quarterstaff technique you exhibited when you were sparring with Sir William.'

Hugh blinked. *'What?'* He pulled back, staring at her. 'What did you say?' he asked, not trusting he had heard her correctly.

Eleanor shrank back slightly, but replied. 'That swipe, turn and bend thing was remarkable, and I wondered…' She shook her head slowly. 'I'm sorry. It was a ridiculous thing to ask.'

Hugh sat up and studied her for a moment. 'Let me understand this.' He dragged his fingers through his dark hair. 'You are asking me to show you how to perform a certain move that you saw me exhibit…' he exhaled '…in combat?'

'Yes,' she whispered. 'I thought I might need to use it to protect myself one day.'

He stared at her for a moment before responding. 'There is no need. I will always protect you, my lady.'

'But there *is* a need—do you not think? One never knows when the situation may arise, and a lady should know how to defend herself, even if it's rudimentary.'

'True, true…' It was Hugh's turn to rub his forehead. 'But really, Eleanor, I cannot believe that this matter is of such importance to you that you had to ask me at this hour.'

She'd woken him up for this?

Eleanor nodded in resignation. 'No…no, you are right.

I'm so sorry to have woken you up. Let's go back to sleep.'
She plumped her pillow and flopped against it.

As if sleep was a possibility now.

He groaned inwardly, thinking how he had misjudged
her and assumed she was bent on more amorous pursuits.

Damn!

Hugh knew he should be shocked at her request, but it
was so typical of Eleanor. He sighed, and after a moment's
reflection said, 'Very well. If it means so much to you.'

'Really? Do you mean that?' She grasped his hand and
held it against her cheek.

'Yes, Eleanor. I do.' Even in the dim light, Hugh could
make out the gleam in her eyes. 'I'll show you on the
morrow, if you like,' he said, shuffling back to his side
of the bed.

'Oh, thank you! Thank you so much.'

Hugh tucked his hand behind his head, smothering the
urge to laugh. 'My pleasure. Now, let's try for some sleep.'

If only it were that easy. Mayhap if he could think of
something to count he might possibly drift off.

The image of what he had planned as her wedding
present popped into his head and he grinned.

Chapter Six

'Sheep? You…you have bought sheep?' Eleanor said quietly. 'For me?' She regarded Hugh blankly.

They were standing together outside the curtain wall of the castle, on the green pasture on the edge of the demesne land that was usually used for growing crops but now was seemingly to be used to rear livestock.

'Ah, but not just an ordinary flock of sheep. This particular breed yields an incredible quality of soft fleece, as you can see—or rather feel.'

Eleanor stared at the soft sheepskin in one hand and the sealed scroll in another. 'I don't understand…'

'There's not much to understand, Eleanor. You are now the proud owner of three hundred and fifty sheep. That is if the tallies are correct.'

'Three hundred and fifty…' She looked at him, incredulous. 'But…but why?'

Hugh chuckled softly. 'It's a wedding present, my lady. Don't tell me you have never received a gift?'

She hadn't. Not since she was a child. But Hugh didn't need to know that. He didn't need to know anything about her miserable past once her father and all her family had perished. Gifts? No, not for her.

His expression softened. 'Well, what do you think?' He raised a brow, waiting for her to respond.

That was just it. Eleanor *couldn't* think when she was around her husband. He deprived her of breath and of thought, which both baffled and bewildered her. Everything she'd thought she knew, thought to be true about men, about what it meant to be married, was slowly changing because of... Hugh.

'I... I don't know what to say.' She shook her head slowly, not knowing whether to laugh or cry at his kindness.

'Say you like it? It may not be the usual thing to give a woman a flock of sheep, but then you're...'

'Different? Unusual?' she asked, raising her brows.

'Well, yes, but that makes you special,' he replied, seeming a little taken aback at what he had no doubt inadvertently uttered.

Eleanor flushed at his words, his lovely, kind words, and laid her hands on his shoulders, lifting herself on her toes and pressing her lips to his.

He looked surprised, and a slow smile spread on his face. 'Well, my lady, does that mean my gift has met with your approval?'

'Yes,' she swallowed. 'It does.'

He curled his hands around her waist and grinned. 'Good. They're yours to do with as you see fit. The quality of wool, itself, could yield a good profit.'

'No one has ever given me anything like this. Thank you.' She choked slightly with emotion as she felt the softness of the sheepskin against her cheek. 'And, yes, it's incredibly soft and would make the finest cloth. Oh, Hugh, the income this could generate will help Tallany's long-term prosperity.'

He watched her for a moment. 'You really care, don't you?' he asked gently.

She nodded unable to voice her response as she touched the soft pelt beneath her fingers absently.

'Well, so do I,' he said.

Eleanor flicked her gaze up to meet his, her eyes wide with amazement. She had done her best to keep her husband at arm's length, but all her defences were crumbling one by one.

It was staggering, the extent of the confused coil that she was in. Hugh was everything Richard had not been. Kind, considerate and patient, as well as a whole host of other things that put her to blush. The way Hugh gazed or smiled at her made her stomach flip. She was shocked by the changes in her feelings towards him, and even more shocked that she was wondering, at times, what intimacy might be like with Hugh.

Sheep, for the love of God!

It made her want to throw her head back and laugh at the absurdity of it all. She couldn't quite believe it. Couldn't believe that her husband would be so thoughtful. For Hugh to gift her something so personal, knowing how much it would mean to her was both touching and unexpected. The thought of being able to manage something that would yield a profit for her people made her feel overwhelmed, if not a little tearful.

Oh, Lord! She swallowed uncomfortably, willing herself to continue with caution and not get carried away with her emotions. She didn't know what to make of his kindness and in truth wasn't sure she deserved it.

'What is it?' Hugh whispered.

'Nothing… I'm just a little surprised by all this.' Eleanor shuffled her feet on the ground, feeling a little self-conscious.

'Don't be. It's perfectly acceptable for a husband to give his bride a wedding present,' he said.

Eleanor nodded absently.

'Besides, I may have an ulterior motive, my lady.'

He winked at her, grinning, then tightened his hold around her waist. A flutter went through her whole body as he drew her a little closer, as if an invisible cord was dragging her to him. He cupped the side of her face, tilting it upwards. Eleanor was startled to see the intensity in Hugh's heated expression. He smiled in that way of his that made her feel a little breathless as he dipped his head and kissed her forehead, her cheeks and her lips.

'You must know that I'm ruthlessly trying to seduce you, Eleanor.'

'With sheep?' Her lips twitched at the corners.

'Naturally.'

From somewhere behind her she heard someone coughing, clearing his throat. She pulled away, and this time Hugh let her go.

'Good morning, my lord and lady, and what a fine and fruitful morning it is.' Sir William's voice was laced with amusement.

Eleanor turned just as he sketched an elaborate bow.

'Ah, Will, impeccable timing as always,' Hugh said sardonically.

'Indeed. I do try to please.' He smirked. 'Now, my lady, am I right that the idea of being a shepherdess is to your taste?'

Eleanor giggled. 'It is—and please call me Eleanor.'

'Thank you.' He raised her hand to his lips. 'And by the same token it's Will. Sir William is far too formal, don't you think?'

'Very well, that's enough of that,' Hugh ground out,

crossing his arms over his chest. 'Be warned, Eleanor, Will is a shameless flirt.'

Will clasped his chest dramatically with one hand. 'You wound me—and when I come bearing yet more gifts.' He lifted the other hand, which held two quarter-staffs.

Eleanor's eyes flicked to Hugh in confusion. Had he told his friend about her desire to learn about using the weaponry the two of them had sparred with yesterday? It was somehow unsettling that he had. Even more so that neither man seemed to be shocked by such a request from a woman.

Hugh seemed to sense her discomfort and leaned in towards her. 'It's all right, my lady, your secret is safe with him.'

Both men laughed with the easiness and understanding that only came with a long-standing friendship such as theirs.

She felt a sudden jolt inside as realisation dawned on her. No, none of her secrets was safe with Sir William, nor even with Hugh. She would do well to remember that.

The cool antechamber, with its high wooden-beamed ceiling and its large ornate furniture pushed to one side, made a perfect substitute for the training ground, since their one and only session with the quarterstaff would take place in private. Combat training not being the normal pursuit of a woman.

'I'm ready and waiting,' she said.

Hugh nodded and handed her a quarterstaff. 'Very well. Now, copy my stance, Eleanor. Put your weight on your legs, slightly apart, and bend your knees. Good, now we can begin...'

He held the long shaft of the quarterstaff across himself and gripped it on either side.

'Hold it in front of you like this and lean in.'

'Like this?'

'Very good—remember your footwork, my lady. Make sure you are light on your feet at all times.'

Hugh started to move stealthily to one side, prompting Eleanor to move too.

'And so begins our dance around each other.' The corners of Hugh's lips curved. 'Very good.'

'Well, I can see now why you're so good at dancing.' Eleanor shook her head and chuckled as her skirts swished against the floor.

'Just so, and the dance of combat is no less intense than any other. Now, concentrate—because at any moment I may strike out.' Hugh lunged forward slowly with his quarterstaff. 'Like this. Now you need to defend yourself.'

Eleanor thrust up her weapon and made contact against Hugh's.

Whack.

'Too excessive. Yield it lightly, Eleanor. But at all times defend, deflect and be ruthlessly dextrous.'

'Surely not ruthless, my lord?' Her lips quirked into a smile.

'Oh, yes, Eleanor. The key to the quarterstaff, unlike other weaponry, is anticipation.'

'Anticipation?'

'Indeed. You must be swift, nimble and quick-witted, but at all times remember to anticipate me….'

The slow smile he gave her almost made her drop her weapon and swoon. Lord, what was happening to her?

She gave herself a mental shake and tried to do as Hugh had instructed and concentrate. The truth was that, although the quarterstaff was new to her, she was well trained in the art of combat. Her father, and after his death Gilbert her steward, had secretly taught her what they deemed necessary skills. The fact that Eleanor was a keen student, and instantly took to being 'ruthlessly dextrous', as Hugh had put it, meant that she was highly skilled and proficient.

Not that her husband knew any of this, and that was a reminder not to give herself away.

So she played down her natural ability and made herself look a little clumsy.

'Very well…now I want to show you the stance you must adopt when you attack. Imagine we're adversaries.'

Eleanor heard Hugh inhale deeply as he placed his quarterstaff on the floor and walked behind her, facing her back.

'Surely not?' she said, disconcerted that he was so close behind her.

Hugh levelled the quarterstaff Eleanor was holding, lifting it higher. 'That's it—keep your weapon at this angle,' he said, covering her hands with his. 'Keep your head forward, tilt your chin a little higher. A bit more. Good, now widen your legs, keeping your balance on your back leg.'

He removed his hands, only to place them either side of Eleanor's waist, making her gulp.

'You need to take a big step forward, pushing through from here,' he said, squeezing her waist gently. 'And, no, I am not your enemy, Eleanor…but imagine that I am,' he whispered, his lips close to her ear, tickling the column of her neck.

She felt the absence of the warmth of his hands around her waist as he detached them and ambled back to face her, picking up his weapon.

'It would be more than my life's worth to cross swords

with you, or in this case a quarterstaff, but let's pretend, shall we?'

He smiled that lop-sided smile that did strange things to her.

'Yes, let's,' she said, returning his smile.

Hugh adjusted her hold on the quarterstaff and tilted her chin up. 'Keep thrusting forward with your weapon to attack.'

'Like this?'

'Good. Now, do that again whilst I show you the defensive stance you need to adopt.'

Eleanor tried not to notice the graceful movements of her husband, or his rippling muscles as he deflected each challenging swipe she made with her weapon.

He stopped abruptly, holding out his hand. 'Now we will switch around and I shall attack whilst you block me.'

Hugh lunged forward, striking with his weapon slowly to allow Eleanor to intercept his attack—which she did ineptly.

'Not bad, my lady,' he said, despite her deliberately bad attempt. Not that Hugh knew any better.

'I'm doing as you instructed.' She shrugged. 'I'm anticipating you.'

'Are you, now?' he said softly. 'As much as you anticipate me, Eleanor, you never fail to surprise me.'

Her heart quickened—and not because of the exercise. 'Is…is that a good thing?'

'Aye, very good.' The timbre of his voice was so low that she felt it rumble through her.

'Take a step closer,' he panted. 'So that we're eye to eye and both our weapons are engaged.'

Eleanor did as he bade and watched him, mesmerised.

'Good. And now…now we must… We need to…' Hugh's voice trailed away.

She was so close that she could see the flecks of gold and amber in his verdant green eyes. They held a raw emotion that transcended anything she had ever seen before. He stilled, and suddenly the very air in the chamber seem to have been sucked out.

Hugh said something under his breath as he gripped her quarterstaff and gently tugged it until she let go. He tossed both weapons to one side. The tension that crackled between them was now a different sort of anticipation. His fingers tentatively reached for her head and unbound her hair, taking out the pins and watching as it tumbled down in waves around her shoulders.

Dear God, he wanted her—and, shockingly, it no longer scared her. When and how had that happened? Even more shockingly, she wanted him too. It bewildered and confused her, but nevertheless it was true.

Her eyes flicked to his lips, smooth and sensual. She exhaled quick hot breaths. Oh, Lord, she really was going to swoon. Hugh's gaze locked onto hers as his fingers curled around her waist, gently pulling her closer until they were almost touching, and she trembled.

Anticipation, indeed!

Without any warning Hugh swooped down and kissed her, open-mouthed. His tongue slid across her lips and plunged in, savouring her hungrily as a soft moan escaped her lips. His other hand slipped into her hair and moved round to the back of her head, anchoring her to him.

Eleanor clung to Hugh and tried to match him with the same fervour, exploring and tasting him as he pressed his body against hers, hard and warm, enveloping her. More and more they fell deeper into the kiss, which now softened into heady exploration. Longing giving way to questioning possibilities.

Slowly Hugh pulled away from her lips and pressed

hot kisses on her cheeks, down the column of her neck. Then he moved back to her lips.

'Eleanor…' he whispered softly against her hair. 'What have you done to me?' He nipped the tender spot just behind her ear.

What had she done to him?

What was he doing to *her*?

Had a kiss ever felt like this? This inexplicable wonder?

'I want you. God knows I do.' He gazed searchingly in her eyes. 'But I understand if you're still not… I mean if you need more time.' He sighed heavily, pulling Eleanor into his arms and stroking the length of her hair.

Oh, Lord, she knew what that meant… But could she? Was she ready?

'Think on it. I will come to you only if you want me to. But…' He swallowed. 'I cannot kiss you or sleep next to you in bed without wanting more.' He pressed his forehead against hers. 'I am only but a man, Eleanor, and a weak-willed man, it seems.'

No, he wasn't. Hugh had honour and kindness coursing through his veins and he was nothing like Richard. It stood to reason that sleeping with him would be different. Besides, he was her husband, and Eleanor knew that they had to cement their union and consummate their marriage eventually.

In any case, curiosity was getting the better of her, wasn't it? No, it was more than that. She *liked* him, and could no longer deny her attraction and desire for him.

She lifted her head and met his quizzical gaze. She smiled. 'Yes, you're right.'

He sighed. 'Exactly. I'll find somewhere else to sleep without causing any suspicion and—'

'No… No, Hugh, that's not what I meant.' She flushed,

not knowing how to put it into words. 'I… I don't want you to sleep anywhere else.'

Hugh pulled back, studying her for a moment. 'Well, now… Does that…? Does that mean what I think it does?' He arched a brow. 'I never did believe that you were repulsed by my kiss.'

'Are you bragging, my lord?'

'Absolutely.' He chuckled. 'I hope this happy event is going to come sooner rather than later, but never fear: I'll wait until you cannot resist me any more.'

She giggled, feeling lighter than she had in a long time. But when had she *ever* felt like this? Hugh was unlike anyone she had met before. He valued her and made her feel special. He didn't deride her or ridicule her for being different, nor did he take pleasure in hurting her… And yet, a little voice warned her, she could get hurt. In more ways than one.

No, she mustn't allow her feelings to get the better of her. She had told him that her heart would never be his. It was the only way to protect herself. Eleanor would do her duty, but no more than that. Hugh was King John's man and he would never forsake his fealty to his liege.

They both jumped as they heard an urgent knocking on the door of the antechamber.

'My lord, your presence is needed immediately,' a muffled male voice said from the other side of the door.

For one of Hugh's men to come so deep into their private solar could only mean one thing—it was something important.

'What is it?' Hugh responded.

'The outlaws have been sighted in the woods outside the demesne!' the voice cried.

'This is turning out to be a good day.' He smiled at Eleanor, then called out to his man. 'Saddle my horse. I will be there presently.'

Chapter Seven

The next few hours were spent in a state of anxious confusion. As dusk settled Eleanor was racking her brain, trying to understand how this calamitous situation could have come about. She was always meticulous in her plans—always. Leaving no detail to chance and never taking unnecessary risks.

But this was different. She had issued no orders to her outlaws.

Had they acted on their own initiative? In which case, why? Had they grown weary? Restless? Since her marriage it had been too dangerous for Le Renard to lead her men in person, so had they taken things into their own hands?

Not that they knew her to be The Fox. No, only three people knew of her secret: her maid Brunhilde, her steward Gilbert Claymore, and of course Father Thomas. The outlaws knew that Lady Eleanor aided and abetted them, but not that she was Le Renard. That would be far too risky.

She twisted the corner of her veil tightly in her hand, her knuckles white. She had to ensure the safety of the outlaws at whatever cost, and had instructed Gilbert to warn them that Hugh and his men were coming after them. It was imperative that they'd got the message, but she had yet to discover whether the mission had been successful or not.

Eleanor stared out of the arched window, leaning against the cold stone wall, and sighed, thinking of the dangers the outlaws—her friends—would be facing.

They were a group of ordinary men, immersed in extraordinary deeds. Local men from all walks of life who had sworn their fealty and allegiance to her when she had helped them survive the hunger and misery that had swept the north. Good, true men. And when they came together in secret to form their band of brotherhood they served Eleanor to eradicate tyranny.

With a little help from their elusive leader, Le Renard, of course.

Her decision to defy the King and his demands for yet more scutage had not been an easy one, and nor had it been taken lightly. Yet, it had been either that or face despair and destitution. Eleanor had had to do *something*, even though it would be incredibly dangerous.

So, with Gilbert's aid, she had formulated a plan. An outrageous plan that had brought like-minded people together for a common cause and to work under a secret leader, Le Renard. A leader whom Lady Eleanor, Gilbert and Father Thomas had vouchsafed to the assembled group of outlaws who had been initially sceptical of an outsider.

The outlaws believed in purging their land of the greed and corruption that had taken root under King John's reign. And they did it by using subterfuge, cunning and guise, making them nameless traitors in the eyes of the law. And being one of them meant that Eleanor's position was precarious, at best.

Yet the need to be Le Renard was as essential to her as the very air she breathed. It was from the ashes of her abusive first marriage that The Fox had risen, giving her purpose, helping her survive. It had meant that Eleanor could bury the shame that she carried and turn it into something good—something that enabled her to fight back. Fight for something she not only believed in but was prepared to die for… Justice.

As a woman she could do nothing, but as Le Renard she could do plenty—and in time she would do much, much more. However, since her marriage, the walls of Tallany Castle had felt as if they were closing in and she'd had to be more careful than ever before. One wrong step and it would all crumble around her.

Eleanor scrambled out of the solar as she recognised the shadowy figure of Gilbert Claymore from her chamber window, riding back into the inner bailey in haste. She grabbed a flame torch and climbed down the dark spiral stairwell, meeting her old steward as he hurried towards her.

'My lady.' Gilbert bowed swiftly. 'You shouldn't be here at this time.'

'Never mind that—what news?'

'We reached the hideout and informed the group of your warning.'

'Thank God!' She exhaled in relief.

'Your lord husband, though…he is a masterful horseman. Faster than any man I have ever seen. He caught up with them as they were getting away and gave chase.'

Having seen him ride effortlessly quickly during their race, she could vouchsafe Hugh's prowess on horseback. This was worrying—very worrying indeed.

'And what of the group? Are they all…? Are they still at risk?'

'I cannot tell, my lady. I had to ride back quickly, for fear of being exposed, but I believe your husband, his friend Sir William and others are returning now.'

'Then I must take my leave of you. I thank you, Gilbert, as always.'

'I live to serve you, my lady.' He inclined his head. 'Let's hope I got there in time and that our friends are safe.'

She scurried back up the spiral stairwell, depositing the torch back into its ornate sconce, and then walked into the inner bailey, which was a hive of activity even at this late hour.

Had it only been earlier this day that Hugh had gifted her a flock of sheep, taught her the art of combat and then kissed her with an all-consuming passion that she could still feel now? How had it descended into this… this mayhem?

A jolt of realisation hit her. Despite the fact that she now liked, admired and was hopelessly attracted to her husband, they did not share the same beliefs. If a line were drawn in the sand, they would always be on different sides.

Eleanor watched Hugh and the others as they rode in through the gatehouse and into the inner bailey, dismounting their horses. She smoothed down her veil, which was chafing at the neck.

'I'm glad to see you return, my lord. Were you…' she swallowed '…successful?'

Hugh bowed and briefly raised her hand to his lips. He looked dishevelled, with mud spattered along his jerkin, braies and boots.

'Indeed, Eleanor. We have caught two of the criminal outlaws.' He gestured, tilting his chin at Will, who was pulling two men bound and gagged down from the back of a horse. 'But you shouldn't be here right now. This is no place for a lady. I will see you in our solar.'

Eleanor glanced at the men without revealing that she recognised them, and schooled her features into an expression of indifference at the sight of her friends, dirty with mud, grime and goodness knew what matted into their hair.

'What will happen now?' she demanded.

He inhaled. 'Justice.'

With that, he trudged towards the hall, following his men.

Justice?

Lord alone knew what that meant—not that she believed Hugh to be cruel.

Eleanor closed her eyes. No, he was a good, honourable man, but she knew what happened to traitors if they were found guilty. She had to do all she could to help her friends Osbert and Godwin, who were also good and honourable. And that meant that they had to be found innocent of any charges they were accused of. She had to find a way to achieve that.

'Hugh—wait.'

Her husband turned, his brow furrowed. 'What is it, Eleanor?'

She straightened her back and met his eyes. 'I want to accompany you when you question those men.'

'Why? This is not a matter for you to involve yourself in.'

Hugh's dark hair flopped over one eye and Eleanor watched him drag it back with his fingers, making her wish that she had done it herself.

She gave herself a mental shake. 'Even so, I am the lady of this castle—the chatelaine—and I have always been involved with matters related to Tallany.'

'I understand, however, this is somewhat different, wouldn't you say?'

'I would. But since I have experience in such matters…'

'Your concern is misplaced, Eleanor.' He tilted his head in irritation. 'As the new Lord of Tallany, I promise they will get a fair trial. Now, if you'll excuse me?'

'Please, Hugh,' she pleaded. 'Please.'

He sighed, giving her a wry smile. 'Very well, if it means that much to you. But this is important, Eleanor. I cannot have interruptions at the proceedings.'

The great hall held a tension that seemed to permeate the night air. The hammer-beam ceiling loomed large and menacingly dark, giving the room an eerie edge. Large flame torches fixed in metal sconces burned throughout the decorative stone walls of the hall, casting shadows light and dark and everything in between.

So different from the raucous celebrations of the wedding feast all those weeks ago.

Hugh sat on the dais with Will beside him, drumming a beat on a trestle table stripped of its usual finery, and on the other side sat Eleanor, resplendent in a green wool dress and a simple cream veil with the intricate Tallany silver circlet on her head.

Not that Hugh understood why his wife insisted on being present at his questioning of the two traitors. She shouldn't be here—it wasn't a place for a woman. He had complied with her wishes in a moment of weakness and he didn't want to quarrel with her—especially now that he was beginning to win her trust. But he didn't have to like it.

Lord knew, he shouldn't expect anything less from Eleanor; his wife was unlike any woman he had ever met.

The steward was standing with a few of the Tallany knights in the corner, and he caught Hugh's eye and nodded.

Hugh stepped down and stood in front the two beleaguered men, their hands bound behind them, kneeling in the middle of the floor on newly strewn rushes.

'I want you to think very hard about what I am about to ask,' he ground out in a clipped, low voice. 'Give us the information we seek about the outlaw bandits you're involved with.'

One of the accused men raised his sagging head and shook it with effort. 'Please, milord, me and Godwin, here, we know of no outlaws—you have to believe us!'

'I don't—as you well know.'

Hugh fixed his gaze on one man and then the other. There was moment of silence which he allowed to stretch as he towered over them, his hands on either side of his waist.

'Well?'

'I beseech you milord…me lady. We know nothing—on my honour.'

'You think you have honour as thieves? I don't believe it.' Hugh knelt on one knee and spoke quietly. 'Osbert, blacksmith of Spalford?' He continued when the man nodded without looking up. 'We know of your involvement with the group as you were chased by us. Come, man, let's put an end to this.'

'It was a misunderstanding, milord. We were at the wrong place at the wrong time. We thought it was due to the late scutage.'

'Why are you protecting your leader? Le Renard is a thief, a cheat and a wanted man. Your whole group is wanted.'

'No, Your Lordship, no—you must believe us. We

knows nothing of him or them outlaws. We ain't p-part of them,' he stammered.

'If you give us names, locations and the whereabouts of your leader, you and your friend will be spared.'

There was a movement at the back of the hall, making the little hairs on the back of Hugh's neck stand on edge. Someone had entered the fray, causing the flames in the sconces to flicker and flare.

'Will they? By whose authority?' a voice filled with arrogant self-importance retorted, interrupting the proceedings.

The company assembled in the hall shuffled and peered to see who had spoken. The voice belonged to a man of medium height who had swept into the hall dressed in chainmail, ready to do battle with a dozen soldiers by his side.

'By mine. Who are you, sir, and what the devil are you doing here?' Hugh roared as the small group made their way towards him with purpose.

The man inclined his head. 'Pleased to make your acquaintance, Sir Hugh. I am Lord Balvoire and...' His lips curled. 'Ah, Lady Eleanor? What a surprise. Delighted to see you, my dear.'

'Whilst I'm sure the pleasure is ours, sir, you have no business here.' He glared down at him, with his arms crossed over his chest. 'And it's *Lord* Hugh—of Tallany.'

'I do apologise, *my lord*,' he said sardonically. 'And I must beg to differ. My dire warnings to King John about the outlaws who have plagued your land and mine have effected a decree from our Sovereign.' He clicked his fingers and one of his entourage stepped forward, handing him a scroll. 'For immediate retribution.'

A muscle twitched in Hugh's jaw. God's breath, this was the obnoxious prig who had sent him his complaints on his wedding day, and now here he was, gloating about whatever it was he'd managed to wheedle out of John. Not that the King would necessarily hold firm with this abominable ass. Still, he would do well to be cautious.

'So, you see, my lord, your business and mine are sadly entwined until we have hunted these disgusting animals down. The reward for their capture is a sweet incentive.' Balvoire grunted. 'And as it happens, I have made a start on the hunt.'

Another man stepped forward and handed Lord Balvoire the large sack he was holding.

'Let's call it a belated wedding present.'

He emptied the sack and two decapitated heads rolled out and fell on the ground in front of Hugh and the two prisoners, who started to tremble uncontrollably. There was an audible gasp, and behind him Hugh heard a soft sob coming from Eleanor. He turned, and to her credit she stilled instantly, swallowing down her distress. He hadn't wanted her exposed to any of this, but he could never have imagined this man's intrusive appearance.

'I do not condone your methods, Lord Balvoire, they are unnecessary before any verdict is made.' He scowled at him. 'I am judge and overlord of Tallany, and as such I will establish a fair system of justice.'

'Let's hope that as judge you will show your mettle, my lord.'

'I do not need your advice, Balvoire. And you'd do well not to cross me.' Hugh glowered.

The older man chuckled. 'Really, we are on the same side, my lord. The side of justice, the iron rule of the land and our Sovereign King, may God protect him,' he said, crossing himself. 'I come in peace.'

'And now that you have delivered your wedding present, as you call it, you may go in peace.'

'You may believe yourself to be above taking advice from me,' said Balvoire, 'but let me remind you that I carry King John's approval for being here. I am his chosen representative and he *will* have his justice.'

'What the hell are you talking about, Balvoire? I have not had any word of this.'

'Haven't you? Oh, how remiss of me.' Lord Balvoire raised the scroll and handed it to Hugh. 'King John wants a clear, resounding message sent to anyone either involved with or harbouring the outlaws. It makes no difference to him either way.'

Hugh knew exactly what that meant and ground his teeth. How in God's name was he supposed to establish fairness in the rule of law if the King sought such brutal retribution? This was not how Hugh wanted these matters to be resolved in Tallany.

He squared his shoulders and glared at Balvoire. 'We have not yet found out anything in relation to the outlaws from these men—nor have we established whether they're even involved.'

'No trials, no verdicts, Lord Hugh. That's what King John has decreed. We are to do what is *necessary*, and you'd do well to remember that, my young lord. Besides, these men are nothing but worthless peasants.' He flicked a glance at Eleanor and sneered. 'As the previous Lord Tallany knew too well.'

By God, he'd had enough of this loathsome man.

Just as Balvoire walked behind one of the bound men, drawing a dagger, clearly about to demonstrate the expected ways of governance, Hugh was there, looming over him, in two easy strides.

'That's enough, my lord. You overstep yourself.'

'Be careful, Lord Hugh,' Balvoire said quietly. 'One would think you *value* these cockroaches. Besides, the

King has requested we work together to capture the outlaws. Mayhap I can guide you?'

'I thank you—but, no,' Hugh said in a low, menacing tone. 'These men are in Tallany, and as judge in this domain *I* will decide. They will be imprisoned until further hearing. Now, Lord Balvoire, I believe you have exhausted your welcome here.'

Eleanor felt as though all the blood in her veins had turned to ice. She screwed her eyes shut and tried to blot out everything she had witnessed as her husband continued in his altercation with the vile Lord Balvoire.

She was vaguely conscious of Sir William's hand covering hers, giving it a squeeze of reassurance, which prompted her to open her eyes and nod her thanks at Will's concern. She was well—or as well as could be expected—but those two prisoners…her friends, men she felt responsible for…were far from it. Not to mention the two other men whose severed heads lay at their feet.

God, how depraved was Lord Balvoire—as was his King…

She stared in horror at the two men crouched on the ground, both shaking violently. Despite the threat of execution, they hadn't given her or the others away—not that she had ever doubted them. Poor brave, selfless men. All of them. It made her stomach recoil, and want to empty itself, but she couldn't betray the feelings of helplessness and guilt that washed over her.

She rubbed her clammy forehead, knowing she had to get out of the hall, and stood abruptly, hoping her feet would carry her. But just as she took a few shaky steps she caught Hugh's anxious eyes and swayed.

'My lady, you do not look well,' he said as he moved towards her with urgency. 'Eleanor?'

She opened her mouth to speak but no words were uttered. It was dry—far too dry. If only she could get something to drink…anything would do…anything to help her regain her composure. Strangely, her body felt as though it didn't belong to her, seemingly drained of life.

Before she could ponder on this, or know what was happening, darkness consumed her.

Eleanor's eyes fluttered rapidly, as she roused herself into consciousness. She felt as though she were floating through clouds, cocooned by a tower of warmth and strength. Ah, blissfully safe…

But then the inevitable jolt of memory flooded her senses with the horrors of what she had witnessed in the great hall.

A feeling of disorientated panic suddenly engulfed her as she pondered on the terrible events and the length of time that had passed since she had fainted.

She didn't know that, or even where she was, so she peered from under her lashes and found that she was in the protective arms of her husband. He was carrying her up the cold spiral stairwell towards their solar. But they were not alone.

'You're right, Hugh, there's no choice in the matter. It is the only way to smoke the outlaws and The Fox out of hiding and get that fool Balvoire off your back,' Will muttered.

He was following them up, lighting the way with a torch.

'The plan would allow a decoy entourage of knights to go ahead with you whilst I, along with a few retainers, guard the actual strongbox and follow, with a measure to separate us. That way, if you are ambushed, we can assist from the rear once we catch up with you. Thus securing the revenue and making sure the outlaws are caught,' Hugh explained.

'That sounds good, but there is a problem. Balvoire has insisted that I impress his demands upon you.'

'Oh? And what does that bastard want?'

'He's an ambitious ass—which makes him danger-ous, Hugh. I'm not sure whether you know or not, but he had been petitioning the King for Lady Eleanor's hand after Millais's death, angling for the huge chunks of Tal-lany land that border his. King John had been close to conceding.'

'And that's so like him to change his mind. And in this case, I'll admit that I'm very glad.' Hugh sighed. 'Which is one reason why the Barons never know where they stand with John.'

'Precisely. And whilst Balvoire has the King's ear he has something to prove—so watch your back, my friend. He means to accompany you with the strongbox to Win-chester, so he can—and I quote—*"make sure you know what you're doing".*' Will hissed as he spoke.

Hugh swore under his breath. 'As long as he under-stands that I am in command then I don't care—especially as his men will swell our numbers, which can only help our cause.'

Eleanor kept her eyes shut as Hugh carried her inside their solar, with Will following just behind. Her head was reeling with all she had learnt from her husband and his friend, but she was alert, focussed and calm.

A clear plan began to take shape in her head. A plan that would avenge those men's deaths at the hands of Lord Balvoire and which, she hoped, would make him suffer. Oh, yes, she wanted to cause Balvoire shame and dishon-our—and although she knew it might also affect Hugh, there was no way of avoiding it.

She reflected once again on what she had witnessed in the great hall of Tallany Castle and wondered whether she could achieve what she'd planned. She sent a silent prayer and swore an oath on her mother's small gold cross.

A flash of vulnerability darted through her mind but she pushed it aside.

This was no time for weakness.

She must have faith and courage and remember that this sacrifice was not about her, or even Hugh, but for the greater good. For justice…and for honour.

Chapter Eight

It had been a few days since the insufferable Lord Balvoire had brought the two decapitated heads to Tallany Castle as his own special marriage gift. Not to mention his attempt to execute Hugh's prisoners, who were now being held in the castle gaol.

Hugh understood Will's caution that night, regarding the man, and now, after just a few hours in his company, since they had left the Tallany gatehouse and the demesne beyond, he was close to wringing Balvoire's neck.

He was an obnoxious windbag who knew nothing of soldiering but had an inflated belief in his own ability. He had to be reminded again and again who was actually in charge of their mission. Lord only knew what King John saw in the man, but no doubt it suited him to have Balvoire toadying to him.

However, Will was right. Balvoire was an ass, but a dangerous one, and Hugh would have to keep his eye on him.

As the new Lord he had to restore peace by upholding the rule of law, and that meant capturing and crushing the outlaws, who were wreaking havoc in Tallany. Taking a strongbox of silver to King John in order to lure the outlaws was a good means to do this, but however Hugh justified it to himself, it did not sit well with him. It made him feel uneasy and pricked his conscience—especially as he was only just beginning to win the trust and respect of the people here.

Hugh sighed, knowing that it wasn't just the people of Tallany but its mistress as well who had been affected by recent events. Since that night in the hall his wife had retreated back into her shell. She had been withdrawn, agitated, hardly saying a thing. Selfishly, Hugh had wanted to continue from where they had left off with that delicious kiss, but everything had changed.

Even this morning, before they had set out on this mission, Hugh had sought her blessing. It had been duly given, but with cool detachment. Then again, it was no surprise that these events had distressed Eleanor. She might be strong but she was also vulnerable, and she needed his care and protection.

He sighed, turning his thoughts to the task that stretched ahead of him. The path they took was on the fringes of the Tallany estate. The woodland, dense with high looming trees, was dappled with thickets and coppice covering a wide span. A blanket of hazy morning fog hugged the ground, making visibility difficult.

Hugh felt twitchy and on guard. His senses were heightened and he was acutely aware of a possible disturbance further along the path as his small retinue of knights and retainers, which included Balvoire and his men, edged further into the forest.

They were a perfect foil for the much larger cortege ahead, with an even larger strongbox as bait to lure the outlaws from hiding. If everything went to plan then they would not only hand the silver levy to King John but also the outlaws, along with their leader, Le Renard. And once the outlaws were caught Hugh would do everything he could to make Tallany and its people prosperous again.

He listened, trying to distinguish any unusual noises as he looked around in all directions. He knew instinctively that something was wrong. He wasn't quite sure what, but the feeling was palpable. It was too still, far too quiet…

A sudden sense of foreboding pierced through him and he gripped the dagger at his waist tighter. It was a feeling that he always had before a battle, and here in this damnable forest he couldn't see the enemy but he could feel them in his bones. They were close—very close.

Hugh bypassed Balvoire and rode to his sergeant at the front of the retinue.

'We need to pick up the pace. I don't want us to be far behind Sir William's cortege or else we risk exposure,' Hugh ordered.

Balvoire rode up beside him. 'No need, Lord Hugh. Surely Sir William will send word if they encounter the outlaws?'

'I have no time for disputes.' Hugh nodded to his sergeant. 'Carry on—and make sure you're vigilant.'

'Yes, my lord,' the sergeant said, and he began to dictate a quicker pace, pulling the whole group into a quicker trot.

'What exactly do you believe will happen?' Balvoire barked, no doubt furious at being dismissed.

'As I said earlier, we don't have time. Now, get your men to the rear, Balvoire. You are leaving it open to attack,' Hugh said through gritted teeth.

But just then, in the periphery of his vision, he glimpsed what he believed was a flash of movement above in the trees ahead.

'What the…?' he muttered under his breath.

Again he saw a shift of movement above him, in the

branches of the towering trees. Outlined shapes darted
and weaved through, leaves rustled, but he still couldn't
really see anything. It could be birds or small animals.
But something in the movements made him reconsider.

'Sergeant, wait!' Hugh thundered—but it was too late.

The men out in front were thrown off their mounts as
a rope tied across the path between two trees made their
horses buckle and fall with a deafening thud.

'Hell's teeth, stop! Retreat! It's a trap!' Hugh bellowed
as mayhem ensued.

He swivelled his neck and watched as chaos erupted at
the rear of the entourage as well. Out of nowhere, ropes
dropped and were pulled and tied together from one tree
to another. Hugh knew he had to protect the strongbox,
but it was no use. He couldn't see his way out of the clearing. They were barricaded in.

At that very moment the hiss of an arrow flew past
him and a succession of men in masks, with hoods drawn
over their heads, swung between the trees and landed in
every direction, surrounding them.

They were ambushed!

Hugh was yanked from his saddle from behind, landing on his back. But he got up on his feet as quickly
as possible, despite the pain. Drawing his sword, Hugh
watched in disgust as one after the other of his entourage
threw down his armour in surrender. He would not. He
had to protect the strongbox.

Just as he was about to engage in combat with a rather
large outlaw a rapid array of arrows swished through the
air, hitting the ground so close to him that he dropped his
sword. He quickly retrieved it and flicked his head back
to see who had executed the attack with such precision.
He knew it could only be one person.

Hugh saw a slight, lean figure standing on a branch.

The man put his bow behind him, grabbed a rope and swung from one tree to another before landing on the cart, hovering just in front of Hugh. He stood with his legs apart, dressed in green braies and tunic, his face hidden under a mask and a hood edged in fur covering his head and shoulders…

It was Le Renard—and he was no more than a boy!

'So, *you* are the notorious Fox?' Hugh drawled sardonically, daring to take a step closer to the cart, clutching the hilt of his sword.

The outlaw waved his hand and bowed in an exaggerated manner. 'At your service, Lord Hugh. But please do not take another step forward.'

'Oh? And why not?' Hugh asked, edging closer.

'Take a look. Your men have all but capitulated; you're completely surrounded, my lord.'

There was a roar of laughter as Hugh looked around to see that his whole entourage had indeed surrendered. His most experienced men, save a few, had been sent ahead with Will and the decoy strongbox that had been meant to snare the outlaw group, but it had backfired…badly.

The plan had been such a good one—Hugh couldn't understand how they had walked into this trap. These outlaws were organised, trained in combat, and they had known they were coming. He felt a cold fury running through his veins but knew he had to temper his emotions.

Instead, he shrugged nonchalantly and smiled.

Le Renard looked him up and down. 'Come, now— yield, Lord Hugh. We've only come for this.' The outlaw dragged off the sackcloth covering the strongbox and kicked the side of it as he spoke.

Hugh's smile evaporated immediately. 'I never yield.' He scowled. 'Especially to a boy.'

Le Renard jumped down from the cart and stood in front of Hugh. 'Yield, my lord. You have no other choice.'

'Never! You will have to kill me first. And whilst there is breath in my body, I will do my duty by my King and protect that strongbox.' He stood tall and proud, emanating as much power and courage as he could muster, and for a moment the younger man stared at him.

'That,' Le Renard muttered, 'is not necessary.'

Hugh knew that, but knew desperately he had to think of something. 'Fight me, outlaw. Man to man. And the victor will keep the coin.'

'Now why would I do something as ridiculous as that? I already have your men and your coin, my lord.' He glanced down at his fingers. 'Not bad for *a boy*, don't you think?'

There was something about the way The Fox spoke that reminded Hugh of something, or someone, but his mind must be playing tricks on him.

He held his sword pointed at the outlaw and gave his head a mental shake. 'So, you're a coward? Is that it? You won't fight with me?'

Le Renard snorted. 'Despite what you think,' he said, clicking his fingers at another outlaw, 'we're not savages bent on violence and destruction.'

The big, burly outlaw Le Renard had beckoned dragged over Balvoire, bound and gagged, and threw him on the ground in front of his leader.

'Not like him,' said The Fox.

Hugh's knuckles were white, his sword arm clenched taut, and yet this outlaw was not interested in taking up arms against him. He was still talking, explaining himself.

'So you see, my lord, we're taking back what is ours.'

'Who *are* you?' Hugh asked.

'No one of consequence, my lord.'

Was it Hugh's imagination or had the timbre in the outlaw's voice risen up a notch?

'You must be deluded. How can the coin possibly be *yours*?'

'This silver has been stolen from us for the coffers of King John and his cronies to pay for pointless wars,' Le Renard growled, and his men roared their approval.

'That's treason!' Hugh spat out, and found half a dozen blades suddenly pointing at him. He stood his ground, even though his heart was hammering relentlessly.

'No, lower your blades,' the leader of the outlaws chided. 'Leave him to me!'

Le Renard glared at his men, but they still held their swords pointed at Hugh and Hugh, in turn, held his firmly pointed at The Fox.

'That, Lord Hugh, is a matter of opinion.' He shrugged as he moved and laid his hand over each of the swords of his fellow outlaws, who lowered them one by one.

'We need to avenge our fallen friends, Fox!' one of the outlaws cried.

'Good, honourable men,' the big, burly outlaw said.

'Honour? You talk of *honour*? There exists none amongst thieves,' Hugh retorted, addressing them all.

'Who you be calling thieves? Those men had more honour in their little finger than you. Than this cur!' the big burly outlaw sneered, kicking Balvoire, who was face-down on the ground.

The rest of the outlaws roared and jeered. 'Avenge our friends!' the outlaw cried, and others shouted out similar chants.

Le Renard stepped back onto the cart and slammed his foot hard against the side. 'No!' he bellowed. 'We have never taken a life and we're not going to start now—

otherwise we'd be no better than *them*.' He flicked his chin at Balvoire and looked at each of his men, who seemed to quieten with his words. 'We have come for one thing and one thing only,' Le Renard said, kicking the strongbox. 'Now, Lord Hugh, I will ask you again to lay down your sword and submit. This is a battle you've lost.'

'Never!' Hugh cried, and he lunged forward and leapt onto the cart, catching Le Renard by surprise.

Hugh brought his blade up, swiping with his sword and meeting Le Renard's with a defensive clang. The outlaw stepped back and jumped off the cart as he defended himself against Hugh's onslaught.

They circled each other as though in a dance—a deadly dance—sparring as their blades criss-crossed each other in a clash. The rest of Hugh's men and Le Renard's men watched the fight unfold, the outlaws still holding the captive men in surrender.

Hugh, being the much taller, stronger and more experienced man, thrust forward in attack again and again as Le Renard lurched backwards in defence.

Hugh had to admit that Le Renard knew the art of swordplay, even though his knowledge was rudimentary and no more than a young squire's. The outlaw had been trained—but by whom and in whose mesnie? He was good—particularly his agility and footwork, which were as quick as his namesake. Mayhap he was as cunning too. Certainly his reputation suggested that was the case.

'Not bad… It seems you have a few hidden talents, Le Renard.'

But Hugh could see that the outlaw had broken out in sweat above the rim of his mask.

'And that surprises you, my lord?'

'You remind me of a few young squires I've trained in the past, nothing more,' he said, 'And, whilst this has been an entertaining diversion, I think it's high time I brought matters to a close—don't you?'

Before waiting for an answer Hugh lurched forward in a quick succession of moves before turning, wrong-footing his opponent and disarming him.

Le Renard looked at his sword on the ground in disbelief before snapping his head back to see Hugh's sword pointing at him, the blade just a flicker away from his face.

Good—now I have you, Le Renard.

'Very good, my lord,' the outlaw said.

'Indeed—now, tell your men to relinquish the strong-box, let go of my men and who knows…? Mayhap I will spare you.'

'And do you think I believe you?' Le Renard laughed softly as he took a few steps back.

'My word is my honour.'

'Mayhap, my lord…' He stepped to one side and then jumped back onto the cart. 'And then again, mayhap not.'

It was Hugh's turn to be surprised and wrong-footed as the outlaw turned away, legs apart and hands on hips. Incredulous, Hugh lunged forth again, but this time the outlaw anticipated him and leapt off the cart, his movements quick and determined.

'Come back and finish this! Come back and fight!' Hugh bellowed.

But Le Renard had climbed the tree he had descended earlier, with the aid of his burly accomplice, who was laughing heartily.

'Whilst this has been a…what did you call it? Oh, yes… *"an entertaining diversion"*, I think now *I* should bring *"matters to a close"*, don't you?' Le Renard mocked as he stood on the branch.

'Get down at once and fight with me! Show me your mettle! Or are you a coward?' Hugh barked.

'Not I, my lord!' He laughed. 'As I said, the time for these games is over. Yield and submit.'

'Never!'

'Very well, have it your way… *Now*, Anselm!'

The big man swung his axe to the ground, cutting through a rope hidden under leaves, which in turn released a heavy leather and rope net from above. This fell over Hugh, making him cower to the ground. And then Le Renard took arrow after arrow from his quiver, nocking each one with precision and then shooting, pinning the edge of the net, imprisoning Hugh beneath.

Le Renard tapped his head in mock salute. 'My lord, it has been a pleasure. You're as valiant as they say you are.'

'I never bargained for trickery, Fox.'

Le Renard ignored him and addressed another of his accomplices. 'Tie the rest of them together—except Balvoire. That one you strip and clothe in the infested hopsack.' He swung round. 'And then we best be gone, before their dissembling cortege suspects something.'

'Wait!' Hugh demanded from underneath his prison. 'Before you go, I want to know why you didn't kill me? You could have speared me with your arrows.'

Le Renard crossed his arms and contemplated his answer. 'I told you—we're not murderers. We do not choose to do what we do and we do not do it lightly, my lord.' He raised himself to address all the captured men. 'We have spared all of you—unlike our fallen friends, who were butchered like animals. Remember that!'

'Fox, we'd better go,' the burly outlaw said.

The outlaw smiled. 'Until we meet again, Lord Hugh of Tallany.'

And just like a puff of smoke they disappeared as

quickly as they'd appeared out of nowhere, taking with them the strongbox filled with the King's silver.

'And when we do you'll not get away from me so easily, so help me God…' Hugh made the oath to himself bitterly as he closed his eyes in humiliation.

Chapter Nine

Eleanor hesitated before stepping around the stretched linen screen in their chamber to see Hugh sitting in a wooden bathtub. He was covered in warm water infused with soap and cleansing herbs, his eyes impassive, his expression hard. And, despite the warmth of the fire that crackled in the hearth, there was a resounding chill in the air.

She exhaled slowly and swallowed down her guilt, knowing full well the reason for his bleak mood.

It had been almost dusk before Hugh and the decoy convoy led by Will had arrived back to the castle keep. Hugh had retired to their solar in a thunderous mood, refusing to see anyone.

And Eleanor didn't blame him. She felt his pain and wished she could have spared his humiliation, wished it could have been avoided, but there had been no other way. What she and her outlaws had done was just. They had taken back what was rightfully theirs, for Tallany and its people.

But, dear God, Hugh...

Her husband had been prepared to protect the King's coin at any cost to himself. He truly had honour coursing through his veins, and it showed the extent of his unreserved fealty to his Sovereign. Eleanor understood that for Hugh, as it had been for her own father, to break a solemn oath that had been sworn before God was to breach a sacred vow. Not that this particular King deserved it…

Hugh would have fought to the death if he'd had to. It had been one of the bravest yet most terrifying things she'd ever seen, and Eleanor had had to deploy all her skills to make sure the situation hadn't got out of hand.

If anything had happened to him it would have devastated her and she would never have forgiven herself. Hugh was a good, honourable man…

But it was more than that—*he* was more than that.

How had she come to care for Hugh in such a short space of time?

He snapped his gaze to meet hers and offered the ghost of a smile briefly before it faded into a slim, compressed line. She walked over to the hearth, picked up the bucket and topped up his bath with more warm water, wanting to be of some use. She tilted her head, trying to catch his eye, but he stared blankly ahead.

'It was not your fault, Hugh,' she murmured after some time. 'You must believe that.'

'I thank you for your concern, Eleanor, but I cannot do that,' he said, looking straight ahead at nothing, clearly lost in his own misery.

She tried again. 'There was nothing you could have done. The outlaws knew of your plans, as you said yourself.'

She fell to her knees beside the tub as he turned to face her.

'Yes, but *how*? How did they know we had the strongbox with the coin? How did they ambush us so easily? They even knew about the decoy cortege, ahead with

Will.' Hugh shook his head slowly. 'I have failed in this mission. I have never experienced failure before and it doesn't sit well with me.'

'Surely the King can't blame you? Why, you've said yourself that the outlaws had targeted him many times before you had even arrived in Tallany.'

'That may be true, but this happened under my watch, Eleanor. It was my responsibility and I failed.' He exhaled. 'One thing is for sure: we have a traitor in our midst. Someone knew of our plan and passed it on to Le Renard and his outlaws.'

'That can't be,' she muttered, trying to mask her anxiety.

'There is no other explanation as to how the outlaws are continually one step ahead of me.' He shut his eyes tightly, his brows meeting in the middle.

Eleanor bit the inside of her cheek. The possibility of Hugh discovering the truth about her—that *she* was the traitor he sought—was real. He was shrewd, intelligent and astute. She had to make sure he never did. It would be an unmitigated disaster. Besides, she couldn't bear to lose his esteem and his respect for her. And, although she knew what she had done had been for right and good, at this moment she didn't *feel* good about it.

She sighed. Watching Hugh, withdrawn and filled with bitter misery, made her want to hold him and make everything better. Again, she felt the weight of responsibility for her actions.

Impulsively, and without being aware of what she was doing, Eleanor reached out and ran her fingers through Hugh's wet hair, pushing it back. She moved closer and touched the side of his face, tracing his strong, angular jaw. He snapped his eyes open and turned to meet her enigmatic gaze, raising his brows in confusion. She smiled at him—a smile of hope and sanguinity.

Her gaze moved from Hugh's eyes to his mouth, and slowly she moved in and pressed her lips gently to his—a soft, feather-light kiss. A kiss of peace…a kiss to heal.

She pulled away and regarded him. Bewilderment was etched on his handsome face as she brushed her thumb over his bottom lip. Eleanor dipped her head to cover his lips again with her own.

As if suddenly awoken from the depths of slumber, Hugh moved his lips against hers and his arms came out of the bath to wrap around her shoulders, pulling her closer and closer until she was pressed against the wooden tub.

Without warning, Hugh leant forward and lifted her up and over, into the bath, making her squeal as she fell on top of him with a splash.

Her eyes widened in surprise and she burst out laughing as she lay on top of him, submerged in delicious-smelling bathwater. He joined in, chuckling at having his fully clothed wife sharing his bath, no doubt.

Then they locked eyes and gradually ceased laughing. Hugh pulled back Eleanor's veil and threw it to the floor, unpinning her bound hair, releasing the velvety dark lengths that tumbled down, their ends doused in the water. He ran his hand through her hair and cupped her face, dripping water.

'What have we here, Eleanor?' he mused, curling his lips into that half-smile, revealing a dimple.

It was astounding how quickly Hugh's mood had changed, and she realised that his temperament was naturally positive. He had an easy confidence that was both attractive and infectious.

Eleanor wasn't sure what to do next but was, nevertheless, aware of her closeness to his body…his very hard, very naked body… She tried not to register the size of his shoulders, or the fact that her legs, although shrouded by the many layers of drenched clothing that covered them, were still nonetheless pressed against his strong, muscly ones. Breathless, she didn't want to admit the other parts of his body were in very close contact with hers too.

Hugh ran his thumb over her bottom lip, imitating what she had done just moments ago. 'You know, you are very beautiful, Eleanor,' he whispered as he leaned in and claimed her lips again, kissing her softly before drawing back, grinning. 'And you're diverting me in the most unexpected way. I thank you.'

He stroked her cheek with the back of his fingers and then pushed up, sitting straight in the tub, jerking her to sit across him.

'But now, if you'll excuse me, my lady, I wish to get out.'

He gripped the side of the bath, indicating that this diversion, however pleasant, was now at an end. He seemed eager to get back to wallowing in misery on his own.

Eleanor knew she was being gently dismissed, but couldn't quite move away. She sat on top of him instead, watching him, exhaling quick puffs of air, trying not to think of his nakedness submerged in the opaque bath water.

Hugh caught her gaze, his eyes narrowing. She felt the hardness of his manhood, even against the many layers of wet clothing, but surprisingly it didn't alarm her. Instead, a rush of heat flooded her senses.

'Eleanor…?' he murmured, looking into her eyes, seeking answers.

His breathing seemed to match hers, slow and gasping, and her heartbeat was pounding in the stillness of the moment as they continued to stare at each other. She caught her bottom lip between her teeth and then leaned in to press her lips to his again. Her response given, Hugh drew her close and kissed her deeply, with such passion and intensity that she felt she was melting into him.

She tried to match him, kiss for kiss. But Hugh eased away from her lips to kiss her cheeks, and then the soft flesh behind her earlobes. Nipping gently, his mouth moved to savour the side of her neck as she trembled.

'Are you cold?' he asked, running his hands down the sides of her shoulders.

She shook her head, unable to say the words, making him smile. His gaze held such intent, such desperate longing, it shifted something deep inside her.

'Eleanor…?' He groaned. 'Is this what you want?'

She watched him, wondering whether his heart was beating as fast as hers.

'Yes,' she whispered. 'Yes.'

In one swift motion Hugh rose from the bath, taking her with him, and set her down close to the hearth, where the fire spread its warmth. He began to dry her with soft lengths of linen cloth, his eyes never leaving hers. Then he dried himself and wrapped another piece of cloth around his waist, securing it tightly. He, too, was breathing heavily as he stepped forward and scooped Eleanor into his arms, capturing her mouth, kissing her deeply.

He carried her to set her down to stand on the rug, and her toes curled into the depths of the soft pile of the wool as warmth flooded her.

'I've wanted you from the moment I set eyes on you, Eleanor of Tallany.' He cupped the side of her face tenderly. 'But I wanted you to come to me yourself, when you were ready. This was always to be your choice.'

She reached out and traced his lips with the tips of

her fingers, making him groan, and then touched her own, swollen with the lingering effects of his devastating kisses.

'It is, Hugh,' she whispered.

She touched the scar that split his eyebrow and placed a kiss where her fingers had been. Then she continued to trace the long, deep battle scars, echoing her own hidden ones, and explored the hard muscles of his shoulders and back.

She heard Hugh's breath catch as her hands caressed the lean, muscular ridges of his chest, biceps and stomach. She gazed, fascinated, at the smattering of hair that drifted over his chest and trailed down his stomach, disappearing underneath the wrapped linen cloth.

She suddenly wanted to know more, wanted to see where the trail would end, and reached instinctively to remove the cloth.

Hugh's hand shot out, clasped her fingers in his, grinning. Then slowly, so exquisitely slowly, he peeled away her layers of heavy, waterlogged clothing, his hands skimming over her, learning the curves of her body, replacing the layers of wet, clinging garments with the explorative touch of his mouth and his hands.

Gradually the outline of Eleanor's body was revealed, until there was only one last layer of clothing. His fingers slowly went to the hem of her tunic, lifting it a little higher. A warning darted through Eleanor, reminding her to be cautious. There were parts of her body she could never expose, knowing they would only disgust Hugh.

She pulled away.

'Do you wish me to stop, Eleanor?' he asked, curling a tendril of her hair around his finger.

'No, no… But…' she took in a deep breath '… I will remove my tunic.'

'A little too late for maidenly modesty, don't you think, wife?'

His eyes smouldered as he raked her from her head to her toes and then back again.

'If you wouldn't mind turning around, husband?'

Hugh chuckled softly with his arms crossed over his chest. 'But I can see all of you anyway.'

'Humour me, please?'

Hugh shook his head but complied, turning his back on Eleanor. As soon as he did so she peeled off the last layer of wet clothing, threw it on the floor and bounded into bed, dragging the coverlet up to her chin.

Incredibly, Eleanor wasn't scared about what was about to happen between them. She was nervous, yes—but not scared. Not any more.

Her heart was pounding as she lay naked on her back under the bedding, but she knew the reason for that. Hugh...only because of Hugh.

'I'm ready, husband.'

'So you are, my lady.'

His eyes glittered with amusement as he strode to the bed and took off the linen cloth before climbing in and sliding next to her under the coverlet.

'Now, what do we have here? A naked wife?'

Eleanor giggled nervously. 'Not such a modest maiden after all?'

'No...' he drawled. 'Not so.'

He kissed her, smiling against her lips, and his hands continued their exploration of her body. Touching, feeling, caressing. Skin to skin.

Saints above!

Hugh's gloriously naked body pressed so close to hers suddenly brought a wave of awareness. Eleanor wanted so much to please him. She would be everything he wanted her to be. And yet she didn't know what that was. These sensations were so new, and so different from what she had previously understood about intimacy, that she was unsure *how* to be what he wanted.

'Eleanor, are you well?'

'Of course—why do you ask?'

'You are rigidly still,' he whispered. 'Am I doing something not to your liking?' He smiled as he stroked and kissed her neck.

'No, no, everything is well.'

'Good,' he said as he grazed his lips over her shoulders, collarbone and chest, moving further down her body.

Her breath hitched.

'You're doing it again,' he said, nipping the inside of her palm.

'I'm sorry. I'm not sure I'm doing this right.'

Hugh stopped and smiled at her. 'Believe me, there's no right and wrong. Not in this and not between us.'

Eleanor returned his smile. 'Are you saying you'd rather I was *ruthlessly dextrous* here as well?'

'Possibly!' He chuckled, a deep throaty sound. 'Tell me, am I to teach you about bed sport as well?'

'Actually, yes,' she said, catching her bottom lip between her teeth. 'I wish to know how to please you.'

Hugh lifted his head and gave her a tender look. 'We could try to please one another.'

'How do I...? Oh... Oh!' Eleanor moaned as he kissed and caressed the tops of her breasts. 'Hugh, it's difficult for me to know what to think when you're doing that.'

He continued to kiss and caress her, moving lower. 'Then don't think.'

'But I don't know...'

'Hush, no more talking.' His mouth brushed over her

breasts, one and then the other, teasing with his lips and his tongue. 'Just trust in every sensation, every feeling.'

'You are still talking…' she said breathlessly.

'I'm allowed.' His hands and mouth ventured further down, following every soft curve of her body. 'I'm the tutor, remember?' he whispered, stroking and caressing.

Every graze of his lips and tongue across her breasts, stomach and thighs wound her tighter as heat spread through her, rendering her speechless and without a single thought. Every touch made her lose herself more in a heady sensuality filled with carnal curiosity and raw need.

She heard a soft moan permeate the room, filled with pleasure, and realised the noise was escaping from her own lips. Her hands needed to explore, needed to feel… They ran down the smooth, hard contours of his shoulders, the sinewy muscles of his back.

He kissed her lips again as he slowly edged her legs apart with his own. 'Look at me, Eleanor,' he rasped, his eyes glittering with emotion. 'We please one another,' he whispered as he entered her, making her gasp. 'Always…'

He stilled, allowing her to get used to him, and pushed aside a strand of hair that had pasted itself to her forehead. He stroked her cheek and Eleanor snaked her hands around Hugh's neck and pulled him towards her.

'Yes,' she murmured breathlessly as she pressed her lips to his and tentatively dipped her tongue into his mouth.

Eleanor heard Hugh growl in response, meeting her tongue measure for measure, and then he started to thrust inside her.

She instinctively wrapped her legs around his buttocks, feeling stretched, arching her back. He was hard and frantic, surging and retreating, gathering pace, taking her to a higher plane, wordlessly asking her to be brave enough to give herself to him as he was to her. It was true and honest, their mutual ardour, and it made her want to shout out from the top of the castle battlements.

'Open your eyes, Eleanor,' he said hoarsely. 'I want to see you.'

He kissed her, nipping and pulling at her plump bottom lip with his teeth so softly that she could have melted as the tension escalating in her body begged for release.

'Hugh!' she cried, and she suddenly felt as though she were floating in a whirl of ecstasy.

He continued to thrust inside her, his eyes locked with hers, holding on to the moment. Eleanor reached out and stroked his jaw with her fingers just as Hugh reached his peak, his body shuddering and collapsing on top of her.

Their bodies entwined, their breathing ragged, they lay there sated in a tangle, unable to move. Until finally Hugh lifted himself off her and kissed the top of her nose. He moved beside her, pulling her close and wrapping the coverlet around them.

A calm silence pervaded the room. The peaceful cocoon that wrapped around them was strangely comforting, and Eleanor was all at once aware of Hugh's nearness—his smell, his touch, his body pressed next to her side. His arms tightened around her waist as she lay on her back, her body still reeling in the aftermath of what had just passed between them. She felt self-conscious, not wanting to expose more than she already had.

'Well, that was...' Hugh took a shaky breath, breaking the silence. 'Unexpected, and yet...wonderful.' He rolled onto his side and watched her. 'Are you well, Eleanor?' he whispered as he gently caressed her cheek.

'Yes, I am.' She turned her head and smiled, meeting

his gaze. 'And now the covenant of our vows is complete. We are truly married.'

'We have been married for some time, sweetheart,' Hugh said, kissing her forehead, 'But, yes, we are truly married.' He rose out of bed, pulling on his braies. 'Stay—don't move, Eleanor. I'm going to see about getting us some food. I have suddenly built up a huge appetite.'

'Wait,' she said, sitting up and then recalling that she was in no state to get out of bed. 'If you allow me to dress, I will attend to it.'

'No, stay where you are. I'll get the trencher that was left in the antechamber. Don't go anywhere.'

He smiled at her before leaving.

As soon as he had gone Eleanor sprang into action, hastily refreshing and readying herself for his return. Pulling a linen chemise over her head, she put on a green woollen kirtle the colour of crisp apples—the exact shade of Hugh's eyes.

She smiled to herself as she reflected on the way his eyes had smouldered, and his lips had left delicious, sensuous imprints all over her body. He had been incredibly tender and given her so much pleasure, making her experience of this new intimacy so, *so* good.

Oh, Hugh...

Eleanor's feelings for him had changed and grown, and yet she had to remind herself be cautious. She couldn't, wouldn't allow herself to get too close to him and she had to stand firm. But it was not easy. None of this was easy.

Hugh returned, carrying a trencher of food: cuts of cooked cold chicken and ham, delicate cheese pastries, soft bread rolls and a small pot of apple and mead pickle.

'I come bearing gifts that should fortify us,' he announced, and Eleanor went to the coffer and poured two mugs of ale, passing one to him and taking a sip out of the other.

'Thank you.' He watched her over the rim of his mug and smiled mischievously. 'But you needn't have dressed, my lady.'

'You would have me behave so wantonly?'

'Aye—but only for my eyes to devour and my lips to savour.' He chuckled softly.

Eleanor felt herself blush and shook her head. 'Really, Hugh, must you tease?'

'Should I not?' he asked innocently. 'Now that I'm a proper husband, I thought it was my prerogative to tease you as much as possible.'

'And there I was, believing you to be a gallant knight.'

Hugh took Eleanor's mug from her and placed it on the coffer, along with his own, and pressed a kiss to her hand. 'My gallantry is always assured.'

She arched her brows. 'Is it, now? Well, I would never want to contradict such strongly held beliefs.'

'Are you by any chance teasing *me*, my lady?'

The corners of her lips twitched. 'Well, as a very proper wife, it is apparently my prerogative to tease my husband.'

He laughed, drawing her into his arms. Close to the bare chest and arms that he had yet to cover. 'You may do so as often as you wish, Eleanor. Rather that, than cross swords with you.'

Had Hugh really said that? It was a very good thing that he could not see her face, hidden against his neck.

She gave herself a mental shake. 'Thank you, but for now if you could help lace up my kirtle…?'

She stepped out of his arms, turning her back to him, and shuddered as his fingers, lacing her garment, grazed against the fine chemise tunic covering her back.

'You make me feel quite underdressed. Either that or I should just untie your kirtle again.'

'No, I think not.' She walked to the coffer, pouring more ale into both mugs. 'Better if you address the situation as I have.'

'Since I am as gallant as they say, I will comply,' he said, fetching a dark red linen tunic and pulling it over his head. 'But you know, Eleanor, there is no need to hide from me.'

Eleanor spilled a little of her drink on the coffer and snapped her head round to meet his eyes. 'What on earth do you mean?'

'Come, let's eat,' he said as he perched on the small bench to one side of the hearth.

Eleanor sat beside him and passed him his mug, averting her eyes, watching the flickering and crackling of the fire as they shared the trencher of food. She felt her heart hammering against her chest, and was finding it hard to swallow down a bite of food.

She took another nervous sip of ale.

She thought he hadn't noticed...

Hugh coughed, clearing his throat. 'I understand why you wouldn't want me to know, my lady,' he sighed. 'But after what we have shared I was going to find out sooner or later.'

Eleanor exhaled, tilting her head to meet Hugh's eyes. 'It isn't something I wish to discuss—especially with you.'

'It is especially with me that you should, Eleanor.' He laced his fingers with hers.

'Don't you see? It is my shame.' She shook her head.

'I don't see. That shame belongs elsewhere.' He cupped her chin and lifted it. 'Show me.'

One moment they had been teasing each other and now suddenly this?

'I can't,' she whispered, unable to say more. No one knew of her hurts—no one except Brunhilde and her steward Gilbert. 'What will you think of me?'

'That you are an amazingly brave woman. Now, show me.' He kissed her fingers. 'Please.'

It seemed Hugh was intent on stripping away every layer, every barrier she had constructed to protect herself. Very well, then—so be it.

She nodded firmly and stood up.

'Come.' He took her by the hand and led her to their bed.

'I warn you, it is quite objectionable to look at. Can you...?'

She pointed to the ties he had laced only moments ago, which Hugh swiftly untied, then pulled the kirtle off her shoulders, allowing it to fall and pool at her feet.

She took a deep breath before she turned her back to Hugh and started to remove her tunic. Feeling exposed, she screwed her eyes shut and waited for the response she knew would come.

It didn't.

Instead Hugh's fingers traced the mangled, corrugated and twisted skin across her back, dipping into the ugly crevices of the damaged rough surface.

'Does it still hurt?' he asked gently.

Eleanor shrugged, shaking her head. 'No, not any more. Brunhilde has a soothing salve that has always helped.' She sighed deeply. 'I'm sorry, Hugh. I hadn't wanted you to see this.'

Eleanor pulled her long linen chemise back over her head, covering herself, and then turned to face him.

'Why?' he asked, his voice rising. 'This is hardly your fault. The blame lies with another.'

'I know. But I wasn't what he—'

'No! You surely cannot make excuses for him.' He caressed her face. 'I'll tell you, Eleanor, that if he were here now I would throw him back to the depths of hell, where he belongs.'

'Thank you.' She smiled, sitting beside him. 'For not judging me.'

'Judge you? No,' he said, shaking his head. 'But I can now fully understand your initial reluctance for our marriage.'

'Not all men are like him.' Eleanor reached over to caress the hard, angular jawline of Hugh's face.

'I'm happy to hear that—but, God's blood, I cannot begin to imagine what it must have been like for you.'

'I was four and ten when I was obliged to marry, and he was ten years older than I. Our union deteriorated very rapidly.' She sighed.

'Why?'

'He was not the man I believed him to be and, as I have told you before, Millais thought I was an unnatural, undutiful wife who needed to be brought to heel.' She shrugged. 'Which he did. Constantly.'

'The bastard!' Hugh hissed, rubbing his temples. 'Was the man so ungodly?'

Yes, he was—he truly was.

If only Hugh knew half of what Richard Millais had subjected her to…

'So now you know that the scars I once spoke of are both visible and invisible, Hugh. And I carry the shame with me always.'

Hugh pulled her gently into his arms and stroked her hair. 'No, it is not you who should carry the shame. These are your battle wounds—just like the ones on my body. And, like me, you have come through your adversity. You have survived.'

She felt a surge of gratitude towards Hugh with those simple yet necessary words. Words that seemed to unlock something deep inside her. Words that she had never known she'd needed until now.

'Thank you for understanding, Hugh. I *had* to survive,' she whispered. 'There was no other alternative. But the choices I made were never easy.'

Hugh sighed. 'I don't doubt that. Sometimes the choices we make may be difficult, but they are essential for us to be able to carry on living.' He smiled down at her. 'And Eleanor...' he said, kissing the top of her head. 'Don't ever hide yourself from me. You don't need to.'

Oh, but she did—she really did!

Hugh led Eleanor back to the bed and held her close, stroking her hair and her back gently, feeling the mangled, coarse skin beneath his fingers.

How could anyone be so cruel as to inflict such terrible pain on someone they were supposed to care for? The thought of Millais hurting her, a defenceless, innocent woman, made his blood boil and made him want to take up arms for her. He would if he had to. He'd protect her until the end of this world.

God's teeth! How desperate must her life have been back then? How terrifying for a lonely young girl, grieving after the loss of her family, to endure such horrors? No wonder she was still wary and suspicious of anyone new in her life—especially someone imposed on her. *Like him.*

What was incredible was the fact that despite it all, after everything she had gone through, her spirit had not been broken. By God, that was one small mercy. She was as remarkable as she was strong, brave and resolute, and he admired her for it. His unusual heiress.

'Kiss me, Hugh,' she murmured, snaking her arms around his neck and pulling him closer.

And he kissed her lips, cheeks, eyes, neck and the tip of her nose before returning to her mouth.

They made love again, and this time he took longer to savour and explore every part of her until she lost herself to him. He made their delicious, languid intimacy stretch until they had both surrendered to it. Until once again she had matched his ardour, his passion and desire. Until they both came undone helplessly in one another's arms.

Hugh felt content, at peace. After such an ominous start to their marriage, being in bed with his wife in his arms was a comforting balm. He needed this, and he was sure she did too. He was grateful, too, knowing that when she had kissed him in the bathtub it had been done out of heartfelt concern and compassion for him after what had happened with those damned outlaws.

It showed that she might possibly care for him.

Through this newly found understanding was there hope for them? Could there be the promise of something more? Of something he had always secretly hoped and longed to find but had rejected, all those years ago? Of contentment, mutual respect and companionship?

Only time would tell whether it *was* a possibility and whether he was prepared to trust another woman again. Not that he dared hope for love. That was something he could not and would not offer. Not even to Eleanor.

'What are you thinking about, Hugh?' she whispered.

'Nothing, sweetheart. Go to sleep.' He stroked her hair and kissed the top of her head.

'I will after you tell me.'

'I was thinking how lucky I am to have you in my arms.'

She nestled closer. 'I believe that is also true for me.'

He realised then, as he held her, that he wanted this—this intimate contentment with Eleanor—and he would fight for it if he had to. He needed it. His hectic life of soldiering was restless, difficult and soulless, and where once he'd thrived on the battlefield he knew now with certainty that he was tired of it all. He wanted to build a home with her—here in Tallany.

'Do you know what I am thinking?' she asked.

He shook his head.

'That I still don't know much about you and I should, Hugh. You're my husband.'

He kissed the tips of her fingers. 'I'm glad we've established that now, but mayhap this conversation can wait for another time?'

'I'm sure it can—but I feel I have been remiss in my wifely duties in more ways than one.'

Hugh folded his arm with his hand beneath his head, staring into the darkness. The truth was that he didn't find it easy talking about himself. Some things in life were best left well alone, never to be thought of again. Yet here, tonight, Eleanor had opened up to him, revealing aspects of her life that were horrific. It must have been incredibly hard to do.

'Tell me, Hugh.'

He sighed. 'What would you like to know?'

'Anything, really—such as where you grew up, whether you have siblings or whether you're an only child… That sort of thing.'

Hugh turned his head and watched the moonlight dancing across her face. 'So many questions to answer in the middle of the night.' He smiled, bemused. 'Very well. I am from the small hamlet of Watamestede, near St Albans. I am the south to your north, Eleanor, and I'm a third son, with two older brothers and three younger sisters. Only three of us survived into adulthood.'

Eleanor rested her chin on his chest. 'I'm sorry. It's never easy losing one's family. Is that why you left to find your fortune?'

'Yes…' He sighed again. 'But that was not the only reason.'

'Oh? What else made you leave your home?'

'I was a poor younger son, but I was ambitious to prove myself. To make something of myself,' he said. 'And I had a reason to as I believed myself in love.'

'Oh, I see.' She wriggled uncomfortably.

'No, I don't think you do, Eleanor.' Hugh shook his head as he laced his fingers through hers. 'It took a long time for me to get where I needed to be, but after years and years of hard work I eventually became a knight. Though finally I was a success, I was only a hearth knight—landless and, in the eyes of Alais Courville, still not good enough.'

'I'm sorry.' She raised her brows. 'What happened?'

'I went home and found that the woman who had promised herself to me—who had apparently given her heart to me—had married my eldest brother. No doubt to become the mistress of the manor,' he said bitterly. 'After that, I never went back.'

'You haven't seen your family since then?'

'No,' he whispered. 'Anyway, it was better for my brother that I didn't go back…and better for Alais.'

'But what about you? It was your home.'

'It was better for me too, sweetheart. To sever those ties and establish myself as a soldier. And I don't have a home. Not any more.'

'She didn't deserve you.' Eleanor squeezed his hand.

'And, Hugh? You do know… Your home is here in Tallany.'

Hugh felt a tightness in his chest, and was gripped with a sudden sense of yearning. He had never shared this with anyone before—not even Will, who knew some of his past—and it felt somehow good to unburden himself to his wife.

'Thank you,' he said, feeling a little self-conscious. 'Come, enough of this morbid conversation, wife. Let us get some much-needed sleep.' He kissed her forehead.

'Hugh?' She reached out, her fingers grazing the sharp angles of his jaw. 'I'm sorry she hurt you.'

He swallowed as he nodded his thanks. 'I realised two things after that whole sorry episode, Eleanor. And as a result I will never repeat such a mistake. I realised that I would never put my faith in courtly love. There is no such thing, I'm afraid.'

She drew back a little, watching him in the dark. 'You don't believe there is? Well, at least you don't make a pretence of that.'

'No, sadly I don't. Love is an emotion that's oppressive, inequitable, and makes people act without reason or sense. It only serves to bring out the worst in people.'

'I see,' she murmured.

'I'm sorry—I shouldn't have said any of that. It was unfair of me. But you and I agreed a while back that affections of the heart were never going to affect us.'

'Yes, I know we did.' She exhaled. 'May I ask what your other realisation was?'

'I hope you don't think less of me for this, Eleanor, but I've realised that there are some things in life that I can never forgive or forget. I know it is a failing.' He frowned. 'But, for me, the betrayal of trust is the worst sin of all. Once my trust has gone, it has gone for ever.'

No, he dared not hope for anything resembling love. It was not for a practical, pragmatic man like him. He would do well to remember that. He'd risked his heart once, and it had turned out very badly. He would not risk it again.

He pulled Eleanor closer and kissed her hair. 'Goodnight, wife. Until the morrow.'

Chapter Ten

The next few days brought a flurry of activity to Tallany Castle as preparations were made for the long journey down south to Winchester Castle, the ancestral home and favourite castle of King John. Even his young son Prince Henry had been born there.

Summons had been received, demanding Hugh, Will and their men to his makeshift court there, the Sovereign needing much support from his allies against the Rebel Barons' new demands on him—especially the auspicious Great Charter of Liberties, or Magna Carta, that they insisted he sign and naturally the King refused to do.

On having had the missive read, Hugh sensed the anger John must be feeling. And his protracted rage at not only having his rule questioned but having to bend to the will of the Rebel Barons, meaning he was unlikely to concede. John was not the easiest of men, and a situation like this was bound to blow up to unparalleled proportions and be an unmitigated disaster. The whole country would end up tearing itself to bits.

And Hugh had no choice in the matter and was honourbound to travel down at the King's request.

His days were spent organising his men, the supplies

and wagons needed for the journey, as well as scouting the demesne lands and local forests with Will for Le Renard and his outlaws—but to no avail. They had once again disappeared as if into thin air. And the imprisoned men hadn't helped much either, swearing they knew nothing about them or their hiding place, adding to Hugh's frustration.

All of which left him little time to spend with Eleanor. Not that he stopped thinking about her. The way she had looked at that precise moment when he had claimed her was now imprinted on him for ever.

Their unexpected closeness was more than he'd ever thought possible with a woman. And when he gazed at her, at those big, brown luminous eyes, that chestnut hair and the intoxicating body that he'd had the pleasure of exploring these past few nights, it made him want to find her and take her back to bed, there and then.

He groaned inwardly. It was more than that—and he knew it. She was witty, spirited and intelligent in a way that captivated and intrigued him. She was both unusual and alluring.

The truth was that he liked Eleanor and enjoyed her company. It was the little things too—such as a shared look or understanding when he caught her eye, trying hard not to laugh at a mutual jest. Or surprising her with a small gift he thought she might appreciate and watching her astonishment at receiving it. He also admired Eleanor's constancy to Tallany and its people. She didn't feel it beneath her to work tirelessly, taking her duty as chatelaine seriously.

Yes, he liked her very well indeed, and all those feelings scared the hell out of him. He knew he shouldn't allow himself to get too close to her. That had never been part of their bargain. But he just couldn't help it. The best thing to do in his predicament was to keep very, very busy and stop his thoughts from wandering to Eleanor. But that was easier said than done.

Just then, as if by magic, Hugh saw her materialise in the crowded castle keep, meandering with her maid, mingling with some of the villagers. Eleanor was handing out silver to a few of them and chatting to an old beggar woman when she spotted him and the corners of her beautiful lips quirked upwards. God, but he lost the ability to think when she smiled at him like that!

He strode towards her and pressed a kiss on the back of her bare hand, no longer covered.

'What a fine surprise, Eleanor. What brings you out into the village at this late hour of the day?' He looked from Eleanor to the older woman. 'Ah, but I can see that I've interrupted you?'

'Not at all, Hugh. This is Aedith, the elder I have told you about, from the small hamlet of Ulnaby on the northern edges. The people there have little surplus food as crops have failed this year.'

'I'm very sorry to hear that, but rest assured that we will do everything we can to help.' He nodded decisively. 'Is there anything else we can do… Aedith?'

The older woman's eyes widened in surprise as she looked from Eleanor to Hugh. 'No…no, my lord. God keep you and my lady safe.' With that, she curtsied and hobbled away.

Hugh turned to Eleanor. 'Why haven't I been informed about these problems before?'

'I only heard about them a moment before I told you.' Eleanor bit her lip. 'I believe that Aedith was unsure whether she would receive the aid Ulnaby needed.'

He raised his brow. 'You mean she was unsure about the intentions of the new Lord of Tallany?'

'Either way, I'm certain that you have now given her peace of mind with your assurances, Hugh.' She smiled. 'Just as you have every other village and hamlet. They know they have nothing to fear in you.'

'Well, thank God for that.'

Eleanor's smile deepened as she regarded him. 'Hugh, there is something else I want to ask you.' She nodded to Brunhilde, who bobbed a curtsey and walked away in a different direction.

'Oh? And how can I help you, my lady?'

'I have been thinking that mayhap I should accompany you to Winchester tomorrow—if you are in agreement?' she said.

'It would be my pleasure to have you come.'

'Good. I think it is about time that I attend court, especially now that I am a married woman.' She shrugged. 'It would also afford me the opportunity to pay my respects at my family's tomb at St Michael's Chapel in Milnthorpe.'

'Of course—and I would be happy for your company, Eleanor.'

'Then it is settled? I can go and arrange everything with Brunhilde for the morrow?' She arched her brows.

'It is and you should,' he said, grinning. 'Go. Get yourself ready, my lady, and I shall see you in our solar later.'

She went on her tiptoes and kissed Hugh on the cheek. 'Yes, but not until much, much later. I have much to do and I am also in need of Brunhilde's tincture, so please do not wait up for me.'

'Very well—but don't be too late, Eleanor. If you send a message to me, I shall be happy to escort you back.'

'Thank you, but there's no need to worry about me. It's not as though I am stepping outside of the village.'

'I know, but it's not a good idea for you to be out so

late—not with dangerous outlaws on the prowl in the area.'

'You have much to attend to, Hugh. I will ask Gilbert to escort me back to our solar. Would that suffice?'

'It would.' His lips tugged at the corners before he pressed them to her fingers again. 'Until later, Eleanor,' he said, and then continued on the dusty pathway in search of Will.

Eleanor stood and watched Hugh walk away before she felt she could breathe again. She put her fingers to her temple and rubbed it, feeling the tightening tensions accumulating there. She sighed, glancing back in the direction her husband had gone, and her shoulders sagged. She hated the fact that she had just lied to him, but there was no other choice.

She scurried away to one side of the inner bailey and waited underneath an arch until Gilbert emerged. He nodded and made a slight bow as she beckoned him over to her side.

'My lady, I await your instruction. Everything is ready and we can take our leave immediately,' the steward whispered.

'Very good, Gilbert—and, yes, we must leave directly. I will go to Brunhilde's chamber to change.'

'Where shall I meet you, Lady Eleanor?'

'Outside the entrance to the undercroft. It grows dark and there will be no one there at this time. Go in haste and please take care, Gilbert.'

'I will, my lady. See you shortly.'

Eleanor watched her steward leave, then turned on her heel and strode towards the far corner of the wide circular inner bailey, her heart beating fast, reflecting on what she had to achieve this evening before embarking on the journey south with Hugh tomorrow.

She rushed into Brunhilde's chamber in a disused private solar and set about getting ready. She was glad that she had been able to gift this chamber to her, and another to Gilbert, to show both of them how much they had meant to her when her family had perished. It was the least she could do for her old faithful friends, who had always been more like family to her than servants.

Brunhilde's chamber was close to the kitchens and the entrance to the undercroft where she would soon meet Gilbert.

Taking off the garments of Lady Eleanor Tallany, she changed into the plain clothing of a castle servant, so that she could pass unnoticed from her maid's solar to the arranged rendezvous with Gilbert. From there, they would continue outside the castle and beyond, to make the necessary arrangements with the outlaws before she left tomorrow. All this had to be done with breathtaking expediency, so that she would not be missed later by Hugh.

Ah, Hugh...

Her husband was seldom far from her thoughts. She loved spending time with him and, if she was honest with herself, couldn't wait until the evenings, when they would be alone in the privacy of their solar; playing chess, sharing conversation, laughter and sensuous intimacies. These last few days and nights had been a blissful revelation to her.

She stared blankly at the hearth and warmed her hands near the flames. Yet the ominous words about trust and betrayal that Hugh had uttered on that first night of shared intimacy troubled her greatly. His words tumbled around her head constantly, making her even more determined that he should never find out about her involvement with the outlaws.

She couldn't bear to think of the consequences—for him to think badly of her and, even worse, for him to believe that yet another woman had hurt him. She cared about him, and enjoyed all the vivid moments they shared. Her feelings had undergone a huge change. Not that she was in love with him…

Besides, Hugh didn't believe in that.

Eleanor sighed as she pulled a plain grey tunic over her head. Not that she did either.

Brunhilde scuttled into the room, her kirtle rustling in the rushes of the floor, wringing her hands together.

'Is everything well?' Eleanor frowned.

'Yes, my lady. Gilbert is ready and waiting for you. But I wanted to say that it's not too late to change your mind about leaving the castle. It's too dangerous to go and come back without getting caught. Please, Lady Eleanor, listen to my warnings.'

Eleanor grasped the older woman's shoulder and rubbed it reassuringly. 'I hear your concerns, but I have to make sure that everything is settled with the outlaws. I cannot have a situation similar to when the others were caught.' She put her hand up to silence Brunhilde, knowing she had more to say. 'At least Osbert and Godwin are still alive and treated fairly, thanks to Hugh. Come, help me with this cloak, Brunhilde. I must be away.'

Eleanor dragged on a long grey cloak and wrapped it around her as her old maid fiddled with the clasp at the front.

'Very well—then I will just say that I think you are the bravest person I know, even though I fret over you,' the old woman said, her eyes filling with tears.

'Oh, Hildy, I will be fine. I promise.'

'I will pray to the Blessed Mary to keep you safe.'
Brunhilde crossed herself and turned her rosary beads
nervously.

Eleanor kissed her wet cheek and smiled softly. 'Please
don't worry about me—besides, Gilbert will be with me.
Now, don't forget that if my husband should seek me here
you must tell him that he has missed me. But I doubt
you'll need to.'

'Yes, my lady, as you wish.'

Eleanor pulled the wide hood of the dark cloak over
her head, so that once outside she'd be hard to recognise.
'Good—now I really must be away. Wish me luck.'

'You are, as always, in my prayers. Godspeed, my
lady. I won't be able to rest until I know you're back safe
and sound.'

Eleanor nodded, giving her hand a squeeze before turning around and walking out of the chamber.

It was going to be a long night, and she would need all
the prayers she could get.

Chapter Eleven

Hugh had been aimlessly strolling around the inner bailey since taking his leave of Will, deep in thought about the coming days. It had grown dark as he had absently reached the furthest corner, and he was about to turn back when a movement caught his eye. It was perhaps an animal, or the rustling of leaves from the old oak tree just outside the castle wall. But, no… The patter of feet and the sound of swathes of material flapping in the breeze put him on guard.

A person…?

But who would be roaming this part of the castle at this hour?

His suspicions raised, he moved stealthily and quietly towards the shifting shape, trying to glimpse the figure without alarming it. It was probably nothing—some hapless drunk taking the wrong turn after leaving the tavern in the village keep—but it would be prudent to be certain.

With Le Renard, his outlaws, and the possibility of a traitor here within the Tallany Castle walls, he needed to be careful, and alert to any unusual behaviour. He had to make sure that Tallany and its environs were safe and impenetrable.

There was no time to get Will's aid, so he had no choice but to follow this person himself.

The figure, hidden within a dark cloak, stopped and looked behind its shoulder—and it was in that brief moment that the moonlight caught the side of her face.

Eleanor?

Hugh exhaled deeply, screwing his eyes shut, rubbing them before opening them again.

Eleanor?

No, he wasn't certain that it was her. Why would it be his wife anyway?

He must follow this figure until he found some answers.

With a sinking feeling and his heart pounding in his chest, he surreptitiously followed, treading lightly, making sure the suspicious-looking person was unaware of him.

Hugh hid in the shadows cast under an archway as the figure reached the entrance to the undercroft, used by the cooks of the castle to keep supplies, and was met by another...

Gilbert Claymore, the Tallany steward!

The two figures slipped inside, as did Hugh, moments later. Making as little noise as possible, he followed them into the undercroft, ensuring a safe distance between them under the low-level arch. He watched as the cloaked figure pulled down its wide hood slowly, to reveal that he was correct after all...

It *was* Eleanor!

But why, for the love of God, why was she meeting Claymore in this secretive manner? Nothing made sense. She had said that the steward would escort her back to their solar, but this rendezvous didn't seem to have anything to do with that. Hell's teeth, what was she up to?

He had the urge to call out to her; ask what in God's name was she doing, but something about the whole situation stopped him in his tracks. He needed to wait and watch.

Hugh strained his ears to hear what they were saying but could only hear muffled voices. He crept closer and crouched down, hiding behind an arch as suddenly Eleanor looked round.

'What was that, Gilbert?' she whispered, and she turned back to her steward, who slowly drew his sword from its scabbard and took tentative steps back the way they had entered, looking in every direction in the shadowy recesses of the large airy chamber. The older man walked slowly, but stopped short of the arch Hugh was crouched behind.

Gilbert looked back at Eleanor. 'There is nothing here, my lady. Mayhap it was a mouse?' He shrugged, striding back towards her.

'Not again. I really wish Cook wouldn't chase all the cats away.' She smiled weakly and turned on her heel. 'Come, we need to hurry, Gilbert. We must be away immediately.'

'Aye, Lady Eleanor.'

They walked to the furthest stone wall. A huge old wooden coffer laden with neatly folded linen cloths and rounds of string leant against it. Eleanor and her steward faced each other and she nodded at him. Then Gilbert slid the wooden door of the coffer across, revealing an empty space large enough for no more than one person to stow themselves away inside.

'After you, my lady.'

He beckoned as Eleanor took a deep breath, crouched low, and curled herself into the space. After a moment Gilbert followed his mistress and crammed himself inside the wooden furniture, sliding closed the door from the inside.

In disbelief at what he had just witnessed, Hugh scurried to the coffer and knelt low, his heart pounding fast, and carefully slid the wooden door open—to find that there was nothing inside.

It couldn't be… He had watched his wife and the Tallany steward get inside, one after the other, and now they had disappeared into thin air.

The only way to find out what they were doing and where they were going was to continue to pursue them.

He imitated what he had dimly seen them do and crept inside the confined space, waiting for something to happen, but nothing did.

Where had Eleanor and Claymore gone?

He scrambled out again and felt inside with his fingers, trying in vain to peer into the dark recess—nothing.

Damn, damn, damn!

Swallowing down his frustration, he gritted his teeth and slid his hands over the back of the coffer. There—this time he felt it. A small gap between two of the wooden panels, so small that it had been easy to miss the first time he had felt his way around.

He carefully slipped his fingers in, but nothing shifted. Taking in a deep breath, he tried again. This time he slid one of the panels and it moved across, revealing a large hollow opening in the stone wall behind the coffer.

He crawled back inside, wedged himself uncomfortably into the enclosed space and closed the outer door so that he was plunged into complete darkness. Sending a silent prayer, he shuffled along so that he was pushing his body into the black void in the stone wall.

Hugh fell from a short height and landed with a thud on his side, onto wet, dank ground. He groaned, rubbing his head, and got up on his feet, blinking a few times. In the distance he saw a glimmer of light darting away and getting fainter and fainter.

Eleanor and Claymore!

He scrambled forward, quickening his pace to catch up with them. As he felt his way along the narrow passage, walled on either side with cragged, sharp slates, he guessed that he was in a maze of hidden interconnecting tunnels, separate from the main tunnels beneath the castle which he knew about—including the gaol. Which meant that these were secret ones.

Dear God!

The further he moved stealthily through the passage the more his heart sank. Whatever they were doing, or about to do, this didn't bode well. It smacked of conspiratorial behaviour. But he had to be patient—had to give Eleanor the benefit of the doubt until he knew what in heaven was going on.

He eventually caught up with them, but kept enough distance to avoid revealing his presence. The winding tunnel dipped and turned in every direction, then became so extremely narrow that he could only squeeze through by shuffling along on his side. The sharp slates on either side dug into him.

Where the hell were they going?

Suddenly, the passage opened out and they came to an abrupt halt.

Claymore knelt down and pushed his hand into a large crevice in the wall, which made a few large slates slide out. The steward then pulled something that Hugh couldn't quite see that was within the wall, which revealed a large hidden trap door, whipping open in the cold night air.

Incredible! If Hugh hadn't been feeling as apprehensive and tense as he was, he might have appreciated the ingenuity of a secret trap door hidden so cleverly.

He continued to watch as Eleanor and the steward crouched down and crawled through the opening and into another space beyond.

Hugh waited a moment before he followed them with caution. He too crouched down, and took in a deep breath before sneaking a furtive look and finding that the space they had entered was actually outside. The steward was opening what appeared to be a rusty iron gate, covered in moss. Once he had achieved this, they were outside in the middle of god knows where!

Hugh followed them in the shadows, making sure he was well hidden, and watched in amazement. Eleanor and Claymore were now walking through the damp woodlands far from Tallany. Remarkably, the secret tunnels underneath the castle, which had seemed so endless, had bypassed the castle, the moat and even the village keep! They were now at the edge of nowhere, deep in the woodland.

Having an ominous feeling about what he was about to discover, Hugh continued trailing his wife and the steward.

After a long time in pursuit of them, weaving around ancient trees casting shadows in the clearings, Hugh watched as they reached what appeared to be a single dilapidated wooden hut. He waited in heightened anticipation to find out what they were to do next.

He hid behind a boulder that sloped above them, with the moonlight offering the only glimmer of visibility in an otherwise dark night. He peered over it and watched as Eleanor entered the small building alone, whilst Claymore stood outside, evidently on the lookout.

Hugh rubbed his eyes, trying hard not to look away

in case he missed something. What was she doing and who was she meeting? Lord, but it was killing him, waiting to find out.

He wiped away the beads of sweat collated on his brow, his heart pounding ferociously as he waited, uneasiness mounting.

Damn and blast, Eleanor! What have you got yourself into?

He couldn't move closer to the hut in case Claymore spotted him, and it was imperative for Hugh that he was not to be discovered. He *had* to know the truth of Eleanor's strange behaviour tonight, however much he dreaded it, and the only way was to remain in hiding.

At last heard the door of the hut creak open and footsteps on the beaten path. Eleanor...? But, no, the silhouette that had come to meet Claymore was that of a man—or rather a boy.

And not just any boy.

The moonlight shed enough light for Hugh to make him out.

It was Le Renard—the outlaw who had outwitted him only just a few days ago, in his signature mask and fur-trimmed hood!

Chapter Twelve

Hugh felt as though someone had punched the air out of him. How was this possible? *How?*

He ground his teeth together and clenched his fists, his knuckles white. He just couldn't believe it. Couldn't believe what he had discovered on this terrible evening. But there was no mistaking it.

Eleanor and Le Renard…

It made his blood boil, just thinking about the implications of this night. All this time *his wife* had evidently been scheming with the outlaw. His wife! He felt like hitting something—or better still someone. The whole thing seemed unbelievable.

Hugh narrowed his gaze at the two figures, Claymore and The Fox, striding together. The steward mounted a horse that had been tethered somewhere, hidden from visibility, and waited for Le Renard, with his own horse, and then they galloped off, deep into the woods.

Hugh knew he should give the pair of traitors chase and find out where the outlaws were hiding. But he couldn't move—couldn't think beyond Eleanor's treachery. He let Le Renard and Claymore go—not that he had the means to follow them anyway.

Eleanor, his wife and Le Renard...

Dear God!

It stood to reason that *she* must be the traitor he sought. It was Eleanor who had passed on information to The Fox and his outlaws. And it was Eleanor who had worked against him from the very start...

What a fool he had been. If he had paid more attention, mayhap, none of this would be such a bitter shock now, but he had allowed himself to get close to her. He'd *liked* her, damn it!

He still liked her...

God, but he should shake himself out of such futile emotions. When he thought of all the nights of delicious intimacies they had recently shared...

Cold fury filled his veins at the thought of her absolute treachery.

Hell's teeth! How could she do this?

It made him sick to the stomach when he thought about that first night of incredible passion... That night after the outlaws and her *friend* Le Renard had thwarted him and stolen the Crown's silver. And it was all because of Eleanor's deceit.

Why? He wanted to scream at her.

'*My castle, my lands and my wealth may now be yours—even my body—but my* heart *will never be.*'

Those ominous words that Eleanor had uttered on their wedding night—the night that had never happened— seemed so full of foreboding now. Had she already given her heart to Le Renard—that man-boy? He didn't know and didn't care—or rather didn't want to care.

He thought of Eleanor as she had lain in his arms, responding to his kisses, coming undone. Had everything they'd shared been an act? Had everything she'd said been a lie? She had been so receptive to his touch and his kisses—but had *that* been a lie as well?

Lord, his stomach was going to empty itself.

Eleanor had come to him that night, after the outlaws had waited for him and his men and taken the strongbox. She would have known full well that it was the information *she* had passed on to Le Renard that had brought about the failure. Had that been a tactical use of diversion to befuddle his senses? Had she felt a pang of guilt? It was impossible to say either way.

Did Hugh even know the real Eleanor Tallany?

Damn! He must stop tormenting himself. Even if she hadn't given her heart to Le Renard, she had still betrayed *him*, still played him false. He should stride down there to that hut and shake some answers out of Eleanor. Congratulate her for playing him for a fool.

But, no. He swallowed down his disgust. He couldn't face her. Not now, and not tonight. Besides, the pragmatic side to his character knew that he had to wait and watch. Now that he knew of both his wife and the steward of Tallany's involvement with the outlaws, he had to wait and see the extent of the disloyalty. For all he knew everyone on these lands—all the Tallany villages and its people—might also be involved.

He could sympathise with the struggles that the people faced. Damn it, he wanted to remedy that. But not like this. Not by breaking the law of the land and consorting with outlaws, for the love of God.

He shook his head and screwed his eyes shut, opening them to fix a cold, hard glare upon the small building where Eleanor was even at that moment, waiting for her friends, and felt his heart blacken towards her.

Damn the woman!

She would never, ever play him false again. Yes, he

would confront his beguiling, duplicitous wife—very soon—but he'd have to wait until after they had got back from Winchester. By then he hoped he would have learnt more, since she was to travel south with him. Not that he wanted her to *now*.

For now, all he wanted was to get drunk—blind drunk. To drown his sorrows in as much ale as he could so he could forget about his problems and forget about his duplicitous wife.

Eleanor, disguised beneath her mask and tunic, pulled forward her fur-trimmed hood and wondered wryly, as she did every time she saw her men, whether they would follow her as they did if they knew their leader was really Lady Eleanor Tallany.

Oh, they knew that Lady Eleanor supported them, but the fact that she was The Fox… No… Only Gilbert, Brunhilde and Father Thomas knew that.

She remembered that ominous day when she had asked Gilbert Claymore to carefully seek local men who would commit to their cause. The day the King's mercenaries had ventured into Tallany demanding yet more scutage they hadn't had to give.

It hadn't mattered that Tallany's coffers were empty—the men had taken everything they could anyway, leaving devastation in their wake. Eleanor had known then that something had to be done. Something that would ensure her people would never have to endure such ignominy again.

Le Renard had been conceived to do just that.

It hadn't been easy. Not at first. The Fox had had to convince the men assembled before him that *he* was the one to lead them, and they had been sceptical at first. They'd had to be persuaded to follow a masked leader, an outsider—even one who had the backing of Gilbert Claymore, Father Thomas and even Lady Tallany. A lean, slight leader more cunning than they could ever have imagined…

In turn, Eleanor had had Gilbert vet the group of men, to discover everything about them—especially if they'd be trustworthy—and then train them secretly to become the outlaws she needed.

Those outlaws had had to learn to work together, trust in each other and follow Le Renard's strategic plans blindly and without question. In return, they were helping to restore something Tallany had lost…something they all needed…*hope.*

Eleanor coughed, clearing her throat and gaining the attention of everyone in the chamber.

'I have called this meeting to bring everyone together and discuss a few pressing matters.' She'd lowered the tone of her voice to sound like one that wasn't hers. 'But firstly—our friends!' She raised her mug as the men followed suit and repeated her toast.

'You should have let me slit the throat of that new Lord of Tallany when I 'ad the chance, Fox. For our friends,' the big, burly outlaw Anselm ground out, and a few others added their agreement.

'And what would that have achieved? Would it have brought our friends back? Would it have honoured them? No. And it wasn't Lord Hugh who murdered our friends but Edmund Balvoire—a man with no principles at all.'

Le Renard glared at Anselm from under his mask, silencing the big man, who sank, disgruntled, back into his chair. 'We have honoured our friends instead by taking this.' Le Renard slammed his gloved hand on the strongbox on the table.

'Verra well, Fox, but what about Osbert and Godwin? Is Lady Eleanor going to help release 'em?'

'You must know that will be risky for her, Anselm, but God willing she will do it soon. And whilst they may be imprisoned, our men are being treated well, I believe. Isn't that so, Claymore?'

'It is.'

The burly outlaw rubbed his jaw. 'Good—let's 'ope it stays that way. What shall we do with the silver this time, then?'

'I want a few of you to take it in batches to the church. Father Thomas will distribute it between local villages and people.' Le Renard nodded at Father Thomas, who smiled and nodded back. 'Some will be given to the poor by Lady Eleanor.' Le Renard paused before continuing. 'But what I want to say is that after tonight we will not be meeting again for some time.'

'What? Why? This is the time to keep going—hit those bastards where it hurts!' Anselm cried.

'No, it is getting too dangerous. We have managed not to get caught so far, but look what happened when we weren't cautious. Two of our own lost their lives and two more were imprisoned because of our complacency. I don't want to risk any more loss of life, so I must have everyone's agreement that we dismantle our group for a short time.'

The outlaws showed their displeasure, grumbling, but Le Renard slammed his mug on the table to get their attention.

'I take the safety of each and every man here very seriously,' he barked. 'And I will not risk anyone until danger is averted. Even now we're being hunted by the likes of Balvoire, who'd have us strung up high, given half a chance. I cannot risk it.'

Le Renard looked at the assembled group, each man as dependable as the next, and felt immense gratitude to each of them.

'We have always come together to address the injustice in our land—to help and protect those in need—but we must stop doing what we do…for now.' The outlaw leader nodded at each one of them from beneath his mask. 'Are we in agreement, then? What say you, my brave and honourable men?'

Le Renard flexed his arm and waited as each man cried, 'Aye!' before placing his hand on top of his until their clasped hands formed a circle of solidarity.

Chapter Thirteen

Eleanor stared at her husband's stiff back as she rode on her young horse behind him as their cavalcade entered a woodland in glorious verdant shades of green on the edge of a small hamlet.

There was something very wrong with Hugh.

Initially, Eleanor had thought that it was the distraction of heading their travelling party, the responsibility of the venture as well as the many duties he had to attend to day and night but…no. Although he was courteous, and had ensured her comfort and that of her women during their journey, there was no mistaking a change within him.

It was perplexing to find that Hugh's feelings had seemingly altered towards her after their growing closeness. It had started the night before their departure, when he hadn't slept in their bed or even in their solar. She hadn't given it much thought, but after three days and three nights on the road he had still not come to her at night.

It was strange behaviour, but mayhap he thought to observe propriety whilst they were travelling and leave Eleanor to her women.

And there was more than that. On the morning they

had left he had put Tallany under the command of one of his most trusted men and effectively retired Gilbert Claymore—which had been shocking, to say the least, as it had been done without discussion with her and in a very heavy-handed manner.

What was wrong with Hugh?

Eleanor had wondered whether her husband had somehow found out about her involvement with the outlaws—or, God forbid, that she was Le Renard—but had dismissed those notions since Hugh had not made any accusations of that kind. Her fear of that had at least abated.

But then it did still beg the question of Hugh's change of behaviour. Could it be that Hugh was worried about getting too close to her? He had warned her on many occasions that he wasn't interested in courtly love. Especially as the only other time he'd got close to a woman it had ended badly for him.

Now he had fulfilled his marriage obligation and finally taken her to bed—many times—there was no reason for him to spend more time than necessary with her.

Oh, but she wished he would. Eleanor missed those tantalisingly private moments they'd shared.

What if he had put her to one side to find someone else to warm his pallet at night? It made her ache inside just thinking about that possibility, but then again it was highly unusual for any husband to be enamoured of his wife. And it was not as if their marriage had been of his choosing.

She tilted her head and peered at Hugh, riding out front on his magnificent destrier, and sighed. The only thing to do was to try and find out what was troubling her husband.

She gently kicked her palfrey's flanks to coax it into catching up with Hugh's horse at the front of the cavalcade.

'Good morning, husband. I hope you are faring well?'

'As well as can be,' he said, without any of his usual humour, looking straight ahead of him.

'You did not come to our tent last night, Hugh.' She caught her bottom lip between her teeth. 'I thought mayhap… Well, now that we have been travelling for the past few days—'

'Excuse me, my lady, but is there anything that you need?'

You—only you.

'I believe we must be getting close to Milnthorpe soon. Do we still have time to stop for a few hours whilst I pay my respects?'

'Yes, if you wish it.'

'I do,' she said. 'It has been a long time since I was there last.'

'Good, that's settled. Now, if there's nothing else, I have other things I must attend to.'

'Hugh, wait. My ladies and I will need to clean off the dirt of the last few days' travel before we offer our prayers.'

'I'm sure you will—and I'm sure we can stop by a stream somewhere.'

'Thank you.' Eleanor inclined her head.

'Now we must press on. So, if you'll excuse me, I have an important matter that I must discuss with Sir William,' he said curtly, setting his horse and speeding ahead.

She tried to keep up with her husband. 'Shall I accompany you?' she asked.

'I really don't think that's necessary.'

She frowned. 'Very well…but when shall I see you?'

Hugh turned his head and fixed her with a hard stare.

'Really, Eleanor, we're not bound together at every moment.'

Stunned by her husband's uncharacteristic rudeness, Eleanor was momentarily taken back. 'I didn't say we were.'

'Go to your women, my lady. I haven't got time for this.'

'Well, *my lord*, when you do find the time, be sure to tell me. It would be of interest to me to know why my husband is behaving like a boorish ass.'

Eleanor was finding it difficult to keep her temper under control, but that stemmed from confusion. She just couldn't understand the change in him.

'I would reflect on your own behaviour if I were you,' he said.

She gasped. 'What…what in heaven's name does *that* mean?'

'Nothing.' He sighed. 'It means nothing. Apologies, Eleanor, but I didn't sleep well last night and as a result I am more irritable than usual.'

'I understand. Is there anything I can do?' She raised her brows. 'Anything that I can help with?'

She'd hoped the look she gave him was one that would tempt him to visit her later that night.

'No,' he replied, before riding out ahead.

Eleanor dropped back to ride beside her ladies whilst she thought on what had just passed between them. Oh, yes, there was definitely something wrong with Hugh and she would do everything she could to find out the reason for his bizarre behaviour. None of it made any sense, but she would be on guard and watchful until she understood everything—even if it ended up hurting her.

Eleanor and her women washed and dressed in clean and sober clothes before arriving in the pretty yet remote hamlet of Milnthorpe. At the church of St Michael she knelt at the altar and received a blessing from the priest, making the sign of the cross before resuming her prayers, conscious of her husband beside her. She was glad of Hugh's presence, since it somehow made it a little easier being in this solemn place.

The sickly-sweet smell of incense enveloped her senses, making her stomach turn on itself. She hated coming here. It brought back the desperate unhappiness and loneliness she had endured after her family had perished, one after the other.

Sometimes she still felt as she had back then—guilty about being the only one to survive. Not that living had been any easier. Her life had been filled with its fair share of difficulty and hardship. The only glimmer of light had been her recent marriage to Hugh, and that seemed to be fading before it had truly begun to shine.

She stood up abruptly, in an attempt to end those morose thoughts, but swayed, losing her footing and finding a pair of strong masculine hands around her shoulders, steadying her.

'You look pale, Eleanor, are you well?'

'Perfectly,' she said, taking in a huge breath. 'Thank you again for allowing me to pay my respects. Coming here always reminds me of how much I have lost.'

'Naturally… I understand.'

Eleanor rubbed her forehead and turned her face away from him.

'Come, you could do with some fresh air.'

Hugh gently guided her by the arm out of the chapel and away from prying eyes, leading her down a cobbled path until they reached a small stone wall overlooking green pasture, with sheep grazing in the field.

Sheep, for the love of God!

It made her think of that day when Hugh had gifted her with her own flock, given with such unbelievable kindness the like of which she had never known. Well, not since her family had been alive.

It had been such a happy few hours or so. She had forgotten about all her problems and enjoyed her husband's company, his humour, not to mention his glorious kisses. Ah, those languid, melting kisses that had left her wanting so much more...

If only she had known then that they would be so fleeting...that he would soon reject her.

Eleanor's eyes darted from the sheep dotted around the field to the young spring lambs nestled beside them and filled with tears. She let out a shaky breath as an ache enveloped her chest.

She wiped her eyes angrily with the back of her hand and looked away. She hated feeling like this—and even worse revealing her weakness in front of another, least of all Hugh. It made her feel vulnerable—something she could never be. She must be strong-willed and resolute; she had learned it was the only way to live. In any case, mayhap she was wrong about Hugh and there was a perfectly reasonable explanation for his behaviour.

'Here, Eleanor, you could do with a drink.' Hugh held out his flagon, offering it to her. 'It's cool water from the stream.'

She took it hesitantly and nodded her wordless thanks, taking a few sips.

'It's not easy to lose someone you care about,' she said, fixing him with a pointed stare.

'No, it's not.'

There wasn't much else to say, and Eleanor didn't feel the need for conversation, allowing the awkward silence to stretch. She realised that she wanted to be alone for a moment, to compose herself and clear her head.

Hugh coughed, gaining her attention. 'How old were you, my lady, when you lost your family?' he asked.

'My brothers and sisters all died through illness one terrible winter,' she whispered. 'For a few years it was just my father and I, until his death when I was in my eleventh year.' A ghost of a smile played on her lips. 'I remember the sound of his laughter. It was so infectious. And he was the most patient man. I could be quite a handful, you see...so eager to learn everything and nothing.'

Hugh chuckled. 'He sounds like a man of true honour.'

Eleanor smiled weakly, nodding in agreement. 'Yes, he was. As for my mother—she died before them all, when I was very young, in childbirth. I barely remember anything about her, although I have been told that I'm much like her.'

'I'm sure you are, Eleanor.' He scuffed his shoe absently against the edge of the stone wall before continuing. 'My mother died in much the same way as yours, although I was much older. Even to this day the smell of lavender and thyme evokes memories of her. She was a gentle, kind soul.'

'I'm sorry for your loss. It's not easy, being left behind.'

He shook his head. 'It's not.'

'That is why I find it difficult to come here. Because it reminds me of the enormity of my loss.'

'I know—but that's why it's important to honour our loved ones in the most fitting way. By living life with grace, dignity...and courage.'

'True... But those high standards are not always easy to live up to.'

'Are they not?' he asked, raising his brow. 'We must

always strive to be better, however hard it is and whatever life throws at us.'

She got up suddenly and smoothed her wine-coloured kirtle with her hand. 'If you don't mind, I would like a little time in solitude. I won't be long.'

'Of course. If there's anything I can do…?'

'Thank you, but, no, you have done enough. Until later,' she said, nodding curtly at him.

Hugh watched as his wife met her maid and quickly hurried away, cloaked under a plain cape with a hood pulled high across her head, similar to the one she had worn that night when he had followed her outside Tallany Castle. When she'd met The Fox.

She stopped and looked over her shoulder, as if making sure they weren't being followed.

Solitude?

Hugh followed his wife and her maid out of the little village of Milnthorpe as she surreptitiously made her way down the narrow, cobbled path with buildings and dwellings on either side. He had been right to wait and allow Eleanor to expose herself rather than make glib accusations straight away.

Where the hell was she going?

After her talk earlier, about her loss, Hugh had wondered whether Eleanor's friendship with Le Renard, or whatever their relationship was, had started after the loss of her family—or possibly during her turbulent marriage to Millais. Not that it made him feel any easier about it, but he could grudgingly understand it.

What he couldn't understand or accept was that she would still risk everything now to see the outlaw.

With his frustration mounting he followed them down

the winding pathway as it opened out into the beautiful rolling countryside.

They continued to make their way until they stopped by what looked like a small stone priory or convent, which must instead be part of St Michael's beneficiary hospital. The monastic institution had been founded by Eleanor's late father. Hugh knew this because the priest had earlier informed him about the good work the sisters at the infirmary did for the sick and the needy.

His wife and her maid went inside the gate and pulled the bell rope and were soon met by an elderly nun who hugged Eleanor, cupped her face and planted a motherly kiss on each of her cheeks.

Together they went inside the walled gardens and through the cloister, where the light danced through the arches and onto the stone floor. Hugh watched as they entered a large chamber with a dozen pallets arranged against the walls, where elderly men and women lay. With the clear lack of beds, some had resorted to lying on sack-cloth on the floor.

The space was basic, but clean, with a hearth on the adjacent wall offering warmth whilst younger nuns milled around, tending to the needy with industrious efficiency.

Hugh stayed at a distance as Eleanor gave three leather pouches of alms to the nun, opening one wide enough for him to see it was filled with silver. No doubt the silver the outlaws had stolen from *him*!

Then, to Hugh's surprise, she went to tend to every in-capacitated person, with purpose—talking to them, holding their hands, even mopping their brows and smoothing down their hair. Her thoughtful kindness and compassion for these poor souls brought a lump to his throat and humbled him as he stood and watched from the doorway.

Hugh had thought the worst of his wife but he had

been wrong. She was not bent on another assignation with Le Renard.

Not this time…

Eleanor lifted her head and caught his eye, frowning. She moved towards him, seemingly not too pleased to see him.

'Hugh? What are you doing here?'

'Ensuring that you enjoy your solitude in safety, my lady.'

Eleanor shot him an exasperated look. 'That's unnecessary. We're not, as you said earlier, always bound together.'

'No, you're right, we're not.' He smiled wryly. How like Eleanor to throw his careless words back to him. 'I will leave you now and meet you for our departure.'

'Wait. Since you're here now, why don't you stay? You can see for yourself all the marvellous work they do here.'

'Yes, I can…'

'This place was founded by my father, in my mother's memory. The whole building was erected for the purpose of looking after the elderly, the infirm and the destitute.'

Hugh looked around and nodded his approval. 'It is a fine legacy, Eleanor, you should be proud.'

She screwed up her face in self-conscious embarrassment. 'There's only so much we can do—people travel from far and wide to come here. We don't turn anyone away, but it's not possible to help everyone in the kingdom. We're only modestly sized, with limited means.'

He nodded at the room. 'That is a difficulty—but I see that they have a very generous patron in you, Eleanor.'

'Yes…' She flushed uncomfortably. 'Come, let me show you around.'

They walked back to the cloisters and then from one chamber to another as Hugh listened intently to Eleanor with his hands behind his back. He saw with astonishment the unique work being done and his wife's quiet satisfaction in taking her role as diligent patron very seriously.

As they passed through all the nuns, as well as the sick and the poor, lifted their heads and turned to greet Eleanor with a smile or a nod of recognition. She was evidently much admired here—but then Hugh could see the reason for that himself.

'It's very impressive. Why didn't you tell me about this place before?'

She shrugged as they stepped out into the cloisters once more. 'I wasn't sure whether you'd approve or not.'

He frowned. 'Why wouldn't anyone approve of this place?'

Eleanor continued to stroll, with Hugh by her side. 'When Richard Millais found out about this place he wouldn't allow me to continue my work here and immediately stopped the precious funds being used for its upkeep. It fell into disrepair for a number of years,' she said, looking thoughtfully at the tranquil gardens in the centre of the cloisters that edged it. 'But thankfully after his death I was able to resume everything, making it exactly as my father would have wished it.'

Hugh sighed. 'I see... And it seems that I have yet to convince you that I am nothing like your first husband?'

'Oh, I know you're nothing like him. I just didn't get around to telling you about this place.'

Like so many things...

'And now you don't have to, Eleanor.'

'No...' She smiled hesitantly.

'It's fortuitous that I followed you here, then, is it not? Otherwise I would never have known.' He glanced at her, watching her reaction.

'I suppose so…not that I think you should skulk around corners watching everything I do.'

'I'm sure you don't,' he retorted, but decided to change the subject…for now. 'What has made you continue your family's legacy?'

Her eyes scanned the garden before meeting his gaze. 'My father always wanted me to continue the work he had established, and he taught me to take my responsibility and duty for our people seriously. Besides, I enjoy it. I feel I am being of some use.'

Hugh tilted his head slightly and regarded her. 'They are lucky to have you.'

'Yes, but it's not enough. There are so many people like this, up and down the country, and far too few nobles who take their responsibilities seriously.'

'Apart from you, Eleanor.'

'And hopefully you too.'

He smiled ruefully. 'I do wish to do more, and I will defer to you on this as my experience in these matters is limited. I'm only a soldier after all.'

'No, you are so much more than that, Hugh,' she murmured, looking away.

He swallowed uncomfortably and gave himself a mental shake. 'I understand your concern, and it does you credit, but the kingdom at large is going through an exceptionally turbulent time. This is one reason we are venturing to Winchester.'

'Yes—and yet with civil unrest and discord between King John and the Barons it's the ordinary people who suffer the consequences. Especially with the King's punitive taxes.'

Hugh inhaled sharply. 'Eleanor, you should not be talking like this. It's both dangerous and seditious,' he hissed. 'And you're not in a position to blame or to pass judgement. You have no idea of the complexities of governance.'

'I suppose I don't—however, I'm not blind as to what is going on in the country.'

'I didn't say you were. I simply meant that no one should pass that kind of judgement. It's not our place.'

She looked at him speculatively before continuing. '*You* can, though, Hugh…as Lord of Tallany.'

He watched her, his eyes narrowing. 'What is it you're trying to say, Eleanor? That I should turn traitor on my King, my Sovereign?'

'Of course not. I mean that you have a voice, so use it. Use it for what is right and just.'

'I may have a voice, as you say, Eleanor, but I am also sworn to my King,' he said in a low tone.

He watched as she played nervously with her mother's cross, the simple piece of jewellery she always wore around her neck.

'Well, then he's indeed fortunate to have a man as honourable as you by his side. But remember what you told me earlier.' She took in a deep breath. 'That we have to live with standards such as dignity and courage. You were right when you said that we could always do better. For me, that is all the work that's being done here and elsewhere in Tallany.' She flicked her eyes at him. 'I hope that you know what it is…for you.'

How had she turned all this round on *him*? Yes, Eleanor might be right in that crippling taxes made life extremely hard, but with England's coffers empty and the country on the brink of civil unrest with the Rebel Barons and the foreign threat from France, how was the kingdom supposed to govern and defend itself effectively?

Eleanor had started to walk away and Hugh caught her wrist and turned her to face him. 'Yes, I do know,' he said, scowling. 'Why do you think I became a knight? Not to prove my valour, or for my own personal gain—even though I did want to make something of myself. No, I wanted to serve my King and country, Eleanor.'

She nodded. 'That is admirable, Hugh, but ordinary people face the harsh realities of a life that you and I will never fully understand.'

'How can anyone travelling up and down the kingdom fail to understand the misery people face? It's something that I'm trying to readdress.' His lips twisted. 'And we *all* have to face the harsh realities of life.'

They stared at each other for a long moment before Hugh turned and walked away.

Chapter Fourteen

They had journeyed for almost two weeks, and had finally arrived just outside the walls of Winchester Castle. Before Eleanor had asked, Hugh had anticipated her request and directed their entourage to the river, allowing them all the chance to clean and wash away the road's debris and dirt. She and her women were around the bend of the river, in a more private, secluded part.

Eleanor...

Hugh had purposely kept her at arm's length, without inviting another exchange such as they had had over a week ago in Milnthorpe. There was still so much he didn't understand or know about her. So much he was confused about.

He knew a few things, though. He knew he didn't want to like her and he certainly didn't want to desire her. He just wanted to be immune to her.

Hugh walked through the dense lush woodland, wondering whether Eleanor had finished her bathing. He tethered his horse to a tree and pulled back a branch. He glimpsed Eleanor in the distance, deep in the slow-streaming river that was edged by tall evergreens.

Her eyes were shut, as she savoured the delights of the

cool water, and her hands ran through her wet unbound hair, and down over her shoulders. The sheer linen tunic she wore clung to every inch of her body. He stood transfixed, watching her bathe, his lips parted, his breathing hitched, knowing he should move…get far away from this enticing creature who had him spellbound.

No one except him was allowed to be anywhere near the women, but right now he wished he too had been barred from the area. It would have been best for his own peace of mind.

Eleanor's maid Brunhilde came forward with another woman, holding up a large linen cloth, and his wife stepped slowly out of the river, her hands skimming the surface as she walked towards them.

Hugh continued to gaze at the scene before him, as Eleanor dried her body, dragging her fingers through her long, wet hair as her women helped her dress. He found it increasingly hard to breathe, felt blood pooling in his loins.

And it was naturally at that precise moment that she caught his gaze and held it, with a faint smile tugging at her lips. He groaned inwardly at his visceral reaction to his wife. Lord, he wanted her desperately—but then he always did.

No, he must find a way to resist temptation and be indifferent to her. He *had* to! He had to find a way to break this pathetic desire for Eleanor and continue to stay away from her.

The woman was an enigma, and every time his thoughts returned to her, and the man she had met the night before they'd left Tallany, he could feel the mist of anger rising. His thoughts and his better judgement were muddled and compounded by her betrayal.

Was she the compassionate patron, the dutiful daughter, or the traitor and temptress? Mayhap a bit of all...

He was torn between anger towards her and this longing to be with her. But he was shrewd enough to know that he needed to be careful not to reveal any of his feelings—it was a weakness he could do without. He had to shroud his anger, and even his desire, and think with his head...watch and learn more about the real Eleanor Tallany and find out who else was involved with the outlaws.

Only then would he know what to do. Well, he hoped he would...

He would conquer this hold she seemed to have over him. He would, damn it!

Eleanor had spotted her husband from afar and wondered how long he had stood there watching her bathe. She'd thought to have seen a spark of desire emanating from him, but the thunderous mood in which he had just left meant that she'd been wrong.

She sighed as she put her arms through the armholes of the green woollen kirtle that Brunhilde had cleaned and brushed down. Her maid then combed through her hair with a special oil that she'd prepared herself, using flower petals and herbs, making it glossy and soft. Ah, the delicious scent always made her smile...

But thinking about the past ten days froze the smile on her face. It had been a difficult trial for Eleanor, since she had barely spoken to Hugh beyond platitudes. She barely recognised her husband as the man she'd thought she knew—the man who occupied her thoughts far too much of the time.

But then what did *she* know about men? Time and time again she had been lulled into a false sense of security and had put her trust in a man, only for him to let her down…badly. She had been taken in much the same way by Richard Millais, although she knew Hugh was nothing like him.

Yet here she was again…alone, confused and forsaken.

She nodded at Brunhilde, who had braided and bound her hair under a gossamer-light veil and put a silver circlet over it.

Whatever was wrong with Hugh, she would find out, and then she would do everything in her power to win him back. And hope to God it was not too late.

Many hours later the Tallany party arrived in Winchester. After the horses were stabled Hugh directed their belongings to be unpacked and settled Eleanor into a small chamber—which he was absolutely *not* going to share with her. He then made his excuses and swiftly left to find Will at the nearest tavern outside the castle.

He had to be apart from her. Even her evocative floral scent had wrapped around his senses enticingly and made Hugh long for her…desperately. If he spent another moment with her today his resolve would crumble away completely—not that it was far from doing that anyway. He needed to drown his sorrows again and he needed to do that *now*.

He found Will with a group of his men, already partaking of a few jugs of ale at the boisterous tavern. Hugh caught up with them and motioned to Will with a flick of his head to come to a more private table.

'What news, Will?' he asked, sitting on a chair.

'I have been well informed that King John is in the foulest of tempers.'

'No change there, then. What's happened now?'

'London is in the hands of the Rebel Barons. The city

opened its gates to them with no resistance, and naturally the King is jumping up and down in rage without taking any responsibility for the situation.'

Hugh uttered an oath as he took a sip of his ale. 'Are you certain?'

'Absolutely—and between us let me say that I have some sympathy with their cause. Many of the Rebel Barons are good men.'

Hugh frowned. 'Even so, where will this all end? Do they believe that they'll be able to make John simply turn and concede to their demands? Hell's teeth, they've all sworn their fealty to him.'

Will raised his brows. 'Ah, but they feel he has left them no choice. And this explains the hurried missive from John demanding our return.'

'It's more than that. The Rebels want him to sign this Charter of Liberties...' Hugh sighed. 'Which John refuses to do.'

Will watched him from over the rim of his mug. 'Tell me, Hugh, is this what has been worrying you? Because that would explain a lot.'

'What is that supposed to mean?'

'It means,' Will said, 'that you have not been yourself ever since we left the north.'

'I don't know what you're talking about.' Hugh frowned.

'Yes, you do. Care to share?'

'No.'

Will shook his head as he poured ale into Hugh's mug. 'Come, Hugh, tell me what's troubling you.'

'Nothing. My life is wonderful. I'm a lucky bastard and I'm deliriously happy.' He stared blankly into his mug, his lips pressed into a thin line.

'You're deliriously something.' Will smirked. 'But happy? No.'

'For once in your life, just leave it. Believe me when I say that there is nothing you can help me with.'

'As bad as that, eh?'

Hugh shook his head and snorted. 'Never get married. It brings nothing but trouble, Will.'

'Oh, Lord. I thought this might have something to do with your heiress.'

Hugh threw his arms up. 'Precisely,' he said shaking his head. 'Did I ask to get married? No. Did I want to get married? No. And yet here I am, married to the most confounding, maddening woman.'

Not to mention reckless, duplicitous and a whole host of other things.

Will sat back and regarded his friend. 'I never thought a woman would capture your heart like this.'

Hugh gave him a disgusted look. 'Know this: Eleanor Tallany has captured no part of me—least of all my *heart*,' he spat.

Will let out soft chuckle. 'Dear me, what has happened? One minute you're wooing your lady with a flock of sheep—which, may I say, was a strange but inspired gift. The next you're playing the part of lovelorn swain.'

Hugh lunged forward and grabbed his friend by his tunic, his jaw clenched tight, his eyes full of murderous intent.

'What the hell is wrong with you?' Will hissed through gritted teeth, and pushed hard against his friend's shoulder.

Realisation of what he was doing hit Hugh like a bolt of lightning. He let Will go, sitting back against his chair, rubbing his head.

'I'm sorry—that was uncalled for,' he said as he buried his head in his hands.

Will stared at his friend in disbelief as he slowly exhaled. 'I've never seen you like this over a woman before, Hugh. What has happened?'

Hugh lifted his head and rubbed his chin. After a long silence he finally spoke in a low voice. 'It's Eleanor.' His mouth twisted. 'She's the traitor we seek.'

Will's eyes widened in disbelief and his jaw dropped. He turned his head in both directions, checking that their conversation was not being overheard, before shuffling closer to Hugh. 'Are you sure about this?' he whispered.

'Unfortunately, yes. I followed her and that old fool of a steward out of Tallany Castle, the night before we left to journey here.' He met Will's eyes. 'She met the outlaw Le Renard.'

'Oh, my God, Hugh.' Will muttered an oath and whistled. 'Is Eleanor aware that you know all this?'

'No, she's not—not yet. But believe me, she will,' he growled. 'First, I have to know who else is involved and how far this goes. And I can only do that if she isn't aware that I know her secret.'

'What are you going to do?'

'I don't know.' He dropped his head and dragged his fingers through his hair. 'What a damnable coil I'm in.'

'You are—but you need to think hard and act quickly, Hugh.'

'How am I supposed to act? Don't you understand what a difficult position she has put me in?'

Will regarded him for a moment and sighed. 'Yes, I believe I can.'

'I'm torn in every direction. If I conceal the fact that

Eleanor is a traitor then it may as well be me holding the traitor's sword against our King.'

And if he didn't, he might as well be signing her death warrant.

'True—except that she is your wife.'

'Except that she is my wife...' Hugh repeated, in a flat, weary tone.

'And you love her,' Will said.

'And I love—' Hugh stopped and flicked his head up, frowned. 'No, I do not!' he snapped, and rose abruptly, scraping his chair against the hard floor.

'Any fool can see you care for your lady.' Will narrowed his gaze. 'Sit down.'

Hugh gave his friend a hard stare before he sat back down and picked up his mug, turning it round in his hand. 'You're asking me to forsake my solemn oath to John?'

'No, of course not,' Will said. 'But listen to me, Hugh. You are no longer a soldier who just follows orders blindly, like I do. You may have given your fealty to the King, but you're also duty-bound to protect your vassals, your dependents, and most of all your lady—whatever she may have done.'

Hugh raised his brows at Will's words, which strangely chimed with what Eleanor had said to him at Milnthorpe.

'I know all this, Will, but her treachery also marks me unless I set her aside.'

'Just deal with the situation yourself, Hugh,' Will said. 'But that's not the only reason you feel "torn", as you put it.'

Hugh frowned. 'What do you mean?'

'It's Eleanor and the outlaw that has you in knots.'

A muscle leapt in Hugh's jaw. 'She betrayed me.'

'Yes, it seems she did.' Will sighed. 'But before you go blowing bluster, Hugh, talk to her.'

'Oh, I shall—believe me. But not yet,' Hugh said. He met Will's speculative gaze and smiled weakly. 'Thank you for your counsel, though, my friend. I appreciate it.'

'Just talk to her, Hugh.' He nodded at his friend. 'Now, let's get drunk.'

Hugh looked at his mug grimly and then back at Will. 'Yes, let's. Blind drunk!'

Chapter Fifteen

Eleanor looked around the beautiful hall of Winchester Castle and bit the inside of her cheek nervously. She should never have ventured here with her husband. Not when this makeshift opulent court was as gloomy and bleak as this. It was a symbol of everything she detested. And being amongst these people she didn't know or trust made her feel wary and unsure—especially as Hugh was doing his best to ignore her as well.

The mood was sombre and grim, even though the courtiers tried to lift everyone's spirits—particularly King John's. She stole a glance at her Sovereign, who had single-handedly been the cause of her grief and unhappiness with one husband and also her short-lived happiness with another.

The King spoke a little to his inner circle of men, amongst them Lord Balvoire, whose lips seemed to be curled into a permanent sneer. There was something deeply unsettling about him, and she wished she was back in her chamber, away from all this.

Eleanor stared at the tender cuts of meat on her trencher and her stomach flipped. Her hunger could not be abated as the fine food she ate was tasteless and the expensive wine bitter.

It was a reflection on everything that she had gleaned since her arrival in Winchester—especially when she considered the obvious wealth on display. When she compared it to the poverty and destitution in Tallany, and throughout the kingdom, it outraged her. She couldn't wait until they were able to leave and travel back north, but when that would be was anyone's guess.

Since their arrival yesterday John had conferred with Hugh briefly, along with all his other noblemen, knights and vassals. The King was understandably furious, since London was now in the grip of the Rebel Barons and was proving to be a matter of great consternation and anxiety for him.

Secretly, Eleanor was elated at the triumph and success of the Rebels, and shared with them the hope that this might prove to be the impetus needed to finally make the King sign the Great Charter of Liberties.

Eleanor hadn't realised she had been staring, when she caught the King's eye. He raised his brows and his silver cup in toast to her. His lips flattened into a mocking thin line and he held her gaze until she inclined her head in a perfunctory deferential bow. He too inclined his head, then looked away and spoke with the man sitting next to him.

Eleanor expelled a huge breath that she hadn't realised she'd been holding and tried to calm her nerves by sipping the rancid wine, her hands shaking in the process. She shuddered and spotted her husband from afar, talking and exchanging pleasantries with a small group of courtiers who were probably acquaintances he hadn't seen since his surprise marriage.

She observed him from under her lashes as his peers

slapped him on the back and shook him by the hand. And she also watched in dismay as the women in the hall followed Hugh's every movement, all stopping to talk, simper or flirt with him.

Since her arrival yesterday they had eyed her speculatively, as though she were a curiosity, and Eleanor realised that this was partly because everything about her was different. The way she dressed, the style of her headdress, even the way she spoke, and not to mention her court manners, were at odds with the way these people believed an heiress should behave.

And all this awkwardness and misery was compounded by Hugh's indifference towards her.

Eleanor noticed a pretty young woman with brilliant blue eyes who was being particularly friendly with her husband. She hung on his every word, repeatedly touched the sleeve of his tunic, smiled and laughed at everything he said. They certainly seemed to be well acquainted with one another. Oh, yes, her husband was indeed popular...

And, yes, Eleanor was indeed feeling the first stirrings of jealousy. A strange, unfamiliar emotion that she had never felt before. She chided herself for feelings that were beneath her, telling herself she preferred not to complicate matters with these futile emotions. She'd also prefer that she was far, far away from this awful place.

Her searching gaze found William Geraint, who had just come into her peripheral vision. He seemed to waver between staying where he was or coming to speak to her. Fortunately for Eleanor the pleading in her eyes must have convinced Will, as he gave her a single nod, said something privately to Hugh and walked over to sit beside her.

He wasn't smiling in his usual easy manner, and something about that unnerved her. Was it her imagination or was Will also behaving differently towards her now? He didn't seem to be his usual, jovial, witty self. Or was she allowing her anxiety about Hugh to colour every single judgement and thought?

Really, now, this wasn't like her. She was The Fox, for goodness' sake!

'Lady Eleanor, I trust you have had a good day?' he asked, quite formally.

'Yes, thank you. But to be honest I have been keeping myself to myself.'

Will's brow furrowed. 'I understand from Hugh that you do not care too much for court.'

She shrugged. 'It's more that I don't know anyone here, Will. I feel like an outsider.'

'Then why you did come here, my lady?' Will asked, without humour.

'I ask myself that every day.' She shook her head before continuing. 'I thought it a good idea at the time, but I was wrong. Very wrong.' She rubbed her forehead, feeling the first strains of a headache.

Will sighed. 'If it helps, Eleanor, I can present you to some ladies of the court whom I think you may like. Not everyone is unfriendly here,' he said, sounding more like his old self.

'Thank you, Will, that's very kind. But I believe that is my husband's responsibility—not that he seems to realise that.'

They both turned their heads to watch Hugh, engrossed in conversation, laughing at something the blue-eyed beauty was saying.

Will regarded her for a moment. 'You care for him, don't you?' he said quietly.

Eleanor was too choked to reply, and continued to look at nothing in particular, her chest feeling painfully tight.

'I just don't understand what is wrong with Hugh. He

seems so different here from the man I knew in Tallany,' she muttered absently.

Will covered her hand with his, giving it a squeeze. 'I cannot say, Eleanor, but for what it is worth I believe my friend cares for you too,' he said. He held up his hands, anticipating her response. 'The only way through this impasse is for you to talk to one another—and soon.'

Hugh was bowing at the young woman, who curtsied in response, giving him a coquettish look before she moved to the centre of the room, evidently readying herself to perform for the entire assembly. He nodded at the young woman and then walked in the opposite direction, towards Eleanor and Will.

Will rose and gave her hand another squeeze. 'I will leave you now, but remember what I said, my lady.' He bowed over her hand. 'Everyone makes mistakes, and some may be bigger than others. I truly hope that you both find a way through your current difficulty. I really do.'

Will passed Hugh and clasped his friend's arm, exchanging a few words with him before continuing to walk in a different direction. Her husband approached and perched next to her wordlessly, without offering a single look or smile, sinking her spirits even lower.

What were the mistakes that Will had alluded to?

Just as Eleanor was about to say something to Hugh, the blue-eyed beauty sat on a low stool in the middle of the hall and started to pluck the strings of a lute. Her elegant fingers worked effortlessly to create the most achingly sweet and melodic music, and when it was accompanied with her lovely voice it brought a lump to Eleanor's throat.

She turned to see that Hugh was equally moved by the captivating music. The song was one she vaguely recalled from when she was young—an ode to springtime and something about a lost love that she remembered her mother singing to her.

It made Eleanor feel so desperately sad and forlorn that she could hardly breathe, with tears filling her eyes. But what made it infinitely worse was that when the music eventually ended Eleanor had to watch in disbelief as the young woman gave such a lingering look to Hugh, as if she had been singing every single word to him.

Oh, Lord, what was happening?

Eleanor felt as if her world was somehow unfolding. She closed her eyes, hoping to shut out those unwelcome thoughts and push away her miserable feelings. She opened them again and rose abruptly, started to walk away, mumbling something about wanting to get some air. She'd had enough!

Needing to be outside, she strode out of the hall as fast as she could and kept on going, practically running until she had put some distance between the hall and wherever it was she had got to.

She had reached a corner of an outbuilding, and she turned and leaned against the stone wall, panting, catching her breath. She loosened her veil and opened the neckline of her dress. The cool night air felt good against her skin, compared to the stuffy, oppressive atmosphere of the hall.

She heard soft footfall and looked around. She grabbed the first thing that she could find—a rake that had been left against the wall.

'Where are you going?' Hugh said, as he rounded the corner.

Eleanor pushed away from the wall and started to stride away, still holding the rake, swinging it by her side. 'Are you following me again? Like you did in Milnthorpe?' she said over her shoulder. 'Didn't anyone ever tell you how incredibly rude that is?'

Hugh walked behind her. 'Yes, but I was worried about you. Are you unwell?'

'Go back to your friends, Hugh. I am perfectly well,' she said curtly.

'If that was so then you wouldn't have left in the way you just did, Eleanor.'

'Leave me, please, to my own contemplations. I'm in no mood for company.' She carried on walking, God knew where, with her husband following behind.

'I can see that, my lady, but what I cannot understand is the reason for it.'

She gave an exasperated toss of her head. 'Mayhap you didn't look hard enough, being otherwise occupied. Now, I'd be much obliged if you'd comply with my wishes and leave me be.'

'What is the matter?'

She crossed in a different direction that brought her to a secluded path.

'Nothing. I'm fine,' she said.

'You don't look fine—you look angry. Which I find bewildering, considering *I'm* the one who should be angry.'

'What is that supposed to mean?' she snapped. 'Are you suggesting that we should compete to find out who merits being the angriest?'

'There is no contest, believe me.' Hugh caught her elbow and pulled her to a halt. 'Where are you going?'

'Back to my chamber, my lord.'

'You're going the wrong way. Come, I'll escort you there.'

'That,' she said, 'is unnecessary.'

She yanked away from his hold and walked ahead.

'Possibly, but it's not safe to go on your own at this time of night.'

'I don't need your help, Hugh. I can look after myself.'

'Is that so?'

She quickly spun and turned the rake round, pointed the end a fraction away from Hugh's face. 'Yes,' she replied through gritted teeth. 'You see, I had a tutor who told me once that I have a natural ability when it comes to defending myself from anyone who wishes me harm.'

Hugh put his hands in the air, his palms outward, and smirked. 'So, do you think that I mean you harm, my lady?'

'I don't know. Do you?' Eleanor pushed the end of the rake against his chest, making him take a few steps back. 'I may not possess any maidenly manners, as you well know, or be proficient at stitching. Nor can I play the lute and sing, oh, so beautifully, like your pretty friend back there, but I can look after myself, Hugh de Villiers.'

His lips curved into that lopsided smile of his. 'Are you...? Are you jealous?'

'Hell's teeth—no, I am not!'

'Are you sure?' Hugh grabbed the end of the rake and started to tug, pulling Eleanor slowly towards him.

'Yes...no. I don't know.' She rolled her eyes, shaking her head. 'What have I to be jealous of?'

Hugh shrugged, continuing to pull her closer even whilst she resisted, pulling back. 'I would not claim to know, Eleanor.'

'Precisely. I don't need to be, since I have the one thing that all those women seem to want.'

'Oh? And what is that?' he whispered, and he yanked the pole sharply, hurtling Eleanor forward into his arms.

'You.'

Hugh's smile widened into a grin as he let go of the

rake and curled his fingers lightly around her waist, drawing her closer. He bent his head and closed his eyes, his lips within a hair's breadth of touching hers, so close that Eleanor could feel the warmth of his breath.

And just when his lips almost brushed against hers, she took a big step back, then swung the rake round and under his feet so quickly and unexpectedly that he lost his footing, flew backwards and hit the ground—hard.

'What the blazes did you do that for, woman?' He made a face, scowling as he rubbed the back of his neck.

She raised her chin imperiously. 'Next time you wish to flirt and carry on with other women have a care not to do it in my presence, will you?'

Eleanor threw the rake down next to him and started to stride away.

'So, you *were* jealous—and I was not flirting or "carrying on" with anyone!' he called after her, getting slowly back on his feet.

'I may not have the appropriate maidenly manners, but I do know that *you*, Hugh de Villiers, are being obnoxious and ill-mannered,' she threw over her shoulder. 'But then you have been both of those since we left Tallany.'

'Is that so, my lady? I beg pardon for my abominable behaviour,' he mocked.

She threw her arms up in annoyance. 'I don't even know why you agreed to me coming on this godforsaken journey to this godforsaken place. Oh, I wish I was back home.'

Hugh caught up with her. 'I'm sure you do, Eleanor. And Lord knows what it is that you get up to when you *are* "back home"—as you so affectionately put it.'

'Have you had too much to drink, Hugh? I don't understand your meaning,' she retorted. 'And, yes, everything I love and hold dear *is* back home—it's also where I belong!'

He grasped her by the arm and pulled her round to face him again. 'Is it, now?' he said, in a low voice filled with barely suppressed anger that surprised and confused Eleanor. 'Have you wondered why I have kept away from you? Why I have not spoken to you in the same manner as before?'

'Why don't you enlighten me, my lord?'

'Very well—but not here.' He grimaced as he let go of her arm and took her hand, marching her towards the guest quarters of the castle. 'This way.'

'Where are you taking me?'

'Back to your chamber—and you had better dismiss your women for the night, as what I have to say to you will not require an audience.'

They walked into the building adjacent and connected to the main castle, which overlooked a pretty herb garden, its blend of evocative aromas permeating the night air. The only sounds that sporadically burst through the silence were the calls of owls and other nocturnal birds and animals in the distance.

Eleanor dug her heels into the ground and stopped walking. 'Why don't you just say what you want to and leave me be?'

'Not here, when anyone could be eavesdropping. Now, come,' he said. 'And I can tell you something, Eleanor Tallany, your prowess with defensive weaponry is not your only talent.'

'Oh? And pray tell me what other talents I apparently possess?' she hissed.

'With pleasure, my lady,' Hugh growled as they reached her chamber.

He swung the door open, surprising Eleanor's women,

who were busy with needlework, seated around the hearth, waiting for their mistress's return from the hall.

Eleanor gave Brunhilde a small smile and indicated with a nod of her head that she wished for her and the others to leave them. Thankfully her maid understood. They all curtsied one by one and left the chamber.

She turned and raised her chin. 'Well? What is it you have to say to me, Hugh?'

She took off her veil and the silver Tallany circlet and placed them carefully on a trestle table covered in one of Brunhilde's blended woven tablecloths. The deep crimson, mauve and evergreen were the colours of Tallany and a reminder of home.

'I wanted to wait until later, Eleanor. This confrontation is not something I wished to face yet,' he said, rubbing his jaw.

She tried to steady her fingers as she took the pins from her hair. They trembled uncontrollably at his ominous words, and her heart was hammering fast in her chest.

What did he mean?

'Eleanor?' he said quietly. 'Let me help you with that.'

His voice had lost all trace of the annoyance and anger it had held only moments ago. He had probably noticed her weakness as she was unbinding her hair.

Dear God, what was happening? Did he pity her?

'Thank you, but no. I don't need your help.'

She glided her hands through her dark locks, making it cascade down in waves. She was ready now for whatever he had to say. She turned to face him and swallowed down her anguish as she straightened her spine and squared her shoulders.

She knew what was about to come.

She'd always known that a man like Hugh would eventually feel like this about her and her *'talents'*, as he put it.

How could she ever have thought that she would be able to hold the interest of this man? A man who would naturally be attracted to someone like that blue-eyed beauty with her melodic voice and perfect manners. Hugh had only ever married her out of duty, and it wasn't as if either of them had *wanted* this union.

Eleanor was headstrong, sharp-tongued and highly opinionated—everything a man, *any* man, would despise. She had always known this about herself, but it was who she was, and she was not about to change. Not for anyone!

'What is the matter, Eleanor?' he muttered, moving towards her.

She took a few steps to one side, wanting to avoid his inquisitive gaze.

'Nothing. Just say what you want and leave,' she said, fiddling with her mother's cross around her neck.

'You have tears in your eyes,' he said, somewhat in disbelief. 'Why?' He frowned.

She rolled her eyes. 'You were right the first time, Hugh. I'm angry and upset.' She turned to face him, shaking her head. 'I knew what I'd got with Richard Millais; he was a man who had no bounds to the cruelty and abuse he inflicted on me—or anyone else for that matter... But you,' she said, jabbing him in the chest. 'You made me like you, care for you, only to reject me and treat me with disrespect.'

'I did no such thing,' he said hoarsely, wiping her cheek with the pad of his thumb.

'If this was the way you wanted matters to be between us, then why, for the love of God, didn't you take my offer that first night after we made our vows? Then you could have found another woman to tend to your needs whilst we made a pretence of our marriage.'

'I could never have done that.' His fingers lingered on her face, wiping her tears away.

'Then why did you make me care? *Why?*' she whispered.

'Don't…please don't cry,' he said gently.

'Saints above, Hugh, I'm not crying!' she replied, throwing her arms up in the air.

But she realised with mortification that her cheeks were indeed damp. She groaned with embarrassment.

What must he think of her?

Eleanor had always been adept at hiding her true feelings and yet here she was, in front of the man she had such conflicting feelings for, totally exposed. Hugh had somehow managed to crawl intrusively beneath her defences and take down every one of her perfectly constructed walls.

Dear God, she wanted him. She needed him. If only just to make this horrible, suffocating ache in her chest go away.

Hugh watched her for a moment and then he sighed, shaking his head. He dipped his head and pressed his lips gently to hers, and this time she let him kiss her.

But it wasn't enough.

Eleanor curled her arms around his neck and kissed him back with everything she had. And then she slipped the tip of her tongue tentatively into his mouth.

Hugh growled as he felt Eleanor's tongue sliding against his. He plunged his fingers into her hair and around the back of her neck, pulling her closer as he deepened the kiss, tasting and devouring her.

By God, he wanted her…

All thought, all his perfectly good intentions about

keeping his distance from her, had melted away the moment she had revealed to him how she felt.

Why did you make me care?

Did she truly care about him? Eleanor was an enigma to him, so who could tell? But there was her anger, the pain that strangely mirrored his own. He had seen it and he'd felt it.

Hugh had purposely kept away from Eleanor and observed her, wondering whether anyone else was involved with the outlaws—even here at court, however unlikely that might seem. But he'd only noted her misery and loneliness and his heart had gone out to her.

He knew he had to be vigilant and watchful, but he'd hated seeing her like that…knowing that he was the cause. So he'd run after her when she had stormed out of the hall.

And now all that was left was a desire so strong that it pulsated through him. All he could think about was his desperate, hopeless need for her. He realised, as he kissed her with every pent-up emotion that he'd thought discarded and ignored, that Eleanor had been hurting just as much as he. She had felt jealous, confused, and so very angry with him.

Without breaking the kiss he lifted her as she clung to him, her legs wrapped around his hips, and carried her to bed.

'I can't seem to stop wanting you, woman,' he whispered, and he nipped her bottom lip, hearing her gasp against his mouth.

'Is that such a terrible thing?' she asked, burying her head into his neck as he laid her down on the soft mattress.

'Yes. Yes, it is. It is not how a sane, grown man should behave.' He broke away, hovering above her.

'If it's any consolation, I cannot stop wanting you either.'

He kissed her hungrily, open-mouthed. 'Good,' he said, pushing his tongue through the soft opening of her lips, seeking and demanding, willing her mouth to spar with his sensually.

'Eleanor...' he groaned, and he got up, his breathing ragged, looking at her with her hair falling in waves around the curve of her neck and down her shoulders. Her chest moved up and down quickly and her mouth was parted: pink, wet and swollen from his kisses.

Hugh groaned again and hurriedly pulled his tunic over his head, then stripped off his braies and hose quickly. In his rush to get back to Eleanor he tripped over the end of his hose, which was stuck to his ankles. He bounced up and down as he pulled it off, a mop of dark hair falling over his eyes.

'It seems that I can't stop falling at your feet either.'

Hugh smiled sheepishly as Eleanor giggled at his eagerness.

'Stop laughing, woman,' he said, shaking his head.

Eleanor covered her mouth with her hand, clearly trying to curb her amusement at his clumsiness. One moment she had been crying miserably and now she was laughing at him. It was a sudden change, so very like Eleanor, and it made her seem achingly young and innocent.

'Turn around so I can help with the ties at the back of your gown.'

With deft fingers Hugh untied her woollen dress and pulled it off her shoulders, his hands gliding down her smooth skin. Eleanor turned back, the laughter now gone from her lips. She inhaled deeply and then pulled her sheer cream-coloured tunic over her head and tossed it on the floor.

She sat there, facing him on the bed in all her naked glory, her eyes never leaving his. He gently pushed her down on the soft cushions and followed, covering her with his body, his hands caressing down the length of her, tracing the soft curves.

She smiled at him, desire swirling in her eyes. She had never looked so lovely, so utterly beautiful. So much so that it made his chest feel tight and his breath catch in his throat.

Hugh pushed those feelings aside and entered her warm, welcoming body, making her tremble visibly. He felt as though he was *home*, somehow, but this too he refused to acknowledge, knowing it was dangerous for him to feel like this.

He pressed his lips to hers, devouring her, familiarising himself again with all the soft contours of her mouth as his tongue stroked hers.

'You beguile me,' he whispered softly. 'My unusual woman.'

He saw a flash of uncertainty pass over her face momentarily before she tightened her hold on him and wrapped her limbs around his, pushing him to the side and onto his back, before straddling him, moving on top of him and proving his point.

Eleanor was indeed different from any other woman Hugh had ever met, and he grinned at her daring—being on top of him, turning the normal way of the world on its head. He found that her shocking behaviour excited him, and even more so because she wasn't even aware she was doing so. This was just who Eleanor was.

'I rather prefer "ruthlessly dexterous",' she said, and smiled, biting the inside of her cheek.

'I'm sure you do.'

He shook his head and locked his eyes with hers as he

moved deep inside her. The image of her sitting atop him, with her dark hair spilling over and covering her nakedness, seared through him, filling his veins with wild fire.

He spread his hand on her chest and slid it down the centre of her body slowly. He curled his fingers on either side of her waist and watched as she tossed her head back and licked her lips. Her reaction to their lovemaking was uninhibited and instinctive, which he found strangely endearing.

Lord, but this woman had a hold on him.

Did she have any idea of the effect she had on him? He wasn't sure, but it made him uneasy. His wife occupied far too much of his time and it must stop.

He wrapped his legs around hers and flipped her, making them both tumble back so that once again he was on top of her, making her take a sharp intake of breath.

'You'll find that I can be just as ruthlessly dexterous.' His lips twitched at the corners.

'I never doubted it.' She dragged her fingers through his hair, drawing it back. 'Although there *are* instances when the student becomes more proficient than the tutor.'

'Is that so?' he rasped, pressing kisses along the column of her neck.

'Yes,' she said breathlessly.

Hugh dipped his head, taking her lips, slanting his mouth across hers and kissing her long and hard. His movement inside her became all-consuming, giving and taking, until it became urgent and demanding. A mix of tenderness and wildness. The past few weeks of anger, frustration and tension were momentarily forgotten, momentarily reconciled. Everything that had gone before seemed washed and swept away on a tide of hopeless longing.

He fell on top of her, panting, complete, and she shuddered beneath him, her fingers moving up and down his back, stroking and soothing. He moved onto his back and Eleanor snuggled close into his arms.

But it wasn't so.

He had wanted this, even though he shouldn't. He had needed this, even though he mustn't. Every rational thought had disappeared the moment he had kissed her, which had led to this intimacy. It was something he should not have done. He had got carried away. He had been so relieved that Eleanor apparently cared for him that he'd thrown caution to the wind and forgotten his duty.

Eleanor was a temptation that he was not strong enough to resist—but, damn it, he must! His honour demanded it.

He untangled himself from Eleanor's embrace and sat up on the edge of the bed, rubbing his hands over his face. It wasn't fair to continually torment himself, and neither was he being fair on Eleanor. He must talk to her and obtain all the answers he sought about the outlaws—but not like this. Not after bedding her!

His eyes darted around the room, without taking in a single thing. He had to leave.

'Hugh, what's wrong?' She sat up in the bed with the coverlet draped around her.

'Nothing, nothing…' He picked up his clothes, strewn in a frenzied mess around the bed and on the floor, and started to dress.

'If that is so then why are you leaving?'

'I have something to attend to, Eleanor,' he replied with his back to her.

'Please don't go,' she pleaded. 'Stay with me.'

He heard the distress in her voice and screwed his eyes shut, trying to dismiss it. Not to allow his wretched feelings and concern for her to pull him back to her.

'I can't, Eleanor,' he whispered. 'I just can't.'

'Whatever mistakes you believe you have made, we can surely overcome them, can we not?'

'Mistakes *I* have made?' He turned, frowning with incredulity.

She clasped the little cross around her neck tightly. 'Don't be angry with him, but Will mentioned it to me earlier.'

Hugh exhaled slowly. 'Oh, Eleanor,' he said, shaking his head. 'He meant *your* mistakes—not mine.'

'I… I don't understand.'

His wife blinked several times, as though she hadn't heard him properly. He folded his arms across his chest.

'Don't you, my lady?' he asked softly, watching bewilderment and confusion flash across her face.

He allowed the silence in the room to stretch for a moment, knowing that finally the time to confront her had come—though it was sooner than he would have liked.

He nodded at her grimly. 'I know, Eleanor,' he said. 'I know you're a traitor!'

Chapter Sixteen

Hugh heard Eleanor gasp and saw her eyes widen in shock. Darts of emotion flickered in her eyes as she finally comprehended him and realised the magnitude of what he had said.

She lifted her head and finally spoke. 'How...how did you know?' she whispered, meeting his penetrating gaze.

At least she wasn't going to deny the accusation.

'I followed you. The night before we left to come here.' Hugh expelled the breath he had been holding.

'You seem to have made quite a habit of following me.'

'For good reason,' he said bitterly. 'And you were not alone, my beautiful wife. Not only are you a traitor but so is your ever-faithful steward Gilbert Claymore.'

'No!' she said, shaking her head. 'Gilbert was only doing his duty by me. As was Brunhilde.'

'I might have known that your maid would be involved as well.' Hugh stood with his arms folded, glaring at her.

'They have nothing to do with it, Hugh.'

'Of course not,' he said sardonically. 'Anyone else?'

'No.'

'Tell me.' He watched her as she gulped and looked away. 'I want the truth now, Eleanor.'

'Only Father Thomas,' she whispered.

'The Tallany priest?' He muttered an oath under his breath as he shook his head in disbelief.

'You must understand, Hugh, that none of them are involved in the way you believe. They're like family to me and were only doing my bidding,' she said, sinking her teeth into her bottom lip. 'It was only ever me. Just me.'

'Your concern for them does you credit,' he said, leaning with his back against the wall, watching her in bed, still naked under the coverlet. 'But don't you see that you have put Tallany itself in danger with your involvement with the outlaws? Everything you have toiled so hard for?'

'Some risks are worth taking, Hugh. They must be taken.' She pulled the coverlet higher up to her neck and lifted her head.

'At what cost, my lady?' His lips compressed into a thin line. 'At the risk of losing everything? What the hell do you think would have happened once you were caught?'

'I did everything not to be.'

'Yet that was always a possibility once we had married, Eleanor, and you're shrewd enough to know that.'

'I know, but sometimes in life there are no other choices.'

'Oh, there are always choices, Eleanor,' he said with a scowl. 'You chose to meet with your steward and go down that tunnel. You chose to meet with that damned outlaw Le Renard. You chose all of it and you chose it willingly.'

'It wasn't like that…'

'Oh? And what am I mistaken in? You lied, Eleanor.' He raked his eyes over her. 'From the very beginning you lied and worked with the outlaws against me.'

'But that was…that was before I knew you,' she muttered.

He laughed mirthlessly. 'What difference did that make? Did you cease your duplicity once you got to know me, oh, so well?' He shook his head. 'No, you damn well did not.'

'As I said, some risks are worth taking,' she said, tilting her chin in the air. 'They must be taken since they're more important than anything and anyone. More important even than you and I.'

He stared at her blankly. 'What a heartfelt speech. And whilst we debate the reasons that have made you lie, cheat and steal to aid a known criminal—an outlaw, for the love of God—there is a very real decision for me to take.'

'What…what is that?'

'What am I to do with you, Eleanor?' he asked. 'Do I look the other way, or do I hand you over to the King? Have you any idea what they will do to your pretty little neck?' he said, frowning.

Her hands shook as she instinctively curled them around her neck. 'No,' she said, as she straightened her spine in an attempt at bravery. 'But you must do what your conscience tells you.'

Hugh noticed her bottom lip wobble, making him want to take her back into his arms, but he couldn't. He must resist the urge to go to her and make everything right between them.

Damn, he couldn't be so weak-willed.

'I will, my lady. I will. Tell me, though, was *anything* about you real? Was anything we shared real?'

She gasped. 'Hugh, how can you say that? Especially after what we just shared on this bed.'

'Easily. It's not as though either of us *wanted* this marriage.'

She balked. 'Yes, but haven't things changed since then?'

'I believed so—I thought so… But not any more.'

Hugh watched Eleanor's eyes fill with unshed tears that she wiped away absently and he winced. He had never wanted any of it to unfold like this. He hated this—hated feeling like this and hated causing her pain. She'd had enough of that in her life…

'At least allow me to explain about The Fox,' she whispered, breaking the silence.

Hugh flicked his eyes at her. 'I don't want to know anything about your friendship with him,' he said in a low voice, his lip curling in distaste. The thought of the outlaw and his wife, even as friends, made his blood boil. He clenched and unclenched his fists and turned his back on her. 'What can you say, Eleanor, about an outlaw you betrayed me for and upon whose head there is a fair price?'

'But you don't understand—'

'No, I don't believe *you* understand, my lady.' He moved towards her and lifted her chin, looking into her sad eyes. 'I too want to do right by Tallany—but not by breaking my allegiance to the King and not by breaking the law.'

'It was and is the only way, Hugh.'

'Is that so, my lady?' He expelled a shaky breath and watched her for a moment. 'Eleanor, you have no idea about what you've done. You have wounded me more than you'll ever know. More than I ever thought possible.'

He walked away and picked up his sword belt, tied it around his waist before walking to the door.

'Hugh,' she called out. 'What will you do?'

He stood rigid, staring at the door. 'I don't know. I really don't know.'

Chapter Seventeen

Eleanor sat on a wooden bench overlooking the herb garden, close to her lodgings at the back of the castle. The gardens were cleverly partitioned by evergreen hedges to separate the medicinal herbs from those of the culinary variety, which were potted and planted closer to the kitchens beyond.

She watched from a distance as kitchen staff intermittently ventured out from the building to take cuttings of the herbs that were needed for their cooking. And even from where she was sitting she could smell the delicious aromas drifting from the kitchens. Not that she could eat a thing. No, but it was good to watch everyday life unfold and carry on as normal. It was a respite from all her troubles and a balm to her wretched, wretched soul.

Eleanor had tossed and turned all night, unable to sleep. Everything that had happened with Hugh, every word that had been uttered, had turned around and around in her head.

Lord above—he'd known about her involvement with the outlaws all this time and said nothing. Stupidly, she had been consumed with jealousy at the thought that his head might have been turned by other women. But, no, it was far more serious than that.

She closed her eyes and took in a huge breath of much-needed fresh air just as she heard footfalls nearby and someone coughing, clearing their throat. She opened her eyes to see that Lord Balvoire had approached. Her heart sank.

Now, what did he want at a time like this?

'My dear Lady Eleanor, I didn't get a chance to greet you properly yesterday. You left the hall so unexpectedly,' he said, bowing over her hand and pressing his slimy, wet lips on it.

She ignored his jibe and resisted the temptation to wipe her hand on her skirts. 'Lord Balvoire.' She inclined her head and got up, not wanting to be seated whilst the odious man was standing over her. 'You find me here alone this morning.'

'I hope that I am not intruding on your reverie, my lady?'

She wanted to say that indeed he was, and that his presence was unwelcome, but instead she said nothing, hoping her silence would be enough of a hint that she did not want his company.

Annoyingly, the hint went over his head and he moved closer to her instead. She saw his skin pockmarked and lined, this close up.

'And why are you alone this morning, my lady?'

'I'm waiting for my husband, Lord Balvoire, so if you don't mind…?' She'd said the first thing that had popped into her head.

'Mind? Why should I mind, my dear? Your forbearance does you credit—especially after the demise of your last husband.'

'Thank you.' She swallowed uncomfortably, feeling her stomach turn at the mention of Richard Millais.

'I hope you don't think I'm prying, my dear, but I couldn't help but notice your distress in the hall last night. I'm sure all is resolved, but one never knows with these soldiers and their wandering ways. I daresay it's the young, handsome ones the most. They do seem to be popular at court.'

Eleanor could tell he wanted to gain a reaction from her. 'Again, I thank you for your concern, my lord, but I really must be going,' she said through gritted teeth.

'I thought you said you were waiting for Lord Hugh?' He raised his brows. 'I'm sorry, I shouldn't have said anything. Please don't leave on my account.'

'I assure you, I'm not.'

'Good, good…because I nearly forgot to tell you how desirous the King is to meet you.'

Eleanor felt bile rise from the pit of her stomach. 'Naturally I would be very honoured.'

'I'm sure you would. And now I will leave you,' he said. 'We cannot be seen together like this without a chaperon or people will gossip.'

He chuckled at his own jest and gave her a leering smile that made her want to hit him. God, he was insufferable.

'You are right, Lord Balvoire. Good day to you.' She inclined her head, stepping away, but he stilled her.

'Ah, what a charming necklace, my dear.'

He reached out and held her mother's cross in his palm, his fingers grazing her skin. Saints in heaven, if he continued this behaviour for much longer she really would end up hitting him.

'It was my mother's,' she said curtly, pulling her necklace from his grasp. 'I always wear it.'

His eyes narrowed as he met her cool gaze. 'I know…' he said, smiling as he took his leave of her. 'Until later, my lady.'

Lord Balvoire left just as Hugh walked towards her, inclining his head stiffly as he passed the slimy fish.

'What did that obnoxious goat want?' Hugh asked.

'And a good morning to you.'

'Good morning, Eleanor.' Hugh frowned. 'That pompous ass puts my hackles up. Be wary of him.'

'On that we agree.' She gave a small shiver.

'So, what did Balvoire want that he sought you out alone?'

'Nothing.'

'More secrets, Eleanor?'

'No, Lord Balvoire was being his usual charming self, and let's just say I was very glad that you came upon us when you did.'

'I see. Come, let's walk.'

Heavens, but this was awkward.

They walked in silence. Eleanor nervously stole sideways glances at her husband as they walked through the beautiful castle gardens. He looked outwardly calm, if a little pale, but his jaw was set hard and his movement was rigid and agitated.

'We have an audience with King John, Eleanor.'

He said it without any emotion, making her suddenly feel anxious. The tone of his voice was somehow ominous.

'He's apparently desirous to meet you.'

Ah, it had finally come to this…

It seemed that Hugh had finally made his mind up. One of the many unsettling things that had kept Eleanor up all night had been wondering what her husband would do about her. Well, now she knew. He was handing her over to King John.

Her heart pounded in her chest and she felt sick with the fear that was taking hold of her. But this wasn't the way to address adversity. Her father had taught her that much.

The thought of him brought a lump to her throat that she quickly dispelled. Eleanor was a noble lady, from a noble family, and she had to carry herself as such. So she pushed away the uneasiness and panic she felt, held her head high, made her back as straight as a quarterstaff with as much dignity as she could muster and walked on.

She fell into step with Hugh and contemplated the fate that would await her, accused of being a traitor in the eyes of the King. But to Eleanor, it was Hugh's eyes, his views and opinions, that mattered the most.

She had wanted to tell him about Le Renard, and her reasons for her part in the band of outlaws, but there was no point. It was too late now. He would still feel the same about her, if not worse. His fealty had never been hers and would never be, regardless of what she said. Besides, it would only serve to make him hate her more.

But her reasons for rebellion were born out of a desperate need to uphold justice and peace in Tallany. To help the poor and destitute with the crippling taxes designed to sink both her and her people.

She would, in truth, do it all again in a heartbeat, except...except for hurting Hugh. When he had confronted her last night, Eleanor had expected scorn and vitriol but instead saw barely disguised pain.

'You have wounded me more than you'll ever know...'

Lord, how those words had speared through her. They had caused an ache so deep and so intense that she could hardly breathe even now...

The guilt and shame Eleanor felt in causing pain to the man she would now gladly give her heart to made her examine her true feelings for her husband. And with sudden and absolute clarity she realised that, yes, her heart did indeed belong to Hugh, whether he wanted it or not. She had never understood or acknowledged her feelings before, always suppressing and fighting them, and yet she could no longer deny them.

Heartsick, she screwed her eyes shut a moment before opening them wide, as if seeing the truth for the first time.

But...in love with Hugh?

She searched within herself and the reality hitting her like a boulder dropping on her head.

Yes, she did indeed love Hugh…and yet he despised her.

Oh, the irony of it was not lost on her. She was in love with a man who was to bring about her downfall. A man who probably hated her as much as his sworn enemy. Eleanor should be jumping into his arms for joy—instead she felt like weeping.

She cast another glance at Hugh's forbidding face, stripped of all emotion. She would rather have preferred his anger to this icy cool detachment. It scared her because with every step they were taking to see the King, Hugh was putting a distance between them that was surely a prelude of what was to come. He was going to wash his hands of her once and for all and was marching her to her treasonous end.

Very well, if that was her fate then she would take her guilt in hurting the man she loved to her grave. Hugh would never know of her true feelings for him, nor why she had acted in the way she had. It didn't matter now anyway.

* * *

Hugh felt consumed with despair and bitter disappointment. He didn't know how he should proceed with Eleanor, his maddening, lying, duplicitous wife—even now, as he walked awkwardly beside her to meet and pay homage to King John at his private solar. He glanced over at her and couldn't help but admire, begrudgingly, the dignity with which she carried herself. She might be a traitor, but she was brave.

She lifted her head and met his gaze, her face ashen, her eyes with dark smudges beneath, and smiled weakly at him. She looked so forlorn, so defeated, that Hugh's heart sank. What did she think he would do? Throw her on the King's mercy?

Something shifted inside him. He might be angry and hurt, but Eleanor Tallany was *his* maddening, lying and duplicitous wife and no one else's. Hell would have to freeze over before he would hand her over to anyone. He would deal with her treachery himself, but to accuse her in front of King John...

Never!

He pulled her around by the elbow, making her stop abruptly. Confusion was etched on her face.

'God's wounds, woman,' he hissed, whispering into her ear. 'Despite everything you have done I'll be damned if I allow anything to happen to you. I will never allow anyone to hurt you, Eleanor. But know this is *not* over between us. Do you understand?'

She nodded, her head bent low, her shoulders sagging visibly with relief. 'Thank you.'

Hugh stared at his wife, looking so young and so deflated that he had to resist the sudden temptation to wrap his arms around her and comfort her.

But although he might not want anything to happen to her, he had meant it: Eleanor had wronged him.

Hugh had thought they had some understanding—he had thought they wanted the same things, especially for Tallany—but, Lord above, not in the way she went about it. Not by consorting with criminal outlaws, damn it. Personally, too, her betrayal had shredded him to bits and he felt strangely exposed—fool that he was.

Will had the right of it. He was her lovelorn swain, whatever she had done.

As for trust? *That* could never be a possibility between them now. And yet… And yet he couldn't help his growing feelings for her, despite everything. He wanted her, yearned for her, even now.

Yes, more fool him!

His gut twisted in pain as he recalled how Alais Courville had dealt him a similar blow, playing him false just as Eleanor had. Was it his misfortune to be attached to untrustworthy women? At least with Alais he had been able to walk away, to lick his wounds privately and never see her again, but that was not possible with Eleanor, was it? He was bound and shackled to her in marriage.

His realisation last night that Eleanor somehow cared for him and had been consumed with jealousy had knocked the air out of him. And the revelation had been such a relief that it had caused the spark that had led them to end up in a tangled heap in bed.

But nothing had changed. Eleanor might care for him, but everything about her was a trick. Her attraction to him contradicted her betrayal, but it hadn't stopped her from committing it. The more time he spent in her company, the more he could sense himself falling prey to her.

He needed to leave. There was no choice in the matter. He had to get away from her. It was the only way he could protect his bruised heart.

He clenched his fists. 'This way, Eleanor.'

He signalled for them to climb the stairs to John's private quarters. The sooner matters were dealt with here in Winchester the sooner he could take his wife back north to Tallany. He would confront her privately, dispassionately, without last night's emotions, and demand that Eleanor reveal where Le Renard and the other outlaws were hiding.

And once he'd caught and brought them to justice he would leave Tallany. Request as many missions as the King would grant so that he would be apart from her. Only then could Hugh hope to break the spell that Eleanor held over him.

Chapter Eighteen

King John's private solar was sumptuously adorned, if hastily decorated, and intricate tapestries depicting past glories of the Angevins covered the stone walls. His standard bearers made it glaringly obvious to all who dared to question it the validity of England's anointed King and Sovereign.

Hugh walked in with Eleanor by his side, appearing to be serenely composed. The only tell-tale sign of nerves that he sensed was the slight trembling of her fingers, hidden in the crook of his arm.

Hugh held himself straight, squared his shoulders and evened out his breath, putting a ready, deferential smile on his lips.

King John's beady eyes watched speculatively as both of them walked near the richly decorated dais at the back of the room where he sat. He did not look particularly well; his face was pale, with sunken cheeks, and there were dark rings under his hooded eyes. His manner emanated irritation with everything and everyone around him as he sat tapping his fingers against the gilded edge of his chair.

Damn, he was in one of his irascible moods!

The chamber felt sombre, just it had when the court had gathered in the hall yesterday evening—as if all life and exuberance had been sucked out of it. And apart from a few retainers and some of John's personal guards—mercenaries paid to do his bidding—there were very few people present.

Hugh noticed Will in the corner, looking uncharacteristically grave, and hovering close to King John was Lord Edmund Balvoire, muttering into his Sovereign's ear.

How that overbearing ass had managed to wheedle his way to John's side Hugh did not know, but Will certainly had the right of Balvoire. He might be an ass, but he was an ambitious and dangerous one.

John must be feeling both vulnerable and outraged at his current situation with the Rebel Barons and the pressure they were putting him under. Especially with their insistence that he signed this Great Charter of theirs. But for the King to be listening to the mutterings of men like Balvoire, who had their own agenda, was not a good omen.

Hugh realised too late that this was not a place to have brought Eleanor. She was the only woman present, and his protectiveness of her did not abate as they reached the dais. Eleanor plunged into a deep, graceful curtsey and he bowed implacably to the King.

'Ah, Hugh, so glad you have come…especially with your good lady here. And so glad to see that matters between you have been resolved.' He smirked. 'New marriages can have their little problems now and then.' John picked at his fingernails and flicked them to the ground.

Hugh gave Eleanor's fingers a little squeeze of encouragement as she flushed next to him. 'Sire, may I introduce my wife, Lady Eleanor of Taliany?'

King John stood abruptly and walked from the dais to meet them, his eyes fixed on his wife.

'Rise, my dear. Your King is very desirous to meet you finally.' He pulled Eleanor up by the hand, his smile curling into a sneer as his eyes raked her up and down. 'Ah, you see, Hugh, how generous I am? For I give you this beauty and receive, alas, nothing. You return here without my silver. Not a very good exchange...' He tilted his head from side to side, inspecting her as though she were a prized destrier.

Hugh clenched his fists at his sides, swallowing down his outrage at John's words and the brazen way in which he was leering at Eleanor. A sense of foreboding took hold of him. What the hell was going on?

'No, sire,' Hugh muttered, not knowing what else to say. He flicked his eyes to Balvoire, who was smirking, seemingly enjoying this exchange.

King John wet his lips as he continued to look at Eleanor. 'And what of these outlaws who have run roughshod over you?'

'We...' he said, looking at Eleanor. 'We are close to capturing all of them and bringing them to justice.'

'The only justice I'm interested in, Hugh, is the capture of these outlaws and in particular The Fox, this Le Renard, or whatever he likes to call himself... I want their heads on spikes. By any means—do you hear?' he said in a low voice, looking around the room. 'Lord Balvoire, here, has some ingenious notions about how to achieve this, so mind you listen to him and work together.'

The King sighed, glancing at his fingernails again.

'I should say that by and by I may concede to these land disputes brought to me by Lord Balvoire on your borders, Hugh... But then again I may not. We must seem fair in all our dealings, must we not?'

This was precisely the sort of behaviour from King John that would enrage the Barons—seeking to find what

would serve him best, never fully promising anything
and pitching one noble against another. Hugh had never
thought to be at the receiving end of it, though.

'Sire,' he said through gritted teeth, understanding the
veiled warning. He was to be tested with Balvoire at his
side, watching his every move, it seemed.

The King spun on his heel. 'Get the outlaws, Hugh,'
he said with a grimace. 'Tell him, my Lord Balvoire, of
your ingenious plan.'

'Yes, sire. The element of surprise.'

'Just so…' The King meandered towards a coffer set
against the stone wall and splashed some red wine into
a goblet.

There was something sinister at play here, and Hugh
had a sudden urge to bundle his wife away to safety.

'While we're at it, I would welcome a way to crush the
Rebel Barons who are against us as well,' the King continued, smiling at Eleanor. 'No matter. I will find a way,' he
said, as though he were talking about an irksome courtier.

John moved close to Eleanor and held out his hands,
licking his lips. 'Come, my dear. Will you not grace your
King with a welcoming kiss?'

Hugh was appalled at the way John was behaving.
His eyes darted across the chamber and registered the
shock on Will's face, the amusement on Balvoire's, the
vile bastard, and Eleanor… Oh, Lord, Eleanor had a look
of horror on her face.

She caught Hugh's gaze, silently pleading, and then
took a deep breath, turning back to face the King, trembling.

King John smiled, seemingly enjoying her reaction.

Hellfire and damnation! What was John playing at?

Just as the King bent his head to kiss her Hugh stepped

in. 'No, sire.' He kept his steady gaze on the King as he gently pulled Eleanor behind him.

'No?' John cocked an eyebrow.

Hugh's heart hammered against his chest. 'No.'

'I don't believe that word is much to our liking.'

'I'm sorry for that, my liege, but Lady Eleanor is not accustomed to court. She does not understand its ways.'

Hugh knew he was on very dangerous ground here, but he would rather die than have Eleanor dishonoured and accosted.

It was outrageous for John to take out on her all his grievances and frustration at Hugh's failure to secure his silver and catch the outlaws. It was clearly his way of warning him that all that he had bestowed upon him could easily be taken away. And God only knew what he would have done if he'd been aware of Eleanor's treachery. But to get to Hugh by intimidating Eleanor, a woman who'd already had her fair share of that, was unforgivable.

A slow smile spread on the King's thin lips. 'You're right—and I must say I think it quite gallant, the way you want to protect your young wife from the evils of court.' He smirked, making Balvoire and a few of his retainers join in with his mocking laughter.

Hugh bowed, never taking his eyes off the King. 'I hope I can protect anyone under my care and anyone I'm duty-bound to…as *you* will know, sire.'

He hoped that John would understand his meaning. Hugh didn't want to remind the King, but hell's teeth, he had to. Without him John would have been ransomed heavily, or dead in some muddy battlefield in Bouvines.

By God, that should mean *something*. Something more than constantly questioning his fealty. Something more than this power-play. Hugh had been prepared to lay down his life for his Sovereign, and not for the riches that might come his way, no. It had been his duty…just as it was his duty to protect his wife.

'I demand your loyalty, Hugh. Do you understand?' the King hissed.

'You have it, my liege.'

He met John's hard gaze, and neither man looked away until the King blinked and nodded at him.

'Very well.' John sipped his wine. 'Very well. We shall see how you do. Now, I have a mission for you to act as emissary with the Scots on your return, Hugh.'

'Sire.'

'And when you take your beautiful lady back to your northern territories remember how very fortunate you have been because of my good opinion. I do hope you will value the treasures I have given you.' King John kept his eyes firmly on Eleanor. 'And once there make them secure. Do you understand me? Let us hope that there are no more insurrections of any kind.'

'Yes, sire.'

Hugh glared at his Sovereign, trying hard to conceal his outrage. He wanted to leave this dangerous place immediately. He needed to take Eleanor back to safety and away from all of this.

One thing was for certain. Despite every contrary feeling Hugh had for Eleanor, and how she had wronged him, he would never, ever allow anyone to hurt her—be they outlaw or king.

Chapter Nineteen

After almost ten days of continuous riding on horse-back Eleanor was fatigued, saddle-sore and emotionally exhausted. She felt empty, bereft, and couldn't wait to get back home...home to Tallany, where she could finally breathe again.

Over the last week and more she had relived everything that had happened in Winchester over and over again in her head. That terrible confrontation with her husband that had broken her heart into a thousand pieces. And then what had happened the following morning, when she'd been presented to King John, and his shocking behaviour.

No wonder the Rebel Barons had risen up against him. She now understood more powerfully the reasons why they wanted to pin the King to his words so that he could no longer break his promises. That was the one hopeful thing to have emerged whilst she had been on this horrendous journey. And she hoped for the sake of all their futures that the Rebels were successful.

Everything she had heard about the King had been confirmed in his behaviour towards Hugh, punishing him for his failure to secure the silver from the outlaws. From Le Renard.

From her.

And, despite knowing of her involvement with the outlaws, Hugh had still stepped in to protect her from the King in that horrible chamber. He'd acted selflessly, without considering the possible danger he'd put himself in.

But that didn't mean Hugh had forgiven her...

Whenever Eleanor considered what she had lost her eyes would suddenly fill with tears, blurring her vision. She had sacrificed her own happiness with Hugh, the man she realised she loved, with her involvement with the outlaws, and even though she knew that she would never regret it...

No, she would never regret her actions as The Fox. Not only had it been a necessity to do what she had done, but her achievements were something she was immensely proud of. Le Renard and the outlaws had given Tallany much-needed hope during very difficult times.

So, yes, despite everything Eleanor was proud of her achievements as The Fox and she must never forget that...

'We shall stop for a while by the river, Eleanor.'

Hugh's voice broke through her musings but she didn't respond, having missed what he had said. He rode alongside her and took her reins, slowly bringing her horse to a halt.

'I think we could all do with a respite, my lady, don't you? Come, you must stretch your legs and partake in some food and ale.'

He dismounted and came to help her, clasping her waist with two big, strong hands, lowering her to the ground. They stood facing each other, eyes locked, before Hugh looked away and broke the contact.

He stepped to one side and escorted her to the side of the riverbank where Will, who would be accompanying Hugh to meet with the Scots, and some of their men, were tethering the horses to a tree. They were joined by Eleanor's women, who helped lay out and prepare a meal of cold meats, bread, cheeses and fruit.

Eleanor sat on the mats that had been laid on the ground and helped pass around trenchers of food and pour mugs of ale from the flagons they had brought with them.

Hugh ate with the men while she sat and nibbled some dried fruit with a handful of nuts and watched him, contemplating her situation, or rather her relationship with her husband, as she always did when her mind wandered.

Hugh was once again being courteous, and showing her every consideration on their journey back, but he kept his distance from her, as before. This time, though, Eleanor knew the reason why. And this time she didn't blame him.

'You have wounded me more than you'll ever know...'

How many times were these words going to spin round and round in her head, compounding her guilt? And yet Hugh had never revealed to King John that she was the one who conspired with the outlaws. For that alone she was indebted to him, even though he wanted nothing more to do with her.

Eleanor had wanted to tell him the rest. About her dissembling as Le Renard. About everything...

But she couldn't do it. If Eleanor had thought Hugh's reaction had been bad when he'd learnt of her betrayal, God only knew what he would do if he learnt the truth about The Fox.

But it did not sit well with her, hiding this—another secret—from him. There was no point, anyway, now that she had all but retired her alter ego. And with everything that had happened it might now have to be an indefinite retirement.

'Eleanor, may I talk with you? Mayhap we could walk

along the river for a moment…if you would honour me?' Hugh said, standing over her.

'Of course.'

They walked along the bank, taking in the winding expanse of river that disappeared into the thickets and hills beyond. Hugh strolled beside her with his hands behind his back as she picked a leaf and twirled it between her fingers.

'You must be happy that we're almost back in Tallany, Eleanor?'

'I am, yes.'

As well as relieved and thankful to be away from the nightmare at court.

'Good, good… And, as you know, once you're safely back I will be leaving for Scotland immediately.'

She did know—but not that he had to go straight away. 'I see. And how long will you be gone?'

'I'm not entirely sure. However long my mission will take with the Scots and their newly anointed King,' he said with a sigh. 'I will make sure that everything is in place before I leave. You will have a few of my best men to stand in my stead, as well as the new steward of Tallany, of course.'

Eleanor looked away and bit her bottom lip at this reminder of having had Gilbert Claymore replaced by someone Hugh could trust.

He regarded her. 'I also want to say that what happened in Winchester with King John was terrible.' He exhaled slowly before adding, 'I have been thinking it over and I hold myself responsible for what *almost* happened.'

Eleanor touched his sleeve. 'But it didn't, and I have you to thank for that.'

'Even so, I should not have brought you into that environment in the first place.'

'From what I have heard, I am not the first woman the King has tried and succeeded in using in that way to get through to good, honourable men…like you,' she said, flicking her eyes in his direction. 'As well as many of the Rebel Barons. They must act with heavy hearts for what they believe. Their decisions cannot be taken lightly.'

Hugh copied Eleanor and picked a leaf off a nearby shrub. 'Yes, these are very difficult times.'

She nodded. 'With many honourable men on both sides in this bitter conflict.'

And a terrible king who was at the centre of it…

'Indeed.'

'I hope that the differences between King John and the Barons will soon be resolved,' she said.

'I do too. It would be good for the sake of the kingdom if matters were finally resolved and the country would come together again as one.'

As it would be good if *they* could come together again… Ah, if only that was a possibility…

Hugh ran his fingers through his hair. 'However, that is not what I wish to talk about. Let me say again that I'm sorry I put you in that hostile situation with John.'

She turned to face him. 'But you didn't, Hugh. The "hostile situation" that we both faced was because of the outlaws and the silver they stole from the King.'

'At least you realise that.'

'I'm not stupid.'

'Oh, I know, my lady. But tell me something: would you have ever stopped your secret assignations with them? With the outlaws?'

She shook her head slowly. 'No, I don't believe I would.'

He regarded her for a moment with the ghost of a smile on his lips. 'I'm glad, at least, of your honesty. And that's what I believed too. Which confirms to me that one way or another, whatever your intentions, I would always have found out about you.'

'If you know anything about me, Hugh, you'll know that I, too, never do anything lightly.'

'And neither do I, Eleanor.' He sighed. 'I have fought all my life for what this kingdom stands for…for our anointed King, for our liberty, and more importantly for the law of the land. Without those foundations holding the country together there will only be madness and chaos.'

'But what if the root of that foundation is rotten?'

'Then you mend it. Listen to me, Eleanor. Whilst I appreciate, now more than ever, the real hardships people face, there *are* other ways.'

'How? Through careful negotiations? The law? Why, even now the Rebels are trying to compel John to sign this Great Charter, to keep him to his word, but he won't do it.'

Hugh exhaled through his teeth. 'Can you not see what would happen if lines were drawn between King John and the Rebel Barons?'

'They already have been.'

He shook his head slowly. 'This is just the beginning— the situation could get much, much worse. It could come to the country tearing itself up, brother against brother. We have to move to broker peace, rather than to full-scale combat. We do not need a hot-headed king and equally hot-headed reactionary behaviour from the Rebels. It would spell disaster for us all—and especially the ordinary people of this kingdom.'

She rubbed her forehead, pondering on everything her husband had said. It was certainly a different view on a complicated situation which was far more volatile than she had believed. Its implications far wider.

Hugh turned and folded his hands on either side of

her shoulders. 'Promise me something, Eleanor. Promise me that you will not be meeting with the outlaws. That you'll stop.'

'Hugh, I wasn't going to.'

'Look what happened in Winchester. And the King doesn't even know about your involvement…for now. Next time I might not be there.'

'I'll manage.'

'That is not enough. I don't want you to just "manage". We'll talk on my return, but I want your word, Eleanor.'

She met his eyes and saw the concern there. 'Very well.' She swallowed. 'You have it.'

'Thank you.' Hugh exhaled slowly. 'Come, let's get back to the others.'

'Wait… Tell me, why didn't you tell the King of my involvement?'

'I could never do that,' he said softly. 'It is and always will be my duty to protect you.'

'Despite what I have done?'

'Despite everything,' he murmured.

Eleanor turned away, not meeting his eyes. 'And you really must leave so soon?'

'I must. The King demands it of me.'

'I know, but is that…? Well, is that the only reason?' Eleanor wasn't sure what had possessed her to ask, nor whether she really wanted to know.

He stopped and clasped her elbow. 'You and I could do with some time apart,' he muttered. 'Who knows? It might be a good thing for both of us.'

He was right. Mayhap they did need time apart. But how was she to make things right between them if he wasn't there? Not that she knew how to…

Eleanor realised with a heavy heart that nothing would ever be the same. Everything had changed irrevocably and they could never go back. It had always been going to end this way once Hugh found out about her involvement, had it not?

They were on different sides and always would be. He would always believe the outlaws to be nothing more than criminals, whilst Eleanor knew that, despite breaking the law, they were a force for good. If only she could make Hugh understand that...

But that was just futile. Everything else might have changed, but that never would.

Chapter Twenty

It had been over a month since Eleanor had arrived back home in Tallany and over a month since she had set eyes on Hugh. But it felt so much longer than that. Her husband had left immediately, once they had arrived back and 'set everything to rights', as he had called it. But everything had not been right…

Since Hugh's departure every disastrous misfortune had befallen her and her people. There had been much lawlessness in Tallany, with looting, thieving, as well as women, the elderly and the frail being accosted.

The culpable group of men who had committed all the lawlessness dressed in a similar way to Eleanor's outlaws, and even wore marks and hoods. Of course it wasn't them. They were trying to pass their crimes off as those of the outlaws—not that anyone in Tallany believed it to be their work, although it had caused much confusion and chaos.

The new steward and Hugh's loyal men hadn't been able to pin the crimes on the outlaws, but why was this happening? Why go to all the trouble of framing the outlaws when they were wanted men anyway?

Eleanor didn't know the reason for that, but couldn't help but think that Lord Balvoire was behind all this and somehow involved. The man was so deplorable that he would certainly stoop this low. And she couldn't help but remember that awful exchange in King John's solar at Winchester, when he'd said that he would employ 'the element of surprise' to catch the outlaws. Was this what he had meant? That he would create havoc in Tallany?

Again, she could not think how this would achieve the capture of the real outlaws—unless, of course, some of them came out of hiding to retaliate.

She was once again in the inner bailey of the castle, pacing back and forth, waiting for news from Gilbert Claymore, who had gone to survey these new troubles that had been reported with Eustace Le Moyne, the new steward, and others.

If only Hugh was here.

Hugh...

Her thoughts were never far from her husband, even after all this time, and even with all the problems that she had faced constantly since he'd been gone. She hadn't heard a single thing from Hugh since he'd left and didn't know when he would return. She couldn't eat, couldn't sleep properly, and the truth was that she missed him desperately. Her life was unravelling fast before her eyes and she seemed unable to stop it.

She lifted her head at the sound of hooves pounding on the cobbled ground as Gilbert Claymore entered the castle gate.

'My Lady Eleanor!' her old steward bellowed. 'It's worse than we imagined.'

'What news, Gilbert?' She could barely get the words out.

'It's Lord Balvoire and he's—he's caught Anselm!' he stammered.

'What?'

'He's bringing him to be hanged here in Tallany!'

Eleanor covered her face with her hands, digging her fingertips into her head. Not Balvoire again. The man had been plaguing her since Hugh's departure and now this.

She had to think and she had to think fast. She was damned if she was going to just stand by and watch her friend hang. There was one thing and one thing alone that she could do, but it was so outrageous, so dangerous, that the likelihood of success was minimal. It mattered not. She had to do it if it meant that she could somehow save Anselm.

First, though, she would have to send secret messages expediently to her outlaw group.

'Come, Gilbert, there's much to do.'

Hugh had been travelling back from Scotland with Will and many of his men for over two weeks. It had been a fruitful and interesting month with King Alexander and if King John had any notions of future peace, he should broker a marriage between the Scottish King and his oldest daughter, once she was of age.

For now, though, the English King had far too many problems in his own kingdom—not that he would get much assistance from the Scots, who preferred to remain neutral between John and the Rebels…for now.

Hugh had been away from Tallany and Eleanor for a long time. It had been mainly out of choice, in the hope that time apart from his wife would allow him to get her out of his mind and loosen the hold she had over him.

But it was useless. Everything at the Scottish court had reminded him of her. Every piece of music; every melody and lovelorn lyric had made him think of her… Her hair, the scent of her skin, the curve of her neck… But it was much more potent than that: he missed *her*…

He missed her funny little quirks… The way she chewed the inside of her cheek when she was nervous or found something amusing. The way she wrinkled her nose when she was thinking. The absurd little things she said that made him laugh. The fact that she preferred to race him on horseback and get instruction in combat rather than stay in the bower and perfect her needlework. The impassioned way she spoke about things that mattered to her, even if she differed from his opinion. The fact that she cared about the plight of ordinary people…

She always, *always* challenged him, with her quick wit and her indomitable spirit. Yet he could never win her loyalty and never have her trust. That belonged to others. To the outlaw and his men.

If anything, the time they had spent apart had made him yearn for her all the more. Ah, but it was no good. His feelings for her were meaningless, complicated, and they had to be suppressed, however painful that would be.

Hugh turned to Will, who had caught up with him on his dappled grey destrier, and nodded at him. 'We've almost reached home,' he said, as they reached the familiar valley that lay beyond the borders.

How long had he been thinking of Tallany as 'home'? It surprised him that he felt that way about the place.

'Thank the Lord! You've been riding like the wind trying to get back—it's been a damned effort keeping up with you.'

'Just putting you through your paces, Will.'

Even before they had reached the expanse of landscape Hugh knew there was something very, very wrong. He glanced at Will, who was suddenly alert and grave, all signs of levity gone, and then flicked his attention back to the scene before him. He noted the pockets of smoke dotted throughout the landscape. They must be the result of a fire. But what had happened here? And more importantly where was Eleanor? He hoped to God she was safe.

Hugh nodded at Will and they bounded down the hill and eventually reached the outer edges of the small hamlet of Ulnaby, closest to the foot of the hill. Had they been attacked? And, if so, why hadn't he been alerted? Or was this some sort of accident?

He felt sick with anger and frustration as he rode into the midst of the hamlet and he gripped the hilt of his sword, taking in the burnt-out shells of what had once been dwellings and the carcasses of livestock.

He could see a group of people huddled together in the hub of the hamlet as he cantered towards them. He recognised the old woman whom Eleanor had introduced to him many weeks ago, when she had been giving coin—no doubt stolen coin… It was Aedith, or some such name…

The woman turned to face him as he and his men dismounted one by one and walked towards them.

'It's Aedith, isn't it? What has been going on here?'

'My lord, you've returned. How thankful we are to see you.'

'What has happened?'

'I don't know. To be perfectly honest, it all started when you left these 'ere parts.'

'All? What do you mean, "all"?'

'Looting, thieving and everything in between, my lord.'

Hugh swore an oath under his breath. 'Tell me how we can be of use.'

Her eyes widened with surprise. 'Bless you, my lord. Anything you can spare. We 'ave children who are separated from their family. And many 'ere haven't eaten for days.'

Hugh nodded decisively. 'We'll give you the rest of our

provisions: food, drink and blankets.' He smiled grimly at her. 'And I swear, as Lord of Tallany, that I will find out who did this here and bring them to justice. Your village will be rebuilt.'

Tired and withdrawn, the old woman looked around the group, wordlessly communicating with them, and then nodded her head. 'Verra well, my lord. Whatever you says.'

'You have my promise, Aedith. Do you have any idea who did this?'

'It were no one local, if that's what you be thinking. And I don't care what anyone says—it weren't The Fox neither.'

Hugh frowned. 'If not them, then who?'

No one spoke as they all looked from one person to the next.

'Couldn't say for sure, me lord,' a young man said, looking away.

'I can,' Aedith said.

The young man shook his head and cautioned her not to continue, but she took no heed.

'I'm an old woman, so I don't care what happens to me, and I will say what I needs to.' She gave the young man a reproving look and flicked her eyes to Hugh. 'I saw one of that Lord Balvoire's men—he was involved with all this.'

'That's quite an accusation.'

'I only knows what I knows... I saw 'im a few times in the village—fancy, too, with Lord Balvoire's colours. He were sweet on our Agnes, you see, and I don't forget a face. I recognised 'im again when they were doing their looting, pretending to be The Fox's men.'

Hugh clenched his jaw. 'Thank you for telling me. And before any of you ask, I promise there won't be any recriminations. You are all under my protection.'

Hugh turned away and rubbed his chin. He could well believe the old woman's assertion that Balvoire's men were involved. The bastard was dangerous, capable of anything to feather his nest, and would grasp what he wanted at any cost.

And what he wanted, since he had been unable to press his suit for Eleanor's hand, was the huge piece of Tallany land that bordered his. Catching a few outlaws was only a means to an end for Balvoire, which was to be in King John's favour.

Needless to say, Hugh needed to tread carefully, as it seemed that every path led to a perilous quagmire that he could easily fall into.

He looked again at the miserable faces of the people huddled together.

'There is something more.' He turned and fetched a small leather pouch from his saddlebag, returning to press it into her wrinkled hands. 'I want you to give silver to everyone in recompense for their loss, Aedith. It's all I can do for now.'

The old woman stared in astonishment at the pouch of silver in her hands and then looked at Hugh and smiled. 'I weren't too sure 'bout yer, with your good looks and being a southerner. Didn't know whether you were good enough for Lady Eleanor. But you'll do. You'll do verra well.'

Hugh's lips twitched. 'I'm glad you approve.'

'One more thing, me lord. There's a rumour that the outlaw Anselm has been caught and is ready to be hanged at Tallany Castle.'

Hugh exchanged a look with Will. 'And do you know who caught the outlaw?'

'I do. Lord Balvoire it was—'im again.'

Indeed…*him again.*

Hugh, followed by Will and his men, left Ulnaby, riding fast through the forest to reach Tallany Castle. His anger was mounting with every pound of the horse's hooves. Damn Balvoire's interference! But Hugh knew that John had given him the authority to be as much of a puffed-up, meddlesome ass as he chose to be.

They reached the castle keep and came to a halt. Will and his men ushered their horses beside his, forming an impressive single unified line. The scene in front of him made Hugh gawp and curse aloud. He pushed forward, shaking his head, a muscle leaping in his jaw.

There outside the castle wall was a temporary wooden canopied dais, where Edmund Balvoire was sitting with all his pomp and self-importance, surrounded by a handful of his men on either side, bearing his standard. To one side were the Tallany men, the new steward and the old, and many of the hearth knights Hugh had left behind.

Hugh darted a look at the Tallany priest, Father Thomas, who had stepped out in front with four guards on either side of the prisoner—the outlaw Anselm. They all stopped, surprised at their arrival.

'Would someone like to tell me what in God's name is going on here?' Hugh bellowed.

Balvoire stood and extended his arms. 'Ah, Lord Hugh. You are just in time to witness the execution of an outlaw—and not just anyone, but Le Renard's right-hand man. The big outlaw Anselm.'

Hugh glanced at the gallows, erected in his absence and surrounded by a crowd of villagers and local folk. And then he looked to the old steward. 'Is everyone safe, Claymore, with these recent disasters that I have only just been informed of?' he asked, before locking his eyes firmly on Balvoire's.

'Yes, my lord. A missive has been sent to notify you about our troubles.'

'I received no such thing,' he said curtly. 'And my wife? Is she…is she well?'

It seemed so long since their parting and now Hugh had to wait to see her.

'She is, my lord, and is inside the castle. She will be glad of your unexpected arrival.'

Balvoire flicked something off his surcoat. 'Yes, it is a shame that Lady Eleanor won't be attending. With the public hanging of such a notorious criminal she really should do so—especially in your absence. Well, never mind… Now you're here, my lord.'

Hugh glared at him. 'Lord Balvoire, can you explain to me why you feel you can march into Tallany and throw your weight around like this?'

'I'm only doing my duty, my young lord, as a good neighbour should—especially with all the difficulties here whilst you were away,' he said wryly. 'And anyway, you will remember that the King asked us to work together.'

'Not like this,' Hugh said through clenched teeth, reining in his anger. 'I thank you for your assistance whilst I have been away on the King's business, but this is a matter for me—not you.'

'Oh, you are full of self-importance, are you not?' Balvoire chuckled softly. 'And I disagree. This is a matter for all of us.'

Hugh dismounted and strode to the dais, growling as he climbed one step at a time until he was towering over the much shorter man. 'Once again you overstep your authority, Balvoire, coming into Tallany like this. Just as you did before in my hall. But, by God, no more.'

'You have much to learn, Hugh de Villiers,' he sneered.

'Not from you.' Hugh jerked his head around and nodded at Eustace Le Moyne, the new steward, and a few of his retainers. 'Escort Lord Balvoire and his men off Tallany, Le Moyne.'

'Yes, my lord.'

He watched as Edmund Balvoire climbed down from the dais. Just as he did so, arrow after arrow hissed through the air, striking as if randomly and yet hitting inanimate objects with absolute accuracy from different directions. Incredibly, the deluge of flying arrows did not strike a single person, but the situation was enough of a diversion to create chaos and everyone dispersed.

Then the outlaw Anselm freed his hands from the rope binding them and punched one of the guards in the face. Damn! The villagers were seemingly helping the prisoner escape into the woods and doing nothing to stop him.

All this had happened in a matter of moments and mayhem ensued.

Hugh turned to Will. 'Catch him and bring him back—but I don't want anyone hurt.'

He turned his head and narrowed his eyes. The arrows had come from many directions, but he suspected only a handful of archers had fired them. Yet there was only one of note. One from a particular angle. One who had shot the most and the fastest arrows. One who had to be the leader. And Hugh knew without hesitation who that must be...

Le Renard.

This time Hugh would get him.

This time the outlaw would not get away from him so easily.

Chapter Twenty-One

It had all happened so quickly. Eleanor had knelt very still, perched high under the branches of an old oak tree chosen for its strategic position and also to conceal her with its expanse of foliage. She had sucked in her breath and nervously tied Le Renard's mask around her eyes and face, hoping that every single one of her outlaws was now in position to play his part in bringing about Anselm's freedom. An outcome which was anything but assured.

Eleanor had watched as Anselm was led out to the gallows by Father Thomas and taken a few more breaths, knowing that the time had come. Father Thomas would have slipped a small blade into Anselm's bound hands before he gave the last rites. She'd hoped to God that there would be enough time for Anselm to cut through the rope.

A few of her men had perched in trees surrounding the area and another handful had made their way into the crowd, blending in with the villagers whilst all eyes followed the prisoner.

She'd watched with bated breath as Anselm was led out towards the gallows…but suddenly a pounding of hooves from a different direction made Eleanor turn her head.

Her breath had caught in her throat.

Hugh...? Could it have been?

Oh, Lord, it *was* Hugh, and he had returned safely to Tallany. Her heart had jumped for joy. He was finally back home. She'd felt like climbing down from the tree and throwing herself into his arms... But, no, she had a job to do.

And she would use this intervention, knowing it would allow her a little more time to put her plans in motion.

She'd moved into range, gripping her arrow tightly and nocking it to her bowstring. She steadied herself, knowing she would have to strike with absolute precision.

The voices at ground level had been drowned out by the rampant beating of her heart. She had felt a tiny bead of moisture on her forehead but had no time to brush it away.

She'd waited for a sign from one of the outlaws in position that Anselm had indeed cut through the ropes that bound his hands.

She would play her part in causing mayhem, helping Anselm to safety.

There was a flash of something in the distance and Eleanor had known it was her sign—the discreet way her outlaws wordlessly communicated with each other.

It was time to act.

She'd struck arrow after arrow with breathtaking precision, sending them flying through the air in different directions, aiming for a wooden post or the branch of another tree. Two of her men had followed suit, adding to the confusion.

She had known the villagers below were intent on aiding the prisoner's escape, and even the Tallany guards seemed reluctant to recapture him. Only Hugh and his men had thrown themselves into the fray.

Eleanor had smiled as she watched Anselm pull a

woollen hood over his head—a similar hood to those worn by every other man around him—before getting away into the woods.

She'd hoped they would all get to safety as quickly. Her smile fell away from her lips and she exhaled, her relief keenly felt.

But this was anything but over, and it was time for her to slip away.

Hugh ran in the direction of where the most arrows had been struck from. He located a tree he suspected had concealed the outlaw, looking above into its branches, but Le Renard had once again disappeared...or had he?

Hugh heard some swishing noises, looked up, and made out a figure swinging from tree to tree ahead in the woods.

Le Renard! It had to be.

Hugh followed on foot and unexpectedly found Eleanor's grey palfrey tethered to a tree. No doubt she was here, waiting for her *friend*, but there was no sign of her or The Fox.

Hugh groaned in frustration. He couldn't have got away, again, especially without a horse. So, where in God's name was the outlaw?

He stroked the palfrey's soft muzzle absently, looking around in every direction, when suddenly something fell onto the horse. Hugh looked up to find that he was face to face with Le Renard himself.

'Greetings, my lord. Thank you for keeping my horse company.'

Le Renard shoved Hugh and grabbed at the reins, pulling the animal to try and get away hastily.

But Hugh was too quick for the outlaw and somehow

managed to hurl himself on top of the moving animal, sitting behind The Fox and getting elbowed for his troubles.

Le Renard applied pressure to the flank of the horse with his legs, making it sprint faster, weaving briskly through the woods.

'Damned impudence! Slow down, boy.'

'No!'

Le Renard careered ahead at breakneck speed, evidently knowing the woods extremely well as he pulled the reins in every direction and missed flying branches. But Hugh now knew them well too, and it seemed the outlaw was going back to the small dilapidated hut he had followed Eleanor and Claymore to before.

Hugh had to think of something. He couldn't reach his sword belt, lodged underneath him, but he managed to filch a dagger from the back of the outlaw's belt. He pushed himself to a sitting position and coiled his arms around Le Renard, pointing the tip of the weapon to the outlaw's neck.

'I swear if you don't stop I'll—'

'Cut me from my neck to my navel?'

The voice of Le Renard seemed different…feminine—in fact it sounded remarkably like Eleanor's… But that was not possible. His ears must be deceiving him.

He gave his head a shake, hoping to clear it.

It couldn't be her…

'It is me, Hugh.'

'Eleanor?' he said, almost falling off the horse. 'It can't be!'

'I'm afraid that it is.'

'I… I don't believe it,' Hugh muttered. 'You must be a decoy for him.'

Le Renard, or rather Eleanor, sighed. 'No, I don't think so.'

'How? How can this be?'

'Please…let's get away from here and I can explain everything.'

Chapter Twenty-Two

Hugh glanced around the small, unassuming hut as he leant against the wooden table with his arms folded. His eyes flicked back to Eleanor, dressed in green hose and tunic with a rope around her waist. He opened his mouth to say something but then closed it again. He had so much to say, so much he wanted to know, that it was difficult to know where to start.

She was dressed as Le Renard, for the love of God.

No, she *was* Le Renard!

'I find this hard to believe,' he said finally. 'Any of this.'

'I know.' She nodded.

'But you...? You are and have been Le Renard?' He shook his head in disbelief. 'All this time?'

'I realise it's not how a lady should behave.'

'That,' he said, 'is an understatement.'

'Precisely—no one would ever believe it. No one would ever believe a woman to be capable. In all honesty, people see what they want to see.' She shrugged.

'Is that what this is about? You showing off your pro-digious talents?'

'No, of course not. This is nothing to do with my being an unnatural woman.'

'You seem natural enough to me, Eleanor—and that's not the issue,' he ground out. 'It is the fact that you lied to me.'

'I know, but it was never intentional. I wanted to tell you…'

'And yet you didn't.' He narrowed his gaze.

'I tried to.'

'Oh, yes?' He tilted his head. 'When exactly was that, my lady?'

'In Winchester.'

True, he hadn't wanted to listen to anything she might have said about Le Renard, but then *never* in his wildest imagination could he have believed that she would be telling him *this*. That his wife was in actual fact the outlaw he had been seeking all this time.

What an idiot he had been…

There was a subdued lull for a moment, before Eleanor broke the silence.

'I had better get out of these clothes.'

'You keep them here?'

She nodded. 'The last time I was here I left a dress.' She moved towards the coffer in the corner of the room and started to undress, slipping into a plain grey dress. 'Can you help me with the laces?'

With deft fingers Hugh helped tie the laces on her dress. 'That must have been the night I followed you,' he said from behind her.

'Yes.'

The night Hugh had been consumed with jealousy and hurt by her betrayal. Yes, he was a damnable idiot…

'You gave me your word that you wouldn't meet with the outlaws again.'

'I couldn't stand by and allow an innocent man to die.'

Hugh bit back a smile. 'Commendable sentiment, sweetheart, but your friend is far from innocent. Anselm's an outlaw, for heaven's sake.'

'We were never just your ordinary run-of-the-mill outlaws.'

'You surprise me.' He gave her a perceptive look. 'Tell me, though, are you a wife pretending to be an outlaw, or an outlaw pretending to be a wife?'

Her forehead creased as she thought of her answer. 'Is there a difference?'

'Oh, yes, Eleanor—since one would suggest that The Fox is not real and the other that everything you and I shared was not.'

'Then I would say neither... I am both Lady Eleanor Tallany *and* the outlaw Le Renard.'

Hugh shook his head. 'It's so dangerous and reckless of you. Why take all this unnecessary risk?'

'I did what I did to survive.'

'But to pursue this for all this time?'

She took a deep breath and met his eyes. 'It all started a long time ago, Hugh, when I was a young girl. My interests, as you might guess, were not the same as other children's. And my father trained me in the art of combat—in secret, of course. I even dressed as a young squire.'

'Your father *encouraged* you?'

'He did it because I was his heir and because I harassed him continually to do so. And he realised that I was an apt pupil.'

'Now, *that* I can believe.' His lips curled upwards slightly and she returned his smile hesitantly. 'But this also has something to do with Millais?'

She nodded. 'Yes. He was a monster.' She swallowed before continuing. 'It wasn't until after Richard died that

I could put everything my father had taught me into practice. And so, in Tallany's hour of need, I didn't hesitate. I couldn't do anything as a woman—as Lady Eleanor Tallany—but as a young man I could. With Gilbert's help and Father Thomas's blessing I got together a group of likeminded local men, bent on redressing the balance and safeguarding those in need.'

'Are you telling me that all those men knew and accepted you as a woman? And that Father Thomas blessed you as…as Le Renard? It cannot be true.' He felt his jaw drop.

'No one knew me as The Fox except Gilbert, Brunhilde and, yes, Father Thomas.'

'The trinity of the faithful,' he said, shaking his head. 'And you were all bent on this madness?'

She nodded. 'Something had to be done, Hugh. People were starving—actually starving—whilst we were sending box after box of silver for King John's coffers with the huge increase in scutage levied for more of his disastrous wars.'

She paused for a moment, clearly recalling, remembering…

'On one particular night I saw the King's soldiers actually laughing and goading the people as they piled up their wagons with silver. One loathsome yob slapped a young girl he'd propositioned and something inside me snapped… Le Renard was born that day.'

Hugh stared at her in disbelief before moving close, resting his forehead against hers. 'Your courage astounds me. When I think of how anyone else would have reacted in a similar situation…' He closed his eyes. 'But Eleanor, you could have got yourself killed.'

'We were never caught because we were always careful, selective, making sure we didn't seize every strongbox moving south. Occasionally we also brought back the Rebel Barons' scutage—meaning we were protected, up to a point.'

'I would never have believed it, but I should have known it was you,' he sighed. 'Racing on horseback, wanting lessons in combat, talented at chess... It was all there, staring me in the face.'

'No one, not even the outlaws themselves, ever realised The Fox was me—because it's outside the realm of possibility for a woman to be able to do all that Le Renard has done. But you...? You would have found out eventually.' She shrugged.

'Not even in my wildest imagination would I have thought of this.' Hugh's eyes widened as he recalled something. 'Oh, God! I even *fought* you—and again you resorted to subterfuge and cheating. From that alone I should have known.'

They fell into silence momentarily. Then, 'What are you going to do?' Eleanor asked, and bit her lip.

'What am I supposed to do?' He rubbed his forehead. 'Whilst everything you have told me seems reasonable— admirable, even—you have not only aided and abetted outlaws but you *are* one. And not just any one, but... Le Renard!'

'I'm sorry, Hugh, but I was doing my duty the only way I knew how.'

'Not that you would have done anything differently even if you had, of course.'

'No. But you have to understand, Hugh, that my first marriage...he... Millais...tried to break me in every way he could. It was a desperate situation. And when he died I put everything—all my efforts—into keeping the people of Tallany, who had suffered with me, safe... As The Fox, I could ensure that no one would hurt us again.'

'Such bravery...' Hugh cupped her face, caressing her cheek. 'You know, Eleanor, he could never have broken you.' He drew her a little closer into his arms. 'When all is said and done, you were stronger than him. Your spirit greater. Your heart constant. He couldn't have changed you, however much he tried.'

Eleanor tilted her chin up and smiled softly. 'But everything changed once I met you. Once I married you.'

His brow furrowed. 'I don't understand...'

'I...' She swallowed. 'I had never met anyone like you before.'

'That is also the truth for me, sweetheart.'

'Well, that's why I...' Eleanor drew in a shaky breath and met his eyes. 'I fell in love with you. I didn't believe it could happen to me, but...but it did.'

If the discovery of Eleanor as The Fox had rendered Hugh speechless, this confession sucked all the air out of him. Yet, he needed to say something. He might be stunned, but his feelings for Eleanor were...were entirely mutual!

Oh, God, they were!

They had been for a long time, if he was honest with himself.

That was why his heart had ached so much when he'd found out about her betrayal. Why he'd needed time away from her...why he'd thought about her all the time and why he'd wanted to come back to Tallany.

Back home...to her.

Yes, indeed, he was in love with her...body, soul and everything in between...and he had to tell her.

Hugh opened his mouth to speak, but Eleanor shook her head and put her fingers to his lips.

'No, please don't say anything, Hugh. Just think about

what I've told you and understand that everything I've said is the truth.'

She handed him the fox-trimmed mask and cape belonging to Le Renard.

'Where are you going?' he asked, finding his voice, but not the words he wanted to say. Eleanor would hear them once she was ready—and once he understood what it meant for their future.

'Back to the castle.'

'Wait. I'll walk you back. It's not safe out there.'

She touched his jaw with the ghost of a smile on her lips. 'I know these woods like the back of my hand, so there is no need to worry, husband.'

And with a nod she left him, to think of all that had just transpired between them in this little hut. This very hut he had followed Eleanor to all those weeks ago.

By God, to think that he had been incandescent with jealousy at the idea of his wife with Le Renard. And she had been the outlaw herself!

He chuckled at his own stupidity as he shook his head. What a fool he had been! He would love nothing more than to get back to what they had once been, and yet everything had shifted. Everything, as Eleanor had said, had changed.

He now knew the truth…

It had been the same when he had found out about Alais Courville and her betrayal. But that woman had thought of nothing but herself, and once the opportunity had come to elevate her position, she'd snatched it without a backward glance.

Eleanor was nothing like her. She was true, loyal and kind-hearted. And being Le Renard had not been a choice but a necessity for her to survive, to heal from past hurts and to be able to protect the people of Tallany.

The irony was not lost on him that a group of outlaws led by a woman disguised as the wily Fox had not only confounded him, but also the King's men.

Eleanor was incredibly brave, and had made decisions that would make most men cower. Not only that but she was courageous and honourable, like the bravest of knights.

Yes, indeed, he loved her...

Hugh looked wide-eyed into his hands. He was holding Le Renard's mask and cape as though seeing them for the first time. He smiled to himself, coming to a decision. He needed to see Eleanor as soon as may be and tell her a few secrets of his own.

Hugh meandered out of the hut and back through the woods on a path in the direction of the castle, still clutching Eleanor's mask and cape in one hand and her bow with the quiver of arrows in the other.

He would send them to King John, as some sort of affirmation that Le Renard was no more, and hope to God that it would suffice in pacifying the King. It would work if Eleanor promised to put a stop to the outlaws' activities, and in time all this might fade away. Then, and only then, would they be able to put their lives back on track.

Muffled noises dragged him out of his musings and he was suddenly alert, his senses heightened. He stopped abruptly and saw shadowy figures flitting to his left. He crept through a clearing and looked around, knowing in his gut that something was not right. Mayhap it was a dog's howling or a horse neighing nearby. But intuition told him that something was wrong. *Very* wrong...

Eleanor's palfrey as well as another horse was tethered to a tree, whilst the old steward's hound barked furiously. A figure was slumped low, facing down to the ground. What the devil was going on?

Hugh calmed the dog and knelt beside the man, his heart beating fast in his chest. He gently pushed the hood off the man's head, gasping as he noted it was sticky with blood on one side. He removed the dirty cloth that had been tied around his mouth and gasped.

It was Gilbert Claymore...

The old steward had been battered, and blood was streaming from his nose. There was also blood from a few stab wounds on his arms and upper chest. Thankfully they didn't seem fatal, but must be seen to immediately. Mercifully, he was still alive.

Hugh eased him gently up and fetched a flagon from the saddle bag, tried to give him a sip of water.

'Gilbert, can you talk? What happened?'

'Balvoire...' His breathing came in short bursts but he managed to say more. 'He was waiting for Lady Eleanor, waiting for me, and I believe he means her harm, my lord.'

Balvoire...

Damn, damn, *damn!*

Hugh felt as though he'd been struck hard in the stomach.

The older man swallowed. 'He knows...he knows *everything* about her.'

This was very bad—as bad as things could get.

'How many men were there? Do you have any idea where that bastard is taking my wife?'

'Just him and one other, and they talked of taking her back to his castle. We need to get to her quickly.'

'You are in no fit state, my friend. You're lucky to be alive. Balvoire meant a slow death for you,' he said. 'Ride back to Tallany Castle and tell Sir William and some of my men to ride out towards Balvoire's castle. This time he has gone too far. I'll take Eleanor's palfrey.'

'Aye, very well, my lord—and take my hound as well.

He'll be useful to track my lady.' Gilbert looked beyond Hugh's shoulders, his eyes widening in surprise.

'What is it?' Hugh's hand reached slowly for the hilt of his sword.

'We have a problem, my lord… It's Anselm, the outlaw who escaped earlier,' Gilbert Claymore muttered under his breath. 'He's just jumped down from that tree and is walking towards us.'

'What the devil is he doing here…? That's all I need at a time like this.'

Hugh drew Le Renard's cape around his shoulders, pulling the hood trimmed with fur forward over his head, and looked down at the mask in his hand.

'Fox! I've been looking for you everywhere,' Anselm shouted from behind him.

Absently, Hugh put on the mask and stood, turning as the outlaw reached them. He had to try and get rid of him somehow.

The huge man looked Hugh up and down and whistled, scratching his head. 'It can't be…' he said, shaking his head. 'Why, you're a fully-fledged man, Fox, so you are.'

'I must have eaten my greens these past few months,' Hugh said wryly.

It was good thing that he hadn't worn his chainmail and was wearing a drab tunic and hose that wasn't too dissimilar to Le Renard's.

'I dunno…' the outlaw said. 'You don't *sound* like 'im.'

'I don't care of what you believe, Anselm, but know this: I *am* him,' Hugh said impatiently. 'And I don't have time for this. Let me help you up, Claymore. Easy, now, easy…'

Anselm swung over to the older man's other side and lifted him. 'I suppose I may as well thank you as any man.'

Was the outlaw addle-brained? Hugh's men as well

as the Tallany guards would still be scouring the woods looking for him. It was incredible that Anselm had managed to evade them as it was. Especially Will.

'You owe me nothing and I must go—as should you. Or else all my effort for your freedom will be in vain.'

'Nothing? He calls it nothing?' he said. 'If it weren't for you I'd be a dead man hanging.'

'Hell's teeth, Anselm! I have to get away immediately and so do you.'

They helped the older man mount his horse before the giant of an outlaw turned and gave him a friendly smile, incongruent with the menacing shadowy bruises on his face and under his eyes.

'Trouble afoot, eh? Where to?'

'It's too dangerous. You're a wanted man!'

Claymore, clutching his chest, decided this was a good time to pipe up. 'Lady Eleanor is in mortal danger... Balvoire has her and is taking her back to his castle.'

Anselm swore an oath. 'And where's 'er fool of a husband?'

'Never mind him,' Hugh snapped. 'I need to go *now*.'

'I'm coming with you, Fox.'

'I said no. Go and get back to your family. You're in no fit state.'

'I *said* I'm coming with you!'

'Damn your impertinence,' he admonished him, but knew he didn't have time. 'Very well, you may be of some use.' He turned to Claymore. 'If he's coming then you'd better forget the guards.'

'Godspeed, my lord,' Claymore said.

Hugh gave the older man a nod and pulled on the reins, galloping away with the outlaw following in his stead.

Chapter Twenty-Three

Eleanor's eyes flickered as she gradually regained consciousness. She groaned in pain, every part of her body aching. Dear God, her head! It felt as though it had split in two. It was throbbing, making it difficult for her to open her eyes, and her stomach felt as though it might need to empty itself.

She touched the top of her head, where it hurt so badly, and felt a lump and a gooey stickiness, through the veil. She felt bitterly cold, and was lying on something soft, yet damp, with the faint murmur of flowing water in the distance.

She gazed through the narrow slits of her partially opened eyes to find that two men stood by the edge of what appeared to be a gorge. One stood with his hands on his hips, and even from this angle, and despite his unusually dark attire, he was very much known to her.

Lord Balvoire...

But why? Why had he done this?

She shifted a little, trying in vain to find a more comfortable position.

'Lord Balvoire?' she mumbled. 'What have you done?'

She rubbed her eyes lightly, trying to coax them to open more.

'Ah, My Lady Eleanor, you're finally with us, are you? Good, good…'

The odious man walked towards her and smiled, making the bile in her stomach rise.

'And that, my dear, is the question I should be asking you.'

'I don't know what you're trying to say…'

'Don't you, my lady?' He crouched beside her.

'No. Your behaviour is as outrageous as it is mad,' she retorted, feeling none of the conviction of her words. She tried again, more forcibly. 'I demand you take me back to my castle.'

'This little misplaced outburst is precisely the reason why I have always liked you, my dear.'

'Misplaced? What are you talking about?'

He sneered, moving closer to her and lifting her chin with his spindly long fingers so his face was level with hers. 'You know, King John should have given you to me,' he murmured, licking his lips, 'You were wasted on Richard Millais, although I admired his persistence in getting you to dance to his tune. Not that you did, of course. *I* would have handled you very differently…'

'Well, that is one thing I can be thankful for. At least the King spared me that.'

'Let's not be too hasty, Lady Eleanor.' He leered at her, running his fingers down her face.

'You forget yourself, sir, and you forget that I'm married. You will mind not to touch me again.' The pounding in her head was now punishing.

'We'll see, my dear. And that new husband of yours will be of no use to you now. You're well beyond his reach.'

She shuddered in alarm. 'Which once again begs the question you have failed to answer, my lord. Why am I here and why have you abducted me in this high-handed manner?'

Eleanor hoped that Lord Balvoire would not notice her growing anxiety. What in heaven's name was going on? She had no choice but to keep him talking whilst hoping to gain some semblance of her strength back, however futile that seemed.

He dragged her to her feet and pulled her round to face the gorge. She could barely stand…still felt so very weak.

'Beautiful here, isn't it? I've always enjoyed coming here. And you see the gorge yonder, Lady Eleanor? Well, the other side of it is my land…my territory.'

'I am aware, my lord, but what has that got to do with anything?'

'Ah, but do you know that this side—this part with the dense woodland—also belonged to my family? The old King Henry annexed it and gifted it to your father, for some nefarious reason of his own, and now, my dear, the time has come to redress that decision.'

'Is that what all this is about?'

'Alas, it is only a means to an end, my dear.' He laughed roughly. 'And now I will ask you the same question you asked me when you fluttered your pretty eyes open just moments ago…' He smiled, revealing yellow-stained teeth. 'What have you done, Lady Eleanor?'

'I'm sure I don't know what you mean, sir.'

'Apologies, my dear. That bang on the head must have been harder than I thought. Allow me to explain,' he said. He leant forward and caught her mother's necklace in his palm. 'Beautiful little thing… And, you know, for all its plain design I recognised it immediately at Winchester.

Clever, really, although I had to wait to have it confirmed and tied up with the outlaw. But then I am a patient man.'

Eleanor swallowed, her heart hammering against her chest. Oh, God, no! This obnoxious, horrible man could not possibly know her secret. She could not betray her emotions. She must not. She had to remain calm and show surprise, even outrage, at his accusations.

'Did you also receive a bang on the head, my lord? You are making little sense. You recognised my cross because I *always* wear it.'

'Yes, and that was why it was quite surprising—shocking, even—when I saw it dangling out of that preposterous outlaw's tunic for a mere moment all those weeks ago. When you ambushed us,' he snarled. 'I thought it odd, because it's such a feminine piece of jewellery. But then I always did think the outlaw had a woman's cunning.'

He pushed down Eleanor's veil, gripping a long lock of hair and pulling it tightly, jolting her forward, closer to him. Closer than she could bear. Her head felt as if it was about to implode.

'It's you, my little Fox, and I have been waiting a long time to catch up with you.'

'You have gone mad. I don't know what you're talking about.'

'Oh, come now, Lady Eleanor. You can do better than that.'

'For goodness' sake, my lord, can you not see how ridiculous this is? I...? Le Renard? It's laughable,' she said evenly. 'As for my necklace—your eyes must have been playing tricks on you. If, say, the sun obscured them or the mud you were face-down in obscured them.'

He smiled slowly. 'Do you know, I do not believe I mentioned being face-down in mud?'

'I—I speculated, my lord,' she stammered, realising her mistake.

'Whilst I am finding this quite entertaining, we need to keep moving.' He signalled to the man he'd been travelling with to tend to the horses, tethered close by. 'I'd rather avoid a full-scale confrontation with Tallany riders or that dolt of a husband of yours.'

'Lord Hugh will have much to say about all this. So, if I were you I would let me go before any possibility of a "full-scale confrontation", as you put it.'

'Oh, I don't think so. I have waited a long time for my plan to fall into place. I must say it was a surprise when your husband returned, much sooner than I expected, but with a little tweaking it has all worked out.'

'What are you talking about?'

'I suspected you would try to set that oaf of an outlaw free somehow—and where better to stage the hanging than Tallany Castle, where I would discover you as The Fox, helping the outlaw. And now, with Hugh de Villiers's overzealous behaviour earlier, practically throwing me out of Tallany, he will once again take all the blame for this.' He whispered in her ear. 'And you are once again to be instrumental in your husband's downfall. Do you really think he will help you when he finds out the truth about you?'

Eleanor's gut twisted tightly. Balvoire was right, wasn't he? She had caused Hugh pain with her duplicity—especially now that he knew everything about Le Renard. It would come as no surprise to her if he decided that she was far more trouble than she was worth and washed his hands of her.

But at least she had told him the truth about how she truly felt.

That she loved him…

What if she never saw him again?

'Come, Lady Eleanor, do not make this more difficult than it needs to be.'

'Where…where are you taking me?'

'Oh, didn't I say? I'm taking you back to my castle, where the real entertainment can start, my dear. I will gain a full confession out of you, and soon not only this piece of land but all the riches of Tallany will come to me.'

'I will never yield to you.'

'Oh, I hoped you'd say that,' he said with another sneer. 'I have means and ways. Let's just say that, unlike Millais, I won't leave marks on your exquisite body. Besides, I need to make you pay for that dirty trick you played on me during your little ambush. Whatever was in that disgusting sack gave me a particularly nasty itchy rash—I do hope I can return the favour.'

From somewhere deep inside, Eleanor had to find her courage—and quickly.

'How dare you, Lord Balvoire?' she said, hiding the panic that was threatening to overwhelm her. 'You are mistaken, but your desperation for my land makes you believe that all your suppositions about my necklace are correct. I tell you they are not. It's all nonsense, and you know it—or else you would not be abducting me in this extreme manner with just one of your hapless minions.'

'Come, woman. I have no time for this!' he snarled, baring his teeth and seizing her by the back of her neck, dragging her towards the horses. 'You are a she-devil, my lady, and I hope you know what happens to *them*.'

His rancid breath was so close to her face that Eleanor gagged.

'Wait, you don't have to do this.'

Fighting her way out of this seemed impossible. Her head hurt, she felt far too weak, but she had to do *some-*

thing. She dragged her feet against the ground, but it was in vain. She was overpowered by his superior strength.

'It would be so much easier if you were to accept your fate more readily, my lady.'

He yanked at her so aggressively that she collided into him, hard, making them both tumble backwards, close to the mossy edge that seemed to fall away to nothing. She heard the sound of gushing water, flowing from the stream some distance below, and steadied herself.

'What are you trying to do? Kill us both, you stupid woman?' he spat.

'That's preferable to what you have planned.'

She pushed herself free and tried to get away, but his arms came around her in a vice-like grip. One hand went to her throat, squeezing softly, and the other moved around her waist, holding her still.

'Don't try that again or I'll hurl you off here myself!' he muttered in her ear, squeezing her neck a little tighter.

Dear God, she was choking. She couldn't breathe. The glorious hues of green in front of her on the horizon reminded her so much of Hugh's eyes but they were fading to nothing…

Her body slumped as she bitterly accepted that all had been lost.

Suddenly she faintly heard something that broke through her desperate thoughts. It gave her hope, even though all hope had seemed lost. It was the distant sound of barking… But, no, she must be imagining things. And yet the hound's barking had become louder and louder, and there was something else… The sound of a horse galloping towards them. Could it be?

Balvoire turned, having also heard the din, and just as he did so an arrow flew past and lodged itself at the centre of his floppy drab hat.

'Let her go,' said a steely low voice that was somehow familiar to her.

Lord Balvoire swung her around, clasping her tightly, pressing her back to his chest, with his dagger drawn and held against her throat. Eleanor peered from under her lashes and was surprised to see the figure in front of her... It was a man whose head and face were hidden under a fox-trimmed hood.

He dismounted effortlessly and prowled towards them, an arrow stretched and nocked against his bow, aimed at Balvoire's chest and ready to be released.

The man was evidently dressed as Le Renard. But that was not possible. Unless...

No, her eyes must be deceiving her.

'I said, let the lady go.'

Balvoire took a small step to one side. 'You...? It can't be... I have the *real* Fox here.'

'I don't think so.' The imposter smirked.

Oh, Lord, could it be...?

Hugh?

'I don't believe you. The outlaw Le Renard is small and wiry. I have met him before,' Balvoire spat, tightening his grip on Eleanor.

'Frankly, I don't care *what* you believe—although it has been known for boys to develop into men,' he drawled. 'Now, I'm going to give you one last chance, Balvoire. Let her go.'

'I don't take kindly to demands, you know...because they make me do *this*.'

Balvoire drew the tip of his dagger down Eleanor's neck, cutting her, making her gasp as she bled.

'The next one won't be so light. Now, this is what you'll do, whoever you are: you will leave quietly and go back to wherever you came from. I will then take Lady Eleanor with me, and you are not going to stop me or follow me. I will otherwise have no choice, sadly, but to kill her.'

'No, I don't think so. This is what *you* will do: you'll step away from my lady and only then will I allow you to leave. But I swear if you come near her, or touch her again, you will be cut from here…to here.'

Le Renard—or rather Hugh—indicated from Balvoire's neck to his navel with the tip of his arrow.

'And I suppose *you* would be the one to do that, eh?' Balvoire snarled.

'Oh, no, not I…' He chuckled. 'But *him*.'

Lord Balvoire jerked his head in the direction Hugh had tilted his head—only to encounter the sharp tip of a sword jabbing him under his chin. And the man holding the hilt of the sword was none other than… Anselm.

'Missed me, my lord?'

'You!' he breathed. 'What are *you* doing here? You have some nerve.'

'As do you, 'olding up my lady, 'ere. And you dare call *me* the villain.'

'Lady Eleanor Tallany is the traitor I've been seeking—as you well know.'

'So, you're dishin' out justice where no one can see what you're about, eh? Truest villain I ever did see.'

'How dare you? When I get my hands on you again, I'll enjoy cutting your entrails out while you're still alive and—'

'Enough!' Le Renard strode forward, closer to Balvoire. 'I said, let my lady go—now!' He aimed his arrow close to the man's chest. 'It's over.'

'Never!'

It happened so quickly.

Balvoire took a small step backwards and slipped on the wet, grassy edge, losing his balance. His eyes widened with shock and he fell, plummeting down below, dragging Eleanor with him.

Hugh hurled himself at her and grabbed her hand just as she felt the ground disappearing beneath her. For a long moment they just stared at each other as she dangled over the edge, suspended in mid-air. But she could feel her grip slipping.

'It's no use, Hugh, I can't hold on,' she whispered.

'I've got you!'

'I'm slipping…'

'Hang on tightly so I can pull you up.'

'It's too difficult to hold on,' she said, as one finger after another slipped away from Hugh's grasp.

'Damn it, Eleanor, I won't let you go.'

He pulled her up with a strength from somewhere deep inside, hauling her back to safety and into his arms.

'I will never let you go, do you hear?' he said softly. 'Never, my love.'

'Balvoire's dead good and proper, Fox.' Anselm looked down to the stream. 'Cracked his 'ead on a boulder.'

Hugh looked up and nodded at Anselm grimly, wrapping his arms around Eleanor, who was shivering, and dropping a kiss on the top of her head. 'Hush, sweetheart. It's over now.'

Eleanor fell in and out of sleep on the ride back to Tallany Castle. Hugh had parted ways with Anselm, who had now paid his debt by helping Le Renard with his rescue mission, and he had left Balvoire's accomplice tied to a tree.

Once the Tallany guards were dispatched they would find Balvoire's body, and the accomplice, from whom they'd get a confession about the attempted abduction of Eleanor.

That was as much as Hugh was willing to do, so as not to expose Eleanor's complicity with the outlaws. And, although it didn't sit right with him that he would have to bend the truth for King John, the alternative was inconceivable.

All that mattered to him was that his wife was safe. When he'd watched Balvoire threaten her, and cut her with his dagger, Hugh had had to use all his resolve to keep himself from pouncing on the bastard. And when she'd almost fallen down that gorge…

It didn't bear thinking about.

Yes, all that mattered was that she was safe and back where she belonged…with him.

'Hugh?' Eleanor muttered. 'I still can't believe that you came to save me.'

'You're awake, sweetheart?' he said gently. 'How do you fare?'

'Tired, sore, and my head is ready to burst—you didn't answer my question.'

'We'll be home soon and then you can rest properly.' He stroked her cheek with the back of his hand. 'You must have a low opinion of me if you believed that I wouldn't come for you.'

'Oh, I have a high enough opinion of you—but that's not what I meant. I can't believe that you came disguised as Le Renard.'

Hugh tugged at the reins, bringing her palfrey to a halt, and sighed. 'A wise woman once told me that sometimes there are no choices when there's a desperate need.' He shrugged, smiling. 'Besides, I thought it was about time you received a few surprises of your own.'

'So now do you understand? About everything that I had to do?'

'For me, there was a much greater need that made me desperate.'

She looked faintly confused. 'A need for what?'

'You, Eleanor...'

'Oh, Hugh.' She wrapped her arms around his neck and kissed him softly on the lips.

'I love you, Eleanor Tallany. I love you, body and soul. You challenge me to be a better man. A man worthy of you.'

'And I love *you*,' she murmured, her eyes filling with tears. 'With all my heart.'

'Ah...is that the same heart that you once declared would never be mine?'

'Yes, the very same.' She smiled, wiping her eyes with the back of her hand.

'Good to know.' He shook his head, chuckling.

'Does this mean that you have forgiven me?' she asked.

'Let's not get carried away, now.' He smiled, raising his brows.

'Well, I'm hopeful that you will. After all, a wise man once promised me hopeful futures that would drown out disastrous pasts.'

'True.' He grinned. 'And now that I hold the constancy of your heart in mine I have no choice but to use it for my own ends.'

'Confounding man! Of all the ridiculous, arrogant—'

Hugh silenced her with a kiss so passionate that it rendered her speechless—if only briefly.

'Hugh?' she said, eventually.

'Yes, my love?'

'You didn't really mean that, did you?' She bit her bottom lip.

'Oh, yes, Eleanor, I meant every word,' he drawled, and bent his head to kiss her again.

Epilogue

Six months later...

Eleanor watched her husband bade farewell to Will as his friend left on yet another mission for the Crown.
The state of the kingdom was incredibly dire, with the animosity between King John and the Rebel Barons now as bad as ever—as Hugh had predicted. It hadn't helped that once again the King had reneged on all the promises he had made, even after the Great Charter—a document that the man had signed himself. No wonder the Rebels found him so difficult to trust.

Eleanor realised that for Hugh it was a difficult balancing act, but at least they were no longer on different sides of this divisive conflict.

With so much strife in the kingdom she knew that her husband felt a huge amount of guilt at being so ridiculously happy and content with Eleanor…as she was with him. And it was the strength of their love and devotion that had slowly restored the trust and faith to their marriage. Something that brought so much joy to Eleanor that it made her heart soar.

And, when all was said and done, that was all that truly mattered…

As for Le Renard—Eleanor had all but retired him… for now.

Hugh was a diligent and effective lord, working with her to re-establish Tallany during these dark times. And even when he was commanded to court, and forced to turn his mind to matters of the Crown, Eleanor knew he safeguarded their land and its people. To her relief, he had also ensured that Osbert and Godwin were freed and returned safely to their families.

And for Eleanor there were now other things for her to focus on. She rubbed her stomach, delighting in the secret she would soon be letting her husband in on.

Hugh strode back towards her and smiled that lopsided smile of his that still managed to make her heart skip a beat. She returned his smile and stood beside him, waving Will off.

Will nodded at Hugh and winked at her, making her smile again. The man just couldn't help being a consummate flirt, but she was inordinately fond of him and, like Hugh, considered him to be like a brother.

'You're going to miss him, aren't you?' she said, squeezing her husband's hand.

'Will seems preoccupied these days. A lot more serious.' Hugh shook his head and sighed, looking down at her. 'I hope that all goes well for him, this time.'

'I hope so too,' she said, tilting her head to gaze at Hugh. She frowned. 'What is that in your hand?'

'Ah, this?' he said, tapping a package that had been wrapped with a thin layer of fabric and tied with string. 'I wanted to give this to you later, but you may as well open it now.'

'What is this? Another present, husband?'

'Precisely, wife. Now, open it.'

Eleanor opened the package to find the most incredibly soft cape lined with an even softer woollen fleece.

'It's beautiful. Thank you.'

'Made from the wool from your own sheep and their lambs.' Hugh's smile widened. 'Not that I believe you are as meek as one.'

'Oh, I would dearly like to know *what* you believe me to be.'

'Well, you're maddening,' he said, kissing her on the lips. 'You're tempestuous,' he said, planting another kiss. 'You're brave,' he said, kissing her once more. 'And I love you.'

'I love you too—but it's no use, Hugh. You cannot make a virtue out of my hopeless qualities,' she said, biting the inside of her cheek. 'Mayhap I am more the cunning fox, after all?'

'Mayhap,' Hugh said as he curled his fingers around her waist and pulled her closer towards him. 'But either way, sweetheart, you have the heart of a lioness. *My* lioness,' he murmured, and he kissed her again.

She giggled. 'Well, your lioness has a little secret.'

'Oh?' He raised his brow. 'And what is that?'

Eleanor shook her head. 'I think my surprise may be best shared later...when we are alone.' She met his smouldering eyes and smiled.

'As you wish, my love, as you wish.'

* * * * *